EROS

HELEN HARPER

EROS

By Helen Harper

Copyright © 2014 Helen Harper

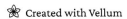 Created with Vellum

PART ONE

'When he had fallen into his first sleep, she silently rose and uncovering her lamp beheld not a hideous monster, but the most beautiful and charming of the gods, with his golden ringlets wandering over his snowy neck and crimson cheek, with two dewy wings on his shoulders, whiter than snow, and with shining feathers like the tender blossoms of spring.'

Source: Thomas Bulfinch, *The Age of Fable; or, Stories of Gods and Heroes* (1855).

CHAPTER
ONE

The man sat slumped at the far end of the bar. Outside the dark night was giving way to a shimmering dawn replete with streaks of brilliant red, which only seemed to tauntingly mirror his bloodshot eyes. The other patrons had yielded to their beds hours before; even Colette, whose winning ways with many an alcohol-sodden tourist rarely failed her, had given up attempting to draw him into conversation and left to find more welcoming comfort elsewhere.

He stared down into his glass. It contained little more than a few half-melted ice cubes so, frowning, he raised it in the air and waved it unsteadily at the bartender.

'I'll have another one.'

No answer was immediately forthcoming. He tried again. 'Hey! I need another drink.'

The bartender looked up from the small sink. 'I think you've had enough.'

'I'll be the judge of that,' he grunted. 'Isn't the customer always right?' As if to illustrate his point further, he shook the glass. The remaining ice cubes clinked together feebly.

Sighing, the bartender walked over. He reached behind and pulled a bottle from a dusty shelf, then turned and began to pour in a finger of expensive amber liquid.

The man waved the glass in the air. 'More.'

Another half inch slopped in.

Grunting, he raised it upwards in an unsteady toast, then gulped down half the contents. Unfortunately, a large quantity missed his mouth and dribbled down his chin instead and onto what had once been a pristine white shirt. The bartender watched with a mixture of amusement and exasperation, taking in the well-cut suit and gleaming gold watch. He may have more money at his disposal than the vast majority of other customers but, when it came down to it, all drunks were the same.

'Lost your heart, have you?'

The man looked up but the words didn't immediately register.

'Huh?'

'I said, have you lost your heart? You've got that look. She's not worth it, mate.'

Scorn lit the man's face. 'You think I'm here because of a woman?'

The bartender eyed him. Even without taking his clothes into consideration, the man's well-groomed golden curls suggested someone who took pains over his appearance. He shrugged. 'Man, then.'

'Spare me the pop psychology. There's no man and there's no woman. Love's a myth. A sham. If you think otherwise, then you've been conned.'

Despite the obvious bitterness in the man's voice, the bartender's reaction was mild. Waiting for him at home was his fiancée. They'd met at a party barely three months earlier, bonding over a disturbingly phallic-looking ice sculpture which had apparently been originally designed as a swan. She'd uttered less than five words before he knew he wanted to spend the rest of his life with her. He'd proposed a week later.

'What would you call it then? Lust? A chemical imbalance?'

'A steaming pile of shit.'

The man took another sip, more carefully this time, and managed to avoid spilling any more whisky. The bartender moved away.

'What?' the man called after him. 'You don't believe me? You think true love exists?' He clasped one hand to his chest. 'That you meet the one and you're stabbed in the heart with a thunderbolt of love?' His hand dropped back down to his glass. 'How is that true love?' he muttered.

'How is it not?' asked the bartender, picking up a glass and beginning to polish.

'Love doesn't work like that,' the man said. 'It can't work like that. Love at first sight is a fallacy.'

The bartender smiled to himself. Catching it, the man opened his mouth to say something before a shadow crossed his face and he clearly thought better of it. Instead, he took another drink. A moment of silence crossed the stale air of the room then he spoke again.

'You feel lust at first sight. And when that fades, you lapse into the comfort of companionship because you think it's better than being alone. Anyone who thinks they're really in love, like in the stories, has been tricked. Smoke and mirrors, my friend.' He eyed the bartender. 'Not that you'd be able to accept that as the truth.'

'And yet there are those who do fall in love. Who marry and grow old, and remain as much in love as the day they met.'

The man's mouth thinned into a grim line. 'They're being manipulated.'

'How can you be manipulated by love?'

The man drained his drink, staring into the bottom of the glass for a brief moment with a morose expression. 'How can you not?'

The bartender opened his mouth to answer but was interrupted by the intrusive beep of an alarm. The man frowned, reaching inside his jacket and pulling out an expensive-looking phone. He stared down at the screen for a moment, a muscle clenching in his jaw, then turned the phone off and put it away, planted his feet onto the floor and pushed back his stool. He dug out a wallet and tossed some crumpled notes onto the bar, squinting back at the bartender.

'That should cover it so far. You're not closing any time soon, are you?'

The bartender raised his eyebrows. 'We're open twenty-four hours.'

'Good,' he grunted. 'I'll be back in ten minutes then.'

The man spun round, swayed slightly and began to lurch towards the door. He veered off to the left, narrowly avoiding crashing into a table, before correcting himself and staggering forward. He stood at the door for a moment, as if suddenly lost in thought, then pulled it open, the sudden flood of sunlight causing him to wince. He muttered something inaudible under his breath and stepped out. The bartender shook his head slightly and scooped up the money, turning to the till to ring it in.

Outside, the man looked up and down the promenade. The early sun glinted off the azure blue of the sea and a few hungry seagulls soared keening overhead. Not too far away, an ice-cream vendor was setting up for the day, opening up a small red- and blue-striped parasol and humming away to himself. The man ignored him and focused instead on the beach. He could just make out a lone jogger approaching along the sand from the east. Other than a figure throwing a stick to a dog down by the water's edge, the area was deserted.

'Fewer witnesses for once,' he muttered to himself, walking across the dull grey cement to where a set of uneven steps led down to the sand.

He supposed that she'd sent him here at this moment because she enjoyed the symmetry of the scene. The poetic justice of the beach's beauty and the soft dawn sunlight. He shrugged, clasping hold of the iron railing at the edge of the steps to avoid falling over, and stumbled clumsily down. It made little difference to him. He'd been doing this for too long to care any more.

When he reached the bottom, he sat down, leaning against the railing. The jogger was getting closer. He could now make out her lurid pink shorts and brightly coloured headband. There wasn't much time left. Closing one eye, he cocked his head towards the man with the dog, both of whom were still completely oblivious to his presence. He was tempted for a moment to let them be. *She* wouldn't like that though. He rubbed his forehead tiredly and reached back inside his jacket, this time pulling out not a phone but a small golden box. He pressed on the lid and the device opened abruptly. Without looking, the man assembled the different parts together, screwing the barrel into place to complete the manoeuvre.

There was a clatter from above as the ice-cream seller dropped something onto the hard pavement of the promenade. The man ignored it and pulled what was now a gleaming gold weapon against his shoulder and aimed the crosshairs in the direction of the animal. He smiled as the dog bounded into the water, completely unaware that he had its heart dead within his sights. Then he swung upwards, switching to the dog's owner. He might be drunk but his aim was true. Truth be told, he never missed.

He watched the other man for several more heartbeats, feeling the pressure of the trigger tight against his fingers.

'For what it's worth,' he whispered, 'I'm sorry.' Then he squeezed.

He didn't need to check to see whether his shot had succeeded in hitting its target. He knew it had; in fact, he was already turning to the jogger.

Now she was closer he could tell she was young and pretty. He allowed himself a moment of reflection about what her life would be like if he chose to let her be. If she'd go on to find someone to marry, to have children with, to grow old with. Not that it really mattered; he was taking all that choice and all that suggestion of freedom out of her hands. The dog splashed through the froth of waves and barked once sharply, as if in warning. Too late. The man pulled the trigger and struck her directly in the heart.

He unscrewed the barrel, clicked off the trigger, and pulled the gun apart, carefully placing each component back into the golden box. Then he stood up, swayed and turned. The ice-cream vendor was crouched down, writing down the day's gelato specials on a small chalkboard. The man slipped the box back inside his jacket, and walked unsteadily back to the bar. He needed another drink. Or two.

Back on the beach, the dog was barking with increased fervour. The jogger had reached both the animal and its owner and stopped. The ice-cream vendor stood up from his writing and spared them a glance. They were inches away from each other and smiling with shy excitement, the deep and sudden knowledge they'd met the one person who could make them truly happy shining out from both of their faces. Meanwhile, pulling himself back onto his bar stool, Cupid, known as Coop to his friends and the God of Love to others, ordered another double Scotch.

CHAPTER
TWO

S kye was sitting at the bar of a small homely coffee shop, chin resting on her hands while she stared out at the grey drizzle of the morning. So far this morning she'd been to the job centre, where the best offering appeared to be working part time in a sandwich shop, scoured the internet for openings and put in an application for temping at a local law firm, as well as registering with yet another recruitment agency. She wasn't being picky; right now any job anywhere would do. The trouble was that all the prospective employers took one look at her CV and immediately dismissed her as over qualified.

'Look, sweetheart,' one helpful woman at an insurance firm had pointed out, 'we are looking for a data inputter. With your qualifications, you'll do this for six weeks then leave as soon as something better comes along. We need someone more long term than that.'

Skye had tried to protest, insisting she would be more loyal. Yes, if a better opportunity came up then she'd go for it, but it had been four months since she'd graduated with a Master's Degree in English Literature and there was absolutely nothing on the horizon. Not even a glimmer of a job for which she was genuinely well-suited. The trouble was that knowing vast amounts about Romantic poets didn't seem to qualify you to do anything at all. And it didn't help that she invariably became tongue-tied and hot cheeked whenever she tried to plead her case.

The sinking feeling in her stomach had been deepening as the weeks had gone past and the last remnants of her student loan had dwindled in her bank account. Frankly, she'd have been more successful if she'd skipped university altogether and taken a college secretarial course. Or learned a trade like plumbing. People always needed plumbers. They didn't need graduates who could quote Keats and point out the symbolic hyperbole of a sonnet. She wondered, and not for the first time, whether she'd made a mistake in coming home. At least in Edinburgh there had been more prospects of employment. In deepest darkest Perthshire there were very few.

She swirled the murky dregs of her coffee around the cup with her spoon. Skye had been nursing the drink for the better part of an hour; sooner or later, she was going to have to buy something else or leave. But there was simply nowhere to go.

'"Human misery must have a stop,"' she quoted softly to herself, '"there is no wind that always blows a storm."'

'Lady Gaga say that in one of her songs?' interrupted the waitress, bustling over to clear away her cup.

Skye coughed awkwardly. She wasn't entirely sure she knew who Lady Gaga was.

'Er, no,' she answered, cursing the warmth she felt lighting up her cheeks, 'Euripides.'

The woman squinted at her. 'Didn't he win Eurovision?'

Skye couldn't think of an answer that seemed appropriate so just smiled half-heartedly.

'You're not looking for help at the moment, are you?' she asked hopefully.

All she got was a sympathetic look in return. 'Sorry, love.'

'Worth a try, I guess,' Skye murmured, pulling out a few small coins and handing them over.

The woman pocketed the money. 'Aye. Don't stop trying, neither. There's jobs to be had for those that look for them.'

Except I am looking, Skye wanted to scream. All I'm doing is sodding looking. Instead, she just nodded politely and scooped up her bag. Maybe it was time to head home after all. It was just possible the postman had already been and there'd be some replies to the many job applications she'd sent out. She'd already checked her email and there had been nothing there other than a plea from an old friend saying she was stuck in the south of France having had all her belongings stolen. She'd begged for a 'small' money transfer to help her get home. Unfortunately for the author of the email, Skye knew her friend was actually currently in Manchester and about to get married. She was most definitely not stranded in the Dordogne. Skye had sent her a quick text informing her that her email account had been hacked – and wondered for half a moment whether scamming unwitting internet users was truly a profitable business.

The rain, which had been little more than a steady drizzle while Skye had been inside the coffee shop, suddenly seemed to pick up force as soon as she stepped outside. She lifted her face upwards, letting the raindrops pelt her bare skin. Despite the shiver of cold in the air and the oppressive clouds overhead, there was something refreshing about walking in the wet. Of course, it would be more fun if there wasn't a hole in the sole of one of her trainers, meaning that the first puddle she inadvertently landed in caused her entire foot to become squelching and wet, but at least it was making her feel a little more alive. In fact, her clothes ended up so sodden that it almost didn't matter when a car drove too quickly round the bend where she was waiting to cross the road and splashed her head to toe in a tsunami of dirty water. By the time she finally made it home, she was completely drenched.

Putting her key in the lock and wiggling it just enough to manage to get the untrustworthy mechanism to turn, she pushed open her front door and stared hopefully down at the doormat. There was indeed a collection of letters. Bending down, she picked them up and quickly scanned each one. Something from the phone company for her dad, an official-looking notice from *Reader's Digest* for her mum, a damp catalogue which seemed to suggest her life wouldn't be complete if she didn't immediately purchase a garden bird-feeder in the shape of the Statue of Liberty, and two letters with her name on.

Her heart in her mouth, Skye took all the letters into the kitchen and carefully dried her hands on a tea-towel before opening the first one. She sighed deeply when she read the contents. It was from the bank, informing her she had gone beyond her overdraft limit. The charges made her stomach drop. Telling herself it would be okay, she turned to the second letter, slitting it open at the top and pulling out the single sheet of expensive-looking paper. 'Dear Ms Sawyer,' it read. 'Thank you for your interest in our company. Unfortunately this time you have not been successful...'

Skye didn't bother reading any further. She balled it up in her hands instead and threw it at the bin, landing it squarely inside.

'Well, at least I might still get a job with the New York Knicks,' she told the empty kitchen, then plodded upstairs to peel off her wet clothes and have a hot shower.

WHEN SHE CAME BACK DOWNSTAIRS, towelling off her hair, her father had come in from work and was sitting at the kitchen table reading the newspaper.

'Hello love,' he said, barely looking up from the sports' pages to acknowledge her.

'Hey. Did they lose again then?'

He didn't answer. Skye smiled to herself. He'd wallow in misery for an hour or two at the not entirely unexpected loss of his beloved football team, before shaking off the defeat as nothing more than a temporary setback. One which would no doubt be repeated again in a week's time. She leaned down and kissed him fondly on the cheek then sat down next to him and began toying with the pages of the catalogue.

The front door rattled, signalling her mother's return. She called out a greeting from the hallway then bustled in with a few heavily laden shopping bags. When she spotted Skye's father sitting dejectedly over the paper, she raised her eyebrows at Skye, who nodded in silent amusement.

'Oh well, better luck next time.'

He grunted in return, and she immediately whacked him on the arm. 'I expect a better welcome than that when I come in the door.'

He gazed up at her with a doleful expression and she laughed. He finally smiled in return and stretched up to hug her. Skye watched the proceedings with a mixture of fondness and envy.

'How about you?' her mother asked, peering round to look at her. 'Any luck on the job front?'

Skye bit her lip and shook her head. Her mother shot her a commiserative glance.

'Something will turn up eventually.'

If only she had her mum's optimism. The guilt she felt at still living at home and sponging off her parents was becoming overwhelming. Skye tried not to think about the letter from the bank and instead looked down at the catalogue, flipping it over to scan the back. Then she frowned. Something was stuck to the underside. Peeling it off, Skye realised it was a postcard with the familiar, statuesque Big Ben and the Houses of Parliament on the front. Turning it over, she read the words.

HEY YOU!

How's life in Bonnie Scotland? Still looking for a job? I'm working at a nightclub that's always looking for new staff. Money's pretty good even if

*the hours are a bit crap. I can put in a good word for you if you want some-
thing to tide you over for a few months. Let me know!!!!*
      Emma xoxo

THERE WAS a phone number scrawled at the bottom. Skye stared
down at it for a moment.

'You're right,' she said slowly, 'maybe something has turned up.'
She passed the postcard over to her mother, who looked down at it,
her brow furrowing.

'A nightclub? Skye, you've got a Master's degree.'

'In English freaking Literature, Mum. Much good it's doing me
out in the real world.'

'Yes, but...'

Skye shot her mother a look. 'I can't stay here forever.'

'You know this is your home. You can live here for as long as you
want.'

Her father eyed her thoughtfully. 'I think what your mum is
trying to say is that perhaps a nightclub isn't really the most suitable
place for you to get a job.'

Skye bristled. 'Why not?'

'Well, nightclubs are generally loud, boisterous places with loud
and boisterous people. And you're...'

'Quiet? Studious? Boring?'

Her mum frowned. 'Skye, that's not what he's saying.'

'Yes, he is,' Skye said quietly. 'And he's right. But beggars can't be
choosers and maybe it's time I stopped being so quiet and mousy,
and started standing up on my own two feet for a change.'

'Skye...'

'Surely even just being in London will make finding a real job
easier. This will simply tide me over, as Emma says.'

'Love, it's not that we disapprove of you working in a nightclub.
Of course we don't. You should do whatever you want to. It's just
that Emma's not you. She's more outgoing.'

'Which means she'll be able to introduce me to lots of people. You never know what might happen or who I might meet.'

'If you want to do this...'

Skye stared down at the postcard. A hot, zippy kick of excitement shot through her stomach. 'Actually, yes, I do.'

CHAPTER
THREE

Coop had chosen to ignore the summons. If she decided she wanted to send him out on another mission to shoot some poor couple in the heart with bolts of love, then she could damned well send him an email about it like she normally did. He had better things to do with his time, and right now they involved lying under a parasol in the sun and hoping his bloody hangover would go away.

It was ridiculous, really. What was the point in being a god if you still had to deal with the after-effects of alcohol? As soon as he felt better, he was going to seek out Bacchus and demand some answers. If the God of Wine and Intoxication couldn't prevent hangovers then Zeus should give the bloody job to someone else. In fact, he thought, stretching out lazily like a cat, he would be the perfect choice. Bacchus could spend a couple of millennia forcing unsuspecting people to fall in love while he travelled the world ensuring his merchandise was of the highest – and, indeed, non-hangover inducing – quality. It would be a dirty job, and no doubt involve a vast amount of sampling and tasting, but he reckoned he could do it. Coop decided then and there he would bring it up the next time he was at Olympus. Not that he was planning to show his face there again any time soon. He had far better things to be doing with his time.

'You know you shouldn't be here, right?' stated a voice from somewhere above his head.

Coop didn't bother to open his eyes. 'I can't think why not. The sun is shining, I've been out and done all the jobs I was supposed to do, and my head feels like it's had Sisyphus's stone thrown at it several times by an angry Cyclops. Until I start feeling better, this is where I am going to remain.'

'You've been summoned.'

'I know.'

'Coop, she's already pissed off enough as it is. If you don't turn up, the whole of Olympus is going to end up hearing about it.'

'Herm, you need to chill out a bit. Take some time off, relax, soak up some rays.' Coop sat up and eyed his old friend. 'Do you want a drink?'

'No.'

'Let me get you a drink. Aria!' he shouted.

'I don't want a damn drink,' said Hermes irritably.

'Of course you do. Aria!'

A voice floated over from the other side of the swimming pool. Hermes looked up, his eyes widening slightly at the sight of the scantily-clad nymph who'd suddenly appeared.

'My lord?'

'Aria, this is Herm. Herm, Aria.'

She curtsied prettily, dipping low enough so that the loose robe which was supposed to be covering her effectively hid nothing. Hermes swallowed.

'Aria,' Coop continued, 'get my good friend Herm here a drink. One of those purple things with swirls in and lots of ice will do. I'll have the same, but,' he added with a wink, 'make mine a double.'

She curtsied again, and left.

'Isn't she marvellous?' he murmured.

Hermes, whose eyes had been following the departure of the sashaying nymph, snapped his half-open jaw shut and refocused his attention onto his friend.

'You seem to be in a good mood.'

'It's true,' said Coop languidly, 'I've been in a bit of a funk of late. But I am indeed feeling remarkably chipper now. Aforementioned hangover aside, of course.'

'And what's brought on this sudden volte-face then?'

'My friend, I've decided to take a holiday. A long, extended holiday. You might call it a sabbatical even.'

'I see,' said Hermes slowly. 'And have you run this, er, holiday by anyone?'

'I don't need to. I am my own man.' He shrugged. 'Or god, rather. In fact, as a love god – as *the* love god – I feel like it's time to put some of my skills into more ardent practice. There are plenty more where Aria came from.'

'I feel faintly nauseous.'

Coop laughed and clapped his friend on the back. 'Join me. You must be bored of all that to-ing and fro-ing to run messages for others.' His eyes gleamed. 'Let's have some fun.'

Hermes shook his head sadly, watching his friend with the expression of someone who was seeing the deep, dark chasm of doom.

'You should probably answer the summons first. Before you make too many plans, that is.'

'She can't stop me.'

A shadow fell across the pair, blocking out the golden sunlight. 'Oh yes, she can.'

Hermes immediately straightened, colour highlighting his cheekbones. He began to cough, although whether it was due to shock or embarrassment wasn't entirely clear. Coop raised his sunglasses, noted the woman in front of him and lowered them again. Other than that, he didn't move.

'Mother. How good of you to visit.'

'Hermes, leave us.' It wasn't a request.

'Certainly! At once,' Hermes stuttered, wheeling round and almost stumbling headlong into the turquoise-blue pool in his haste to get away.

Aria, who was just entering with two tall glasses perched on top of an elaborate silver tray, caught sight of the new visitor, paused for a fraction of a second with her mouth dropping into a perfect circle, then abruptly turned and left.

'You're frightening everyone away,' Coop murmured.

Aphrodite stared down at her son, her face a frozen mask of wrath. 'Apparently I don't seem to be having the same effect on you. That's unfortunate because if you don't pull yourself together, put on some clothes and present yourself properly at Olympus within the hour then, so help me, I will not be responsible for the consequences.'

Coop raised his sunglasses again. 'What?' he asked, with a mocking edge to his voice. 'You mean you'd do something to hurt your beloved son?'

The answering look in Aphrodite's eyes would have sent many a lesser being to cower behind the nearest rock.

'I have other children. And all of them are a damn sight more responsible and trustworthy than you.'

'I fail to see what the problem is. I was working yesterday, doing your bidding. Today I am taking some time off to relax and recuperate. Tomorrow I may just take off some more time.'

'You idiot,' she hissed. 'You have absolutely no idea, have you? Do you remember the assignment in Kos last month?'

Coop frowned, as if deep in thought. 'Hmm. Kos, you say? To be honest, I don't.'

'Well, let me jog your memory. You had to shoot the couple on the beach just after dawn. You spent most of your time drinking in some dive of a bar.'

He smiled, a dimple appearing in his cheek. 'Oh, I remember now. Good whisky.'

'Maybe if you hadn't spent so much time concentrating on what was in your glass and worried more about what you were supposed to be doing, we wouldn't be in this mess.'

'I really have no idea what you're talking about.'

'You got it wrong,' Aphrodite said flatly. 'The beach was deserted and you still managed to screw it up. Do you have any idea how complicated it's going to be to straighten out your mess?'

'Mother, dearest, my aim was true,' Coop began.

'Oh, yes,' she said sarcastically, 'you hit your mark alright. It was just the wrong mark.'

He raised himself onto his elbows, a furrow suddenly creasing his forehead. 'What do you mean?'

'You shot the wrong man, you fool.'

Coop began to lie back down on the lounger again as if in dismissal. 'No, I didn't.'

In a sudden fit of uncharacteristically physical anger, Aphrodite kicked the foot of the sun lounger, causing it to collapse with a clatter. Coop, landing with a heavy thud on the ground, scowled up at her. 'That was completely uncalled for.'

'Get up.'

For a moment he considered ignoring her completely but there was a tinge of angry disappointment in his mother's eyes, which he'd never seen before. And besides, his arse hurt from dropping so unexpectedly onto the hard concrete of the pool's edge. With a sigh, he pulled himself up to standing height, towering over Aphrodite's shorter frame.

'Shoot the man on the beach,' he said finally, giving in to the inevitable. 'That's what your email said. I may have been drunk but I remember it quite clearly.'

'By,' she replied shortly.

'Huh?'

'Shoot the man *by* the beach. Not *on* the beach.'

'There was no man by the beach. It was barely dawn, Mother, the place was deserted.'

She didn't even blink, just stared up at him, a tiny muscle flickering in her cheek. Coop looked back at her, his face the picture of innocence. There had been no-one else at the damned place, just the jogger, the man with the dog and the...

He blinked. 'Oh.'

'So you didn't remember quite as clearly as you thought you did?'

Coop raised his index finger in realisation. 'The ice-cream guy. He was the one?'

She sighed. 'Yes. He was by the beach. Not on the beach. By the beach.'

'On, by, to be honest it's a very small difference.' He shrugged. 'Easy mistake to make. Besides, what does it actually matter? I'll find some other poor girl for Mr Rocky Road to fall in love with and everyone will be happy. It's not a big deal.'

Aphrodite slapped him across the cheek. 'How dare you?' she spat. 'You know very well it doesn't work like that.'

The answering look of cynicism in her son's face was clear. 'If they were meant to be together, then they would be.' He raised a hand to his stinging cheek for a moment and looked Aphrodite directly in the eyes. 'My intervention wouldn't be necessary if it was true love. Except true love doesn't exist. So whether the jogger ends up with an ice-cream seller or a local with a dog, who cares?' He shrugged. 'They'll be happy either way.'

There was the faintest slump in his mother's body. 'When did you become like this?'

'Like what?'

'Like someone who is so disgusted with the world that they'll ignore the natural order and throw every sensible thought and caution to the wind.'

'Natural order?' he scoffed. 'How is it natural if I need to shoot them for them to realise how they feel?'

'You know very well that sometimes a little push is required. You've forced the wrong two people to be together and, unless I sort out your mess, they'll be unhappy for the rest of their lives. All because of you.'

'Thanks to me,' he pointed out, 'they're now in love.'

'With the wrong person.'

'There's no such thing as the right person, Mother. It's all smoke and mirrors.'

'The stars...'

'Screw the stars. Screw fate. And screw love.'

Aphrodite stiffened then pulled back her shoulders in a dignified gesture. 'You cannot spit on everything I stand for, Coop. I will not allow it.' She took a step forward and stared up at her son. 'Present yourself at Olympus before the sun sets or I will not be responsible for my actions.'

With that, she turned on her heel and left, her back ramrod straight. Coop watched her go, a scowl marring his handsome features. She had spent too long as the Goddess of Love, he decided, and her vision was clouded by her ridiculous belief that some people were just destined to be together. She simply couldn't grasp the fact that if it was truly their destiny, his services wouldn't be required. She probably needed a long holiday too. He'd suggest as much to her later when he turned up at the seat of the gods. Of course, he was only going to appear at Olympus because, as his mother, she deserved a modicum of respect. He certainly wasn't afraid of her. Bending over, he returned the sun lounger to its original position and lay back down. There was still time for a little nap.

CHAPTER

FOUR

The trouble, Skye was starting to realise, was that it was all very well deciding to be more lion than mouse and up sticks to the big city, but the theory was an awful lot easier than the practice. Emma had stayed true to her word, not only helping her get a job in Nemesis, the same nightclub as herself, but also putting her up in the house she already shared with two other girls, Joy and Chrissie. Skye had felt welcome from the outset, even though the room she was sleeping in was more cupboard than actual bedroom, and the three of them were fun to be around. But, almost three weeks into her big move, and she still felt like a fish out of water. A floundering, flailing fish out of water.

Working at the club was fun, if bewildering. It was a vast space encompassing a range of different 'rooms', which pumped out diverse music, allowing patrons to enjoy whatever they were in the mood for. There were at least a hundred employees, many of them a similar age to herself, who worked as everything from waitresses to dancers. As the newest recruit, Skye had been designated the Chill-out Room, a small space filled with ambient music where weary clubbers could relax. Considering that the majority of Nemesis's customers went there to dance energetically or to see and be seen, few ended up in her area. Skye was secretly grateful for that; she enjoyed finally having some work to do but she found the crowds that frequented the nightclub vaguely terrifying. And that was to say nothing of the club's owner, a gruff, large bear of a man who barked out orders and stared hard at anyone who didn't immediately jump to his bidding. In her one and only meeting with him, she'd found herself completely tongue-tied and red cheeked. It was just as well Emma had already vouched for her.

Still, she got one day off a week, which she spent searching for other jobs more suited to her qualifications. Nothing had turned up as yet but she remained optimistic. Despite the late nights, she managed to rise early and use her time fruitfully. Emma, however, was somewhat baffled by her efforts.

'Skye, you need to live in the moment,' she kept insisting. 'The wages at Nemesis are fantastic, the lifestyle is beyond brilliant and you get to meet all manner of people.'

Emma's eyes had gleamed at that last comment and Skye was fully aware what kind of people she'd been referring to. Just the previous evening her friend had been flirting incorrigibly with a group of men who'd travelled in from the States on business and had come to the club to wind down and experience some of London's nightlife. She'd finally tottered home at about ten o'clock in the morning, bleary-eyed, and headed straight for the warmth and comfort of her bed.

Skye envied Emma's relaxed manner and open, easygoing nature, which allowed her to make new friends at the drop of a hat. Whenever a customer spoke to Skye, she was professional and polite but she couldn't strike up conversations like Emma. Socialising was an art form, Skye decided, and most definitely one at which she did not excel. If she was going to get anywhere in life, however, she was going to have to work harder at it.

With that thought in mind, she decided she would begin by winning over her colleagues. Life at Nemesis meant antisocial hours, but that didn't mean it was an antisocial environment. Skye might not find it particularly easy to force her way into conversations in the spacious staffroom during her breaks, but she knew she could get to know other people besides Emma, Joy and Chrissie. And the best way to do that was by baking. After all, she figured, everyone loved cupcakes, and they were definitely something she knew how to make. That was the reason why she was foregoing her usual afternoon trawl for job opportunities and concentrating on swirling the intricate Nemesis logo in icing on top of a range of chocolate, red velvet and lemon cakes.

The radio was humming softly in the background and, while she moved from one delicate cake to another, she imagined the response in her head.

'Wow, these cupcakes are amazing!' the tall, Amazonian and slightly scary-looking Brazilian dancer Marina would say. 'Who made them?'

'Oh, just me,' Skye pictured herself replying airily. 'I had some free time this afternoon.'

'Darling, we simply must be best friends straight away.' And Marina would extend a graceful arm out towards her while planting several air kisses above Skye's cheeks.

A sleepy voice interrupted her reverie. 'What on earth are you doing, Skye?'

Half turning, she spotted Joy and grinned, holding a single cupcake aloft and waving it in her direction. 'I'm creating a conversation starter.'

'Cake?'

'Yeah, do you want some?'

Joy arched an eyebrow in her direction. 'You realise that if I eat it, I'll be too busy cramming it into my mouth to talk?'

Skye hesitated for a beat before recovering. 'But when you've finished it, then you'll be happy to chat to the master baker who provided it.'

'Hmmm...' Her flatmate's response was non-committal.

'Everyone loves cupcakes,' said Skye firmly.

Joy shrugged, reached into the fridge and pulled out a carton of orange juice. 'Sure.'

Dismissing her lack of enthusiasm, Skye turned back to her sugary art work. 'I just need a way to get to know other people, that's all. You guys are great. I barely know you and you've been so welcoming and made it so easy. But I find it harder at work. There are more people and I clam up and then...' Her voice trailed off.

'Hon, you've just got to talk to them. Have a chat, shoot the breeze, chew the fat, you know?'

'Talk the talk and walk the walk, you mean?'

Joy grinned without a trace of self-consciousness. 'Too many idioms in a row?'

Skye smiled back. 'Yeah, maybe.'

'Hey, we're not all masters of the English language like you.'

'If I was truly a master of the English language then I'd be able to speak it without automatically blushing,' Skye muttered to herself.

'You just need more practice, Skye,' said Joy gently. 'Leave those cakes alone for a moment and come and sit down.'

'I need to finish these off,' she protested.

'They'll wait.' Joy took her by the elbow and pulled her onto one of the wooden kitchen chairs. 'Now, imagine I'm one of the bartenders. We're in the staffroom and it's just the two of us. What will you say?'

'Er, hi?'

'It's not supposed to be a question, Skye. Try again.'

'Okay, yes, you're right.' She took a deep breath. 'Hello.'

'Hello.'

A moment of silence passed, while Skye shifted awkwardly in her seat.

'You're going to need to say something else at some point,' Joy nudged.

Skye chewed on her bottom lip. 'Um, do you come here often?'

Joy's shoulders started to shake and her face contorted in a spasm. The kitchen door opened and Emma appeared, still in her pyjamas despite the late hour. She began to lift a hand in sleepy greeting then stared down at Joy in some alarm. 'Are you okay?'

A tiny snort escaped from Joy. She clamped both her hands over her mouth but it was clear nothing was going to prevent the explosion. A single tear rolled down her cheek before she finally erupted into gales of laughter. Emma looked completely nonplussed.

'What's going on?' she asked Skye, who was watching Joy with a look of resigned amusement.

'We're having an imaginary conversation,' she explained. 'Joy is a bartender in the staffroom at work and I'm me.'

Emma looked even more confused.

'Small talk practice,' wheezed Joy through her giggles.

A look of dawning comprehension spread across Emma's face and she grinned. 'Brilliant! Who can I be?' She didn't wait for an answer but instead snapped her fingers. 'I know, I'll be Helios.'

'The owner?' Skye squeaked. 'Why would he be in the staffroom?'

Emma shrugged. 'Maybe he's checking up on his newest recruit.' She deepened her voice. 'So, how are you finding things at our little club then?'

Skye sighed and gave in. 'They're fine. Things are fine.'

'Fine?' Emma boomed. 'Is that all you can say?'

Pushing her chair back, Skye stood up and walked back to the kitchen counter to pick up a cupcake, which she held out. 'Cake?' she asked.

Joy burst into another round of giggles.

Skye shook her head. 'This is no help.'

'I'm sorry,' Joy gasped. 'I'll be serious. Instead of the staffroom, imagine I'm a customer. Someone important.'

'And devastatingly handsome to boot,' added Emma.

'In fact, you've taken one look at me and you know I'm Mr Right. How are you going to approach me?'

'Mr Right? At Nemesis?' Skye tugged at her ponytail. 'I suppose I could ask you if you wanted a drink.'

'Go on then.'

'Would you like a drink?'

'No, not like that!' Emma licked her lips slowly and blinked. 'Hello,' she cooed. 'I'm Skye and today I'll be your waitress. Is there anything you desire?'

Skye's cheeks flushed. 'I'd never say that.'

'Just try.'

'Hello. I'm Skye and today I'll be your waitress. Is there anything you'd like?'

'Is there anything you *desire*,' prompted Emma.

Skye sighed. 'Is there anything you desire?'

Joy smiled like a predator. 'Only you.'

Skye rolled her eyes. 'This is ridiculous.' She turned back to finish her icing.

'Don't knock it till you've tried it, hon.'

'It's just not me.'

'Promise us you'll try it just once tonight. See what happens.'

Emma nodded. 'What's the worst thing that could happen if you do?'

'The ground will open up and swallow me whole.'

'Skye...'

'Fine. I promise, okay? Anything to get you two to leave me alone.'

'Perfect. And it'll be extra quiet in the Chill-out Room tonight anyway, so it'll be easier.'

Skye wasn't convinced that anything would make it easier but she was slightly perplexed. 'Why will it be quiet?'

'Haven't you heard? Orpheus are playing tonight.'

'The place is going to be rammed,' grinned Joy. 'It's so exciting. I'm going to try and weasel my way into helping backstage. Maybe I'll even get to meet Oz in person.'

'Oz?'

Skye received a light punch on the arm. 'The lead singer, of course!'

'Of Orpheus?'

Emma shook her head. 'You've never heard of them, have you?'

Skye just looked at her blankly.

'Despite your master's degree, your education has been severely lacking. I'll get my iPhone while you finish off those cakes.' She grinned. 'We've got some serious work to do.'

CHAPTER
FIVE

I t was late in the day by the time Coop finally made it to the heavy gates of Olympus. In times gone by, the stronghold had been located on the summit of Mount Olympus in Greece; however, with the advent of tourism the gods had shifted slightly to a pretty cedar and pine-tree forest further down the slopes and close to the picturesque town of Litochoro.

The sprawling complex was still carefully concealed from most human eyes by some kind of clever manipulation by Hera. It had once been a fairly simple operation but the advent of air flight, not to mention satellite technology, meant that the concealment methods had become more and more complex over the years. Hera had attempted to explain it to Coop one afternoon and he'd done his best to listen politely. She was, after all, the Queen of the Heavens. Actually it was rather tedious stuff and he would be hard-pressed now to even begin to understand how it worked.

Coop wasn't entirely sure why they bothered trying to hide it. Plenty of humans were aware of their existence; in fact, one of the reasons why he ventured into Olympus so rarely was the number of supplicants who arrived daily, asking for some boon or other.

His mother had told him patiently that if most of the world lacked faith, it was because believing otherwise would complicate their lives and muddy their understanding of how they thought things worked. In other words, knowing there really were gods on earth would create so much chaos and confusion that it was easier to maintain their existence was a myth.

Coop had barely stepped foot through the door and he already felt annoyed. Sweeping through the marble hallway was Apollo, with a ridiculously large entourage trailing after him.

When he caught sight of Coop he shouted, 'Cupid! I hear you've been a naughty little boy.'

Irritated, Coop balled up his fists and strode up to the Sun God. 'Well, you know what they say about all work and no play,' he replied evenly.

Apollo smirked. 'Are you trying to suggest that I'm a dull boy? I'm off out tonight in London with a few friends. Orpheus are playing in Helios's nightclub. If you really want to find out what fun is, you should come along. Maybe I could teach you a thing or two about holding your drink. You know, so that you don't screw up your one and only job because you're too drunk to see straight.'

A muscle jerked in Coop's cheek. Apollo leaned in, lowering his voice to a whisper. 'Are you about to throw your toys out of the pram? I always wondered why you're depicted as a naked baby. It seems those artists actually knew you rather well, after all.'

Hermes appeared out of nowhere at Coop's side. 'Your mother is waiting.'

Apollo's eyes gleamed. 'Yes, you'd better run along now.'

A growl emanated from Coop's throat.

'Coop,' began Hermes warningly.

'I'm coming,' he said shortly, using every ounce of willpower to turn on his heel and not punch the smug bastard in the face.

'You shouldn't let him get to you,' said Hermes, once they were out of earshot.

'Just because he's Zeus's bloody progeny doesn't make him special.'

'Actually, it kind of does,' Hermes pointed out.

'Whose side are you on?'

'I'm not going to bother answering that. And your mother is waiting. Let's not annoy her any further.'

The pair of them strode out through a small walled courtyard area. Harmonia, one of the spirits, was sitting on a small marble bench with a book in one hand and a brightly coloured bird resting on the other. She glanced up as they walked through. Coop sent her a wink. She smiled shyly back at him.

'If I winked at her, she'd probably run a mile,' grimaced Hermes.

Coop shrugged. 'You need to work on developing some more winning ways with the ladies.'

'And perhaps making myself look like I'm the God of Love,' Hermes said, with an envious look at his friend's golden good looks and well-toned physique.

'Believe me, I'd rather have your job. It's not all it's cracked up to be, mate.'

'And therein lies the problem.'

Coop looked up and sighed dramatically when he realised who had just spoken. 'Mother. You have developed the most irksome habit of showing up out of nowhere and interrupting my conversations.' He gestured expansively, stretching out his arms into the air. 'Come on then. Tell me off again for making a simple error, so I can get out of here.'

Aphrodite raised her eyebrows. 'Oh, it's not me you're going to talk to. I think I've made my feelings quite clear on the matter.' There was a particular edge of ice to her voice.

'So who am I going to talk to?'

She pointed over to the large double doors on the left-hand side of the hall. They were engraved with serpents and monsters, each caught in a position of frozen wrath.

'Go in and find out,' she said softly, flicking a quick glance at Hermes. 'It's probably better if you stay outside.'

'Gladly, my lady.'

Coop glanced from one to the other and back again. Then he straightened his shoulders. 'Whatever. Bring on your worst.'

A sad smile touched Aphrodite's lips as he sauntered over to the doors, dramatically pulled them open and walked into the other room. Then she followed him in.

The room was a vast, empty, windowless space with black marble floors that glinted and shone. A robed figure was waiting at the far end.

'Great,' Coop muttered, without breaking his stride.

He continued forward, walking as arrogantly as he dared. When he finally reached the figure, he pasted on a smile and waved his arm around. 'Is this supposed to intimidate me, Lord Zeus?'

The King of the Heavens stared at him expressionlessly. 'You fucked up.'

Coop blinked. 'Okay, yes, I admit it. I made a mistake. It's hardly the end of the world though.'

'Your attitude is causing your kind mother considerable concern.'

He almost laughed aloud. Kind mother? That would be the day.

'So give me my penance and be done with it,' he drawled.

'This is not about punishment, boy. This is about learning a lesson.'

'Then I am yours to teach.'

Aphrodite sucked in her breath at the faint hint of mockery in her son's voice.

Zeus didn't react to it. 'What is the issue?'

'I beg your pardon?'

'The issue. The problem. Why are you so blasé about your job and your position?'

Coop looked him directly in the eyes. 'It's a lie. You're asking me to go around changing people's lives on the basis of a lie. I've had enough of it.'

'You've had enough,' Zeus repeated flatly. 'You've had enough of making people happy.'

'What I do to them, what I make them feel, it's not real. It's not fair. On the basis of some whim, I have to make them fall in love.'

'Some whim? You know very well these are couples who are destined to be together. What you do gives them nothing more than a push in the right direction.'

'If they're destined to be together, then they don't need me.'

'You are trying my patience. People don't get happy endings without a little bit of work first. You just make that work easier.'

Coop shrugged. 'Whatever.'

Zeus's eyes turned stone grey. 'I am going to put you into isolation. Maybe that will help you appreciate how important it is to be with another person.'

'Excellent. That sounds like a brilliant idea, my lord. I've been meaning to take a break.'

'You mistake me.' Zeus folded his arms. 'You will still do the job you have been tasked with.'

'Forgive me, but I'm hardly going to be isolated then, am I?'

'No-one from Olympus or from the human world will see you, Cupid. From this moment on, until I deem otherwise, you will be invisible. You'll still be able to do your job, but no-one will see you to interact with you. Perhaps it will make you realise how devastating it can be to feel lonely. It will also make it considerably harder to order drinks.'

Coop mulled it over. 'I think I'll manage,' he said finally.

'None of your friends or lackeys or hangers-on is allowed to visit your place of residence either.'

'Hold on, that's not fair,' Coop began to protest.

'The order is already in place. And as soon as you leave here, the invisibility will take effect. You will still do your job and complete the orders given to you by your mother.' Zeus looked briefly at Aphrodite. 'Fuck up again and the consequences will be more permanent.'

'But...'

'Now go.'

Coop stared at him. This was a bit extreme, considering it had only been one teeny-weeny little error. However, despite the fact it was meant to be a punishment, being invisible opened up all manner of possibilities. He aimed for a hangdog look.

'Very well,' he murmured, then turned and walked out.

Both Zeus and Aphrodite watched him go.

'You realise he thinks that being invisible is going to be fun,' she murmured.

'It may well be for the first few days. I don't imagine he will be feeling quite so happy about it in a few weeks' time.'

'He's so immature,' Aphrodite sighed. 'And yet so cynical at the same time. I hope this works.'

Zeus permitted himself a small smile. 'Oh, it will work, believe me.'

Outside, Hermes was slumped against a wall. He straightened up abruptly when Coop came out. 'It was Zeus, wasn't it? What the hell happened? What did he do?'

Coop snorted. 'He thinks by making me invisible I'll learn that being lonely is a bad thing, being in love is a good thing, and forcing people to feel that way is even better.'

'Invisible?' Hermes started. 'Seriously? That's so cool!'

Coop grinned. 'Yeah. And I know just where I'm going to start. There's a certain Sun God who needs taking down a peg or two.'

'Er, is that really such a good idea?'

'Herm, my friend,' Coop answered, clapping him on the shoulder, 'it's more than good. This punishment may well turn out to be the best thing that's ever happened to me.'

CHAPTER
SIX

Skye smoothed down her black skirt and gave herself one final glance in the mirror. She'd already deposited the full tray of cupcakes on the table in the staffroom, managing to transport them all the way to Nemesis without any of them getting too crushed or lopsided. She was feeling good about this evening. Joy and Emma had played her numerous songs from Orpheus's last album and then Chrissie, her other flatmate, had wandered in to join them. Before long they were sitting in the kitchen using all manner of utensils as makeshift microphones and singing off-key at the top of their voices – until their next-door neighbour had started banging on the wall and shouting at them to shut up.

Despite not having heard of the band until a few hours ago, Skye hoped she'd be able to catch them singing at least one song during her break. Then she'd still have time to hop into the staffroom and enact her cupcake plan to be more sociable with her co-workers. She even felt good about her promise to the girls to try and flirt with a mysterious stranger. Things were definitely looking up.

She headed out, ready for the ambient beat of the chill-out room, when she realised Helios, the club's owner, was coming towards her.

36

'You!' he said, jabbing a finger in her direction. 'You're that new girl, right?'

Skye nodded, her tongue suddenly cleaving to the roof of her mouth.

'You're going to be in the Rock Room tonight. It's all hands on deck with Orpheus in attendance. I've got a lot of special guests coming in and I want to make sure they're all happy. You got me?'

She nodded again, feeling her cheeks heat up for what seemed to be no reason at all. Damn her inborn shyness.

Helios stared at her. 'Well, what are you waiting for?' He shooed her off. 'Go!'

Skye squeaked out something which might have been a 'yes, sir' if it had been audible and scooted off in the opposite direction. Clouds of nervous butterflies flew around her stomach. It would be beyond busy and crowded in the Rock Room. She hoped the crush of people wouldn't start making her feel claustrophobic, although at least as a waitress she'd be in the slightly more spacious VIP area.

Nervously, she opened the door to the bar of the Rock Room. The other members of staff were already busy setting up for the night. Spotting who she presumed was the head barman, she squared her shoulders and walked over. It was okay. She could do this.

She cleared her throat and he turned round. He glared at her. 'What?' he barked.

Trying not to let his unfriendly attitude faze her, Skye smiled and stuck out her hand. 'Hi. I don't think we've met before. I've been working in the Chill-out Room but Helios told me to come here tonight.'

The barman's eyes travelled down her body and up again, making her feel rather grubby. He jerked his head up to the gallery area, the only place where tables and chairs were set up.

'You'll be up there. Tables six to fifteen. Treat them well and don't get in my way.'

He turned and walked off.

'I've made cupcakes,' she whispered after his back. 'They're in the staffroom. Please help yourself.'

'Hey!' Emma bounced up. 'What are you doing here?'

Skye explained and her friend beamed back. 'Brill! We'll have so much fun! Joy's over the moon too because she's backstage in the Green Room so she'll definitely get to meet the band.'

Skye grinned. 'Lucky her!' She looked up and realised the barman had turned back and was glowering at her from under his bushy eyebrows. 'I'd better go and make sure the tables are set up,' she said hastily.

'See ya!'

Skye weaved her way up to the gallery, leaving Emma behind. She straightened a few napkins and made sure all the tables were spotlessly clean. She might not have bothered; everything was already ready. She checked for errant pieces of rubbish on the floor or chewing gum stuck under the tables. She might be nervous about having been moved out of the relative comfort of the Chill-out Room, but that didn't mean she wasn't determined to do the very best job she could.

Soon the first customers began trickling in and, although the VIPs in Skye's section didn't start showing up until just before Orpheus started their set, she busied herself making sure everyone was comfortable and happy. There was a definite buzz in the air and a thrill of electricity in the atmosphere that Skye found contagious. She bounced from table to table, taking orders and ensuring no-one was left without a drink or nibbles. She even managed a little bit of banter, joking with a group of well-heeled girls about the fact that Oz, the lead singer of Orpheus, was apparently still single.

Despite the fact her feet were beginning to hurt, it occurred to Skye that she was genuinely enjoying herself. This was better than sitting curled up on the sofa watching soap operas and reality television. John Keats had once said, 'Oh for a life of Sensations rather than Thoughts,' and, for once, Skye realised she might actually understand what he meant.

She'd only just delivered a tray of fizzing cocktails to one table when she noticed that Helios had suddenly appeared and was hovering around the entrance to the gallery. He was fidgeting with a large ring which sat, squat and heavy, on one of his fingers. Startled at the thought that the brash club owner might actually be nervous, she sidled over to get a better view of what was going on.

A large group of newcomers was just entering the room. Every single one of them was dressed to the nines. Skye gawked at them. So this was what the other half actually looked like, she thought, suddenly realising how cheap and ill-fitting her clothes were in comparison. She watched as Helios wiped his hands on his clothes then strode forward to greet them. A large man emerged from the throng, clearly the alpha male of the group. He was just a fraction taller than the others, with hair which looked like spun gold even in the darkened club. He held himself with a poise and confidence that screamed of a life of privilege, making Skye wonder whether he was some kind of celebrity.

There were a few gasps and some stifled giggles behind her. Skye half turned and registered that the group of girls she'd been bantering with were staring open-mouthed in the man's direction. She grinned to herself. It appeared that the band weren't going to be the only thing providing this evening's entertainment.

One of the women beckoned her over. 'Who is that?' she shouted over the music to Skye.

Skye shrugged, 'I don't know.' Clearly, whoever he was, he wasn't a particularly famous celebrity after all.

'He's so hot,' one of them shrieked. 'And he's heading over in this direction. Oh my God!'

'Can you find out his name?' the first girl asked.

Skye bobbed her head. Anything to keep the customers happy. Holding her tray by her side so as not to bang into anyone, she walked over to the stairs, then stood to the side as the man and the rest of his friends came up with Helios next to them.

'I'm so pleased you made it, Apollo,' Helios was saying. 'It's a real honour to have you here.'

Skye noted something of a curl to the guest's lip. 'Well, I hope you have the best table picked out for us. After all, we don't want to be bothered by the riff-raff.'

As if feeling Skye watching him, his cool blue eyes suddenly flicked over her then slid away in abrupt dismissal. She could feel her cheeks reddening in response. He might look like he could give Michelangelo's David a run for his money in terms of sex appeal, she thought, but he was clearly a prick in real life. Somehow it made her feel a bit better about herself. She straightened up and, once the group had passed, returned to the group of still-staring girls.

'His name's Apollo,' she told them.

'Ooooh, Apollo!' The shrieker smiled broadly. 'Do you think he's Italian?'

'Too blond,' said her friend dismissively, eyeing him up as he settled down in a corner of the gallery.

Noting that the customers at a nearby table had almost emptied their bottle of champagne, Skye left the gaggle of women to it. From what she'd seen of this Apollo's character, she rather hoped that none of them decided to get a bit closer to him. At least they'd be distracted when the band came on.

Busying herself with making sure all her tables had their glasses topped up, Skye forgot about Apollo. There was a single man leaning against the balustrade and staring fixedly down into the crowd. She was tempted to check whether he was allowed to be in the VIP area, but decided against it when she realised he looked abjectly miserable. It was the bouncers' job to worry about trespassers, Skye figured.

The man was wearing a poorly-fitting wig. She felt a wave of sympathy towards him. He was probably trying to disguise a bald spot or something. She asked him if he wanted a drink and he just shook his head, before suddenly grunting as if in pain. Weird. Skye decided to leave him to it.

It wasn't long before it became apparent that Orpheus were about to come on stage. There was a lot of movement on the darkened dais at the front of the Rock Room and then, abruptly, the entire club was plunged into darkness. Skye had just collected another tray of drinks from the bar and struggled to keep her balance as the crowd of people surged forward, eager to get close to their heroes. She was jostled and jabbed from various angles, and had to push her way through to get back up to the gallery just as the stage was flooded with multi-coloured lights and the strum of a bass guitar sounded.

Skye quickly delivered the drinks and moved to the side to watch the band as they plunged into their first song. It was one that Emma and Joy had played for her earlier that day – and one which the patrons of Nemesis clearly knew well, as they all immediately began singing along to the chorus. Oz, the lead singer, cupped the microphone with his hands, flexing his tattooed arms with their well-defined muscles as he lifted up the whole stand.

Emma joined her. 'Aaaaaah!' she shouted. 'Aren't they amazing?'

Skye grinned at her friend, nodding in agreement and watching the audience as they jumped up and down in time to the beat. She could get used to this. With the customers at her tables more concerned about watching Orpheus than drinking, she had time to enjoy the music properly herself. She watched awestruck as Oz leapt around the stage, feeding on the crowd's energy. What must it be like, she wondered, to have so many pairs of eyes staring at you with such adulation? Strobe lights flickered across the room and she could feel her heart beating in time to the music. The heat was tremendous and, even from where she was standing, she could see the sweat slick on Oz's skin. He used the corner of his pristine white wife-beater to wipe his brow, displaying a rippling tanned stomach as he did so.

'Off! Off! Off!' the audience began to chant.

He grinned at them and made a show of lifting his shirt further to reveal more of his body. 'Is this what you want?' he yelled into the microphone.

There was a roar of approval. The singer let go of the microphone and began to pull the top over his head, just as Skye's view was blocked by someone passing in front of her. The rather supercilious Apollo, she noted, heading off for the restroom.

Emma nudged her. 'Wow, did you see that guy?'

Skye rolled her eyes and leaned over. 'Yeah, he's a bit of a wanker, though.'

'Language!' Emma admonished in mock horror. 'Although,' she paused, 'if you don't like him, he should be the one you practise your lines with. It won't bother you if you get the brush-off then.'

Skye swallowed. It had been too much to hope that her friend had forgotten about her promise to find someone to flirt outrageously with. Emma was probably right, however. She didn't want to get to know the arrogant Apollo, so it wouldn't matter when he ignored her and her skin turned flame-red. And at least it was dark.

Sounding much braver than she felt, she heard herself answer, 'Alright, then.'

Emma punched her arm and beamed. 'You can do it, girl! I'd better go check on my tables but I want to hear all the gory details later.'

Skye nodded weakly. 'Sure.'

She turned round to see whether her customers needed anything. If they wanted more drinks she'd hardly be able to take time out to try and chat. Unfortunately, their glasses were all full, and every single one was focusing on the stage in front. Bugger.

Steeling herself, she twisted round to face the restroom door. How hard could it be? It was three sentences. Less than five seconds of her life. You want to become more confident, Skye told herself. You'll never manage it unless you try.

The door opened and her stomach lurched. Apollo emerged, a small smile playing around his lips.

'Do it,' she whispered, and walked right up to him and smiled.

'Hello, I'm Skye. I'm a waitress here at Nemesis. Is there anything you desire?'

He looked her up and down with his cornflower-blue eyes and smiled disarmingly. 'Well, hello, Skye. Actually there is something I desire.'

An alarm bell began ringing in Skye's skull. Uh-oh. Apollo leaned in towards her. He smelled of musk and masculinity. 'What I really desire is,' he said, pausing for effect.

'Yes?' Skye breathed, suddenly terrified.

'For you to get the fuck out of my way.' He leaned back, his smile disappearing. 'My sights are set a little higher than on a serving girl.'

Stunned beyond words at his rudeness, Skye stepped back. He pushed past her, returning to his group of friends. She watched as he gestured towards her and said something. There was a wave of laughter from the group as they turned towards her. Feeling sick, she blinked rapidly and almost ran down the stairs. She squeezed through the people to the bar and shouted to the barman that she was taking her break. He gave her a brisk nod, as if irritated that she was bothering him, and Skye sprinted off to the sanctuary of the quiet staffroom.

She headed straight into the bathroom and stared at herself in the mirror. Her face was flushed and hot. Don't be an idiot, she told herself firmly. You knew what kind of person he was; what did you expect would happen? She turned on the cold tap and let the water run under her fingers for a moment before splashing her face in an attempt to cool down. She grabbed a couple of paper towels and dried her skin, then took a deep breath and walked back to the door. Opening it, she realised that there were a couple of other staff members inside.

'Where on earth did these come from?' It was Marina, the Brazilian dancer, holding up a cupcake.

'Goodness knows,' came the answer.

Marina tossed the small cake down onto the table. 'Must be some idiot who thinks that eating a mound of sugar, then dancing for an hour in a cage is a good idea.'

Her friend giggled. 'Yeah, I can just picture you vomming all over Orpheus.'

'Honestly,' Marina said scathingly, 'some people are just so stupid.'

Skye closed the door quietly and walked into one of the cubicles. She flipped the lock, lowered the toilet seat, sat down and began to cry.

CHAPTER
SEVEN

Coop and Hermes arrived late at Nemesis, squeezing in behind a couple who were holding hands. Coop rolled his eyes and pointed to them, forgetting for a moment that his friend could no longer see what he was doing. He nudged him instead.

'Look at those two,' he said irritably.

Hermes jumped. 'At least they're happy,' he muttered. 'I look like I've got no mates and I'm coming to dance on my own.'

'You're wearing a disguise,' Coop reminded him.

Hermes scratched at his wig. 'Yeah, a bloody annoying one. I should have asked Zeus to make me invisible, too.'

One of the bouncers walked into Coop, shoving him against the wall. He cursed, while the bouncer looked momentarily confused, glancing around and trying to work out what he'd just banged into.

'It'd be a lot more fun if people didn't keep smashing into me.'

'I'm not sure any of this is fun,' Hermes said grumpily. 'Tell me again why we're here.'

'As I have already told you, you'll soon see,' Coop said as they walked into the Rock Room. 'Now, be a mate and go and get me a drink.'

'I can't,' Hermes replied flatly. 'You can't be invisible and have some drink floating in front of you and expect no-one to notice.'

Coop scowled. 'Fine.' He looked around, spotting the quieter gallery area. 'Let's go up there. I'll be less likely to be walked into there.'

'Up where?'

'There.'

'Coop, I can't see you pointing, remember?'

'The gallery, up to the bloody gallery, alright? That's where Apollo will be anyway.'

Hermes closed his eyes for a second. 'I'm not sure that...' He didn't have a chance to finish his sentence before his friend grabbed his elbow and began yanking him over in the direction of the stairs. A startled looking waitress passed him, obviously wondering why he seemed to be walking with his arm out in front of him.

'This is a really stupid idea,' he hissed.

'Chill out,' Coop drawled, climbing up the staircase and pulling Hermes over to the side. 'Look, Apollo's over there with all of his fawning minions.'

'Yeah, so?'

'We watch and wait.'

'Can't I just enjoy the band?'

'We're not here for the music,' was the terse reply.

Hermes leaned against the railing and stared down at the crowd. He registered a small clear voice saying something next to him and half turned, realising it was a pretty waitress asking if he wanted a drink.

'No, thanks,' he muttered.

Coop dug an elbow into his ribs and he groaned in pain. The waitress looked alarmed and he managed to grimace a smile. Fortunately, she turned away and left him alone.

'Don't do that!' he hissed.

'What? I want a drink.'

'And I already told you that you can't have one. Coop, let's just go.'

'No chance.'

Ignoring Hermes' protests, Coop turned round and watched Apollo. There had to be at least eight people surrounding him. Coop recognised a few of them as hangers-on from Olympus. None of them had any real power to speak of, probably because it made Apollo feel more important if he surrounded himself with weaklings.

Coop also noted Helios hovering anxiously downstairs, flicking nervous glances at the Sun God. Because, heavens forbid, Apollo shouldn't have his every whim pandered to, thought Coop irritably.

Even when Orpheus came on and began belting out their first song, he didn't turn back round. He was waiting for just the right moment which, fortunately, didn't take long. Barely three songs in, Apollo pulled himself up and began walking towards the men's restroom. Coop grinned to himself and pushed off from the railing. It was time to have some fun.

'I'll be back soon,' he said casually to Hermes, who muttered something inaudible back.

Coop trailed after Apollo, dancing behind him and pulling faces. Okay, it was pretty childish but it was still fun. As soon as they were in the bathroom, he set his plan into action. Apollo unzipped himself at the urinal while Coop carefully turned on a tap until it was barely dripping. He caught some of the water on his fingertip and flicked it at the urinating god. Apollo jerked and turned around as if expecting to see someone there; of course all that was visible was the seemingly empty restroom.

Coop smirked and flicked more water at him. Apollo cursed and this time looked up at the ceiling as if he expected to see a leak. As soon as he did so, Coop carefully picked up one of the foul-smelling yellow urinal cubes and flung it at Apollo's back. Apollo spun round, arcing a stream of urine onto the floor and making Coop laugh aloud.

A look of comprehension spread across Apollo's face. 'Let me guess,' he said slowly, 'the little God of Love is here to spread some mischief. I'd have expected no less. Did you really think I wouldn't hear what my father has done to you?'

The smile disappeared from Coop's face. 'You'd better watch your back, you know. You'll never be completely sure whether I'm around spying on you. You might call it mischief, but I'm going to be having a hell of a lot of fun.'

'Really?' Apollo asked drily. 'Do you think I should be worried that you're following me into the men's room to flick water on me? Frankly, my little cherub, if that's the most exciting thing you have to do with your time, then feel free. And feel free to spy on me whenever you want. All you'll discover is that my life is considerably more interesting than yours.' He zipped up his trousers and walked over to wash his hands.

'I'm going back out now,' he announced. 'You can come and join us, you know. You can have fun watching all these human girls fall over themselves to be with me.'

Coop snorted. 'You know very well that they prefer me.'

'Not when you're invisible, they don't,' smirked Apollo. He raised a hand in the air and waved it in a mock salute. 'Toodle-do, Love.'

Apollo walked out. Coop remained where he was for a moment, seething. Okay, flicking water in the toilets was an immature thing to do. He was man enough to admit that. But it didn't mean he was finished by any means. He stalked out after the Sun God, just in time to see some poor waitress's face crumple as Apollo obviously said something insulting to her.

Coop watched as Apollo sauntered back to his friends and rubbed salt in the wound by encouraging them to laugh at her. Coop's hackles rose. He wasn't above some petty mischief but he wasn't about to stoop to a level where people actually got hurt. He turned back to see the girl run off down the stairs and suddenly knew exactly what he was going to do to teach Apollo a lesson.

Spotting Hermes in the same spot where he'd left him, he walked over. 'There's something I need you to do.'

'Coop, there's always something you need me to do.'

'Yeah, but this time it's important. That waitress? The one who asked you if you wanted a drink?'

'You're not getting any alcohol, Coop.'

'No, no, it's fine, I don't want a drink. But Apollo does.'

'Huh?'

'When that waitress comes back, tell her you want to buy Apollo a drink. Send over a bottle of champagne. But she has to deliver it personally. She won't want to do it but you need to make her.'

'Why would I want to make someone do something they don't want to do? I wouldn't want to wait on that smug bastard either,' Hermes complained.

'Trust me. This will be worth it.'

It seemed an age before the girl came back to the gallery. When she did, Coop noted the drawn look on her face and felt a wave of sympathy. It was okay though: he was about to make her feel a hell of a lot better about herself. He grinned. Everyone needed an ego boost from time to time. He nudged his friend. 'There she is. Go and get her over here.'

'Coop,' Hermes began.

'Please.'

Hermes sighed heavily. 'Fine.' He beckoned the waitress over.

'Yes, sir?'

Hermes eyed her. She appeared very subdued, especially against the buoyant energy of the crowd.

'I'd like to order a drink,' he said gently.

'Of course. What would you like?'

'Champagne, please,' he said. 'A full bottle. But it's not for me.' Hermes pointed over to where Apollo was sprawled across a chair. 'You need to give it to him.'

The girl's face dropped and she blushed. 'Um, I, can get you the champagne,' she started to stutter, 'but maybe it would be better if you delivered it yourself.'

Hermes felt awful, but he could feel Coop jabbing him in his side. 'No, I'd like you to do it.'

She stared at him, emotions openly warring on her face. Then, finally, she nodded. 'Okay.'

Hermes watched her turn and head down to the bar to make the order. 'If you're doing this to torture that poor girl, Coop...'

'You know me better than that. I don't mess with innocents.'

'I don't think I've ever seen anyone look less inclined to do something.'

'Perhaps. But the "flower that smells the sweetest is shy and lonely."'

'Huh?'

'Wordsworth. He was a poet.'

'I know who Wordsworth was,' Hermes growled, as the girl returned with a tray.

She barely looked at him as she passed although Hermes carefully followed her progress. When she reached Apollo's table, the Sun God looked up at her, amused. He said something to her and her face flamed while his friends laughed uproariously.

'Coop, this is really bad.'

Coop wasn't paying any attention. He'd pulled out his little golden box and was already assembling its contents. He stepped to the side to get a clear shot and trained his sights down onto Apollo's heart. The Sun God wouldn't know what had hit him.

As soon as Coop was positive that Apollo was looking directly at the girl, he squeezed the trigger and struck him directly in the heart.

CHAPTER

EIGHT

Skye was standing in front of the table, wondering whether it was possible for things to get any worse. The man called Apollo was gazing at her with such a look of derision that she felt physically sick. She should have stood up for herself and told that man to get someone else to deliver the sodding champagne. Except this was her job, and she had to remain professional and do it to the best of her ability. But the palpable mockery in Apollo's eyes at her return for more humiliation made her wish the ground would open up and swallow her.

He raised his eyebrows. 'You're hot,' he said, licking his lips slowly. Then he cast his eyes around at his friends. 'Isn't she? She's blushing like a virgin at her first orgy.'

The whole table began to laugh as if he'd just told the funniest joke of all time. Skye wished she could think of a witty retort which wouldn't lose her her job but her mind was blank.

'The gentleman by the stairs would like you to have this champagne with his compliments,' she said stiffly.

Apollo's brow furrowed and he leaned over to see who she

meant, then looked back at her. 'It's really from you, isn't it? You're trying to impress me.'

Skye opened her mouth to make an angry reply but suddenly a spasm crossed Apollo's face and he blinked up at her. 'You're beautiful,' he said.

She stared at him. What was he trying to pull now? He patted his knee and gestured towards her. 'Come and sit down.'

Skye was unable to keep the loathing out of her voice. 'The champagne is from the gentleman by the stairs, sir.'

She put the tray down on the table and turned to leave. Apollo, however, was up in a flash and standing in front blocking her way. He reached out and gently touched her cheek. 'Don't go. Stay and have some champagne with us.'

Skye ignored him and side-stepped to the right. He moved with her. Then she side-stepped left. He mirrored her movements again.

'I'll get rid of all these people,' he said. 'Then we can be alone.'

Skye gritted her teeth. He was going to an awful lot of trouble just to humiliate her even more. Before she could say anything, however, he jerked his hand over at his friends. 'Leave,' he said, keeping his eyes trained on her face.

There was a moment of silence from behind him. Then someone snorted and Apollo hardened his voice. 'Now.'

It was clear there wasn't to be a discussion. Without further objections, all of them stood up and walked past her. A few gave her curious glances, while a couple seemed openly hostile.

Again, Skye tried to move with them and escape. Again, Apollo blocked her path. 'You keep trying to get away from me,' he said. 'But I want you to stay.'

Something inside Skye snapped. 'That's enough,' she yelled. 'I'm just trying to do my job. Just because I'm a waitress doesn't make me less of a person or less worthy than you. I can't help the fact that I blush. I guess it means that I have feelings. Except you wouldn't know anything about that, would you? Clearly, the only feelings you've ever had have been of puffed up self-importance. You think that because you've got money you're better than me. You think that because you've got good looks, everyone should fall down at your feet and worship you. Well,' she paused for a moment then looked him straight in the eye, 'well, screw you.'

For a heartbeat, Apollo didn't speak. Then he leaned in towards her, until his face was almost touching hers. 'You're magnificent.' And he planted his lips onto hers.

Skye jerked up her knee and slammed it with all her might into his groin. He doubled over in pain. Within a flash, Helios was there, glaring at her. 'Get your stuff and get out,' he snarled. 'You're fired.'

Apollo moaned something. Skye stared down at him and up at Helios. Then she gathered the very last scraps of her dignity and walked out.

THE NEXT MORNING, Skye lay in bed and stared at the peeling floral wallpaper. Her adventure in the Big Smoke had ended in abject failure. It was ironic, she figured, that in finding her voice and her spirit she'd managed to end up getting herself sacked from her job.

It had taken the security staff at Nemesis all of five minutes to escort her to her locker to collect her stuff and then shove her out onto the street. She turned over listlessly. She'd just have to go home with her tail between her legs. Her parents were too kind to say 'I told you so', but she knew that's what they'd probably be thinking.

Skye hugged her knees to her chest and sighed. Well, being a waitress was only ever a temporary option anyway, she told herself. Something else would turn up soon.

The doorbell rang. Skye ignored it and curled up into a tighter ball. A moment later, it rang again. She swore to herself. Aware that her flatmates had enjoyed a much later night than she had, she pulled herself out of bed and padded downstairs, wrenching the door open and blinking out into the bright sunshine.

'What?'

There was a teenager standing in front of her, thrusting out a huge floral display. Skye stared at it uncomprehendingly.

'Flowers for you,' he trilled.

They're obviously not going to be for me, Skye thought irritably, taking the heavy bouquet and scribbling her signature on a piece of paper before closing the door and taking them into the kitchen. The bloody thing weighed a ton. It contained all manner of roses: deep succulent reds, delicate pinks, sunny yellows. While she'd been traipsing unhappily through the streets of London, someone else had clearly garnered themselves a rich admirer. She shrugged and began looking for a vase to put them in. All she found in the cupboards was one small chipped glass affair, so she ended up separating the flowers into all manner of receptacles, from an old Pepsi bottle to a grubby but tall mug. Then she stood up to go back to bed and return to both her duvet and her misery.

Before she had taken three steps there was a muffled ringing sound from her bag, which she'd dumped in a corner of the kitchen. Hoping it wasn't her parents calling to check up on her, she dug the phone out and looked at the screen. Unknown number. Great. It was probably someone cold-calling to sell insurance or something else that she couldn't afford. She hit the green answer button and held it up to her ear.

'Did you get my flowers?' a deep voice asked.

Skye held the phone away from her face and stared at it. The voice spoke again. 'Hello? Can you hear me?'

Slowly, she brought it back to her ear. 'Who is this?'

'Apollo, of course. Did you get the flowers? I hope you like roses. I wasn't sure if you would or not.'

Skye hung up. How in the hell had he found her number? And more to the point, why was he calling and sending her flowers?

The phone rang again. Skye looked at it for several moments, then answered it again.

'We got cut off,' Apollo said. 'Are you okay?'

Skye found her voice. 'How did you get my number? And my address?'

'Helios gave it to me, of course. Would you like to meet me for lunch?'

'What?' she screeched. 'How dare he give out personal information right after firing me! There must be laws against that kind of thing.'

'I'm sorry you lost your job,' said Apollo solicitously. 'But you're better than that anyway. And now you're not working, you'll be able to spend more time with me.'

Skye hung up again. The whole world had gone crazy. Any minute now she was going to wake up and realise all this was just a terrible dream. She pinched the skin of her arm. It hurt. Bugger.

The phone rang once more. She answered it and immediately began shouting. 'Stop calling me! I don't want anything to do with you, do you understand? I don't know what it is you think you're doing but you can't mess with people's heads like this.'

'Ms Sawyer?'

Skye's mouth dropped. It wasn't him. 'Er, yes,' she said cautiously, her stomach dropping in horror.

'This is Love and Associates calling. We received your CV via a recruitment agency.'

Her eyes widened. 'You mean Pendleton's?'

'Yes, from Pendleton's. We were quite impressed at your background.'

Skye couldn't keep the scepticism out of her voice. 'I'd have thought Master's Degrees in English Literature were two a penny.'

'Oh, quite the contrary,' said Coop, scribbling down English Literature on a piece of paper and holding it up for Hermes to see. 'We often find that English graduates have a lot to offer.'

Skye blinked. Was this for real? If it was, and she'd answered the phone like that...

'I'm sorry. When I answered I thought you were someone else.'

'Oh, that's quite alright. It happens all the time. Now,' he said, looking at Hermes' own written response and grimacing, 'we were wondering whether you were still looking for a position.'

Skye sat down heavily on a nearby chair. 'What kind of position?' she asked cautiously.

'Personal assistant for a client of ours,' Coop said, keeping his fingers tightly crossed. 'A writer. He's a bit of a recluse. It's likely that you won't even see him as he likes to keep himself to himself. Nevertheless, he's looking for someone to help him out. Sort out bills, do some typing, that kind of thing.'

For a moment, Skye didn't reply. Was it possible that at the very moment when she'd thought all was lost, she had been saved by pure providence?

'Ms Sawyer?'

She took a deep breath. 'It sounds … nice,' she said. That was an obvious understatement. It sounded more than nice, it sounded perfect. 'Is it in London?'

'Ah, no,' replied Coop. 'It's in Greece, a live-in position. That won't be a problem, I trust?'

Skye's heart sank. In Greece? Where she didn't speak the language? It would be even harder there to make friends than it was here. She should have known it was too good to be true. She opened her mouth to decline the offer, when the doorbell rang again.

'Sorry,' she apologised, 'there's someone at my door. Would you mind terribly if I called you back in five minutes?'

'No problem. In fact, I'll call you back.' Coop hung up.

Hermes was watching the seemingly floating phone through narrowed eyes. 'Is she going to bite?'

'I'm not sure,' Coop answered. 'If she does though, it'll be perfect.'

'In what way?'

'She'll come to my home and live there. My darling mother and the King of Heavens have expressly forbidden anyone from Olympus from visiting, which means that Apollo, who is now madly in love with her, will be driven insane at not being able to see her.' The satisfaction in Coop's voice was obvious.

Hermes remained doubtful. 'But you're invisible. Won't she think that's a bit strange?'

Coop dismissed his reservations. 'I'll work around it. She'll never know. The shy and reclusive Ms Sawyer will get a job, a wage and a good reference when I'm done with her so she can go on her merry way and be happy. And Apollo will be tortured at every turn to know that she's with me.'

'If Aphrodite finds out...'

'She won't,' Coop said confidently. 'Apollo is too arrogant and concerned with his self-image to want to tell anyone he's found "the one" until she's actually in his arms. And that will never happen.'

'If the girl doesn't agree, then this is all for naught.'

'She'll say yes. I can feel it in my bones.'

Skye, meanwhile, had opened her door and was staring unhappily at the man on her doorstep. Apollo had obviously decided that sending flowers wasn't enough. This time, he'd come in person.

'Hello, my darling,' he said throatily.

Skye moved to shut the door in his face, but he jammed it open with his foot. 'You can't escape me, you know. I won't rest and I won't leave you alone until you are mine.'

She gazed at his handsome face. He looked – bizarrely – like he was telling the truth.

'If you don't leave, I'll call the police,' she said, with more conviction than she actually felt.

Apollo laughed. 'Don't you know who I am? The police can't stop me.'

The worst thing was, Skye reflected, that she believed him. She had no idea who he really was but something about him emanated a sort of shivering power. The kind that made her want to hide under the bed. She thought quickly, then made a decision. Why the hell not?

'Okay,' she said. 'But I'm busy today. Let's meet tomorrow instead.'

'I'm not going to wait that long,' Apollo uttered implacably.

'If you want to spend time with me, then you'll just have to.'

He clasped his chest. 'You leave me no choice, my lady. Tomorrow it is.' His eyes glinted for a moment. 'But before I go, you must grant me one kiss.'

'No.'

'I won't leave without it.'

Skye sighed. She'd never see him again, and if it meant he left her in peace...

'Fine.'

Apollo smiled as if there had never been any doubt that she would grant his request. He leaned in, his lips touching hers and his hand curving round her waist. Skye felt his tongue pushing against her lips and tried not to recoil. After a few moments, she pulled away.

A smile lit his perfectly sculpted lips. 'I knew you'd be a great kisser,' he said.

She tried to avoid rolling her eyes. Given that she'd stood stock still and not moved a muscle, she'd hardly provided him with a passionate clinch.

'You said you'd leave me alone now.'

Apollo's eyes smouldered. 'Only until tomorrow.'

Skye forced her mouth into a vague semblance of a smile. 'Of course.'

'Adieu, sweet princess.'

'Goodbye,' Skye replied and firmly closed the door.

The telephone rang again. This time she practically ran into the kitchen and scooped it up. 'Hello?'

'Yes, this is Love and Associates calling again,' said Coop. 'Have you made a decision? I realise it's very short notice but our client is rather desperate.'

'I'll take it,' Skye said, throwing all caution to the wind. 'But only if I can leave tonight.'

The corners of Coop's mouth turned up. 'Excellent,' he purred. 'We'll send a car around seven o'clock to take you to the airport. Goodbye Ms Sawyer.'

Skye put the phone down. If someone had told her yesterday morning when she was in here baking a few cupcakes that she'd be moving to Greece today, she'd have thought they were crazy. She blinked rapidly. Everything was happening so fast. Then she glanced at the clock on the wall and realised that if she was going to pack she had better get a move on.

CHAPTER
NINE

By the time she finally arrived at the palatial mansion in Greece where she was going to live and work, Skye felt incredibly weary and travel-worn. It had been difficult saying her farewells to Chrissie, Joy and Emma. Emma in particular had been sceptical about the job. 'But you don't know anything at all about this man!' she'd protested. 'What if he turns out to be some kind of serial killer stalker?'

Skye had refrained from pointing out that she'd already found her own stalker right here in London and merely murmured that it was a great opportunity which had come along at just the right moment. Joy was adamant she could get Helios to change his mind about sacking her but, the more her friends protested that she was being rash and putting herself in danger, the more determined Skye had become to see it through. It might have been a coincidence that she'd been offered this job only hours after losing her last one, but she wasn't about to look a gift horse in the mouth. Besides, Skye had to admit, she'd been treated like royalty from the moment the shiny limousine had pulled up outside their small London terrace.

She was driven directly to the airport where there was a first-class ticket to Athens waiting for her. And as soon as she emerged from the bustle of immigration and customs, there was another driver waiting to collect her. It was a long drive and, as darkness had already fallen by the time she clambered into the car, she'd been unable to work out which direction they were travelling in. However, the car was thoughtfully equipped with a mini-bar and television screen and the journey had been more than comfortable.

She attempted to engage the driver in stilted conversation about her new employer, but he said that he'd never met him: this was a last-minute contract job. That made Skye feel rather nervous although she reminded herself of Shakespeare's words in *Macbeth*: 'Screw your courage to the sticking place and we'll not fail'. Of course, the tragic Macbeth's success had been famously short-lived but that didn't mean the sentiment should be ignored.

The driver helped her take her luggage into the house and then left. Despite the fact that the place was bathed in warm orange lights, it seemed entirely deserted. Skye wandered from room to room until, finally finding a large living room area complete with vast leather sofas and a carefully positioned chaise longue, she came across a note.

WELCOME.

Please make yourself at home as much as possible. Help yourself to food from the kitchen. I have taken the liberty of making you a small snack in case you are hungry after your long trip. There is a bedroom for you down the hall – third door to the right. You have free access to the premises apart from the east wing, which I must ask you not to enter. I value my privacy and require peace and quiet in which to work.

KAMADEVA

. . .

THE WORDS WERE ETCHED in ink in an elegant looping script. Skye spent some time reading and rereading the note. Kamadeva was certainly an unusual name. She wondered whether her new employer was of Indian descent. Despite Love and Associates' warning about his reclusive nature, Skye was surprised he'd not appeared to greet her. She had no way of even knowing whether he was in the house or not.

Shrugging to herself, she wheeled her luggage down the corridor to her bedroom. The floor beneath her feet was cool marble, without a speck of dust in sight. She felt like she was in a luxurious five-star hotel rather than someone's home. Even so, she was stunned when she cautiously pushed open the door to her room. She'd suspected it was going to be a far cry from her cupboard at Emma's place in London, but nothing had prepared her for this. That whole house could have fitted into this room.

She stared around, mouth half open. There was a huge king-size, four-poster bed, with billowing silk sheets hanging down from the wooden frame and plump pillows atop a pristine white coverlet. Taking a step forward, Skye realised it was embroidered with birds, bees and butterflies, each one apparently individually hand-crafted because no two were alike. She traced her fingers over its soft, smooth surface and took in the rest of the room. There were gigantic splashes of colour from the artwork on the walls and beautiful teak furniture. As well as the door through which she had entered, there were two others on opposite sides. Skye opened the first one and entered an en-suite bathroom, tastefully tiled in matte black, with a huge old-fashioned bathtub and rain shower. The second door led into a walk-in wardrobe. Skye glanced ruefully down at her suitcase. Her small wardrobe would look rather pathetic hanging up in there.

Leaving her bag, she wandered onto the balcony and peered down. The first thing she saw was the turquoise-blue of the swimming pool, illuminated by cleverly placed lighting. Skye wondered whether she'd be allowed to use it. She'd not brought a costume with her though, so it probably didn't matter. She bit her lip and stared out over the gardens. Whoever her new employer was, he certainly wasn't short of a bob or two.

Coop, hovering in the doorway, watched her lean over the balustrade and rest her face in her hands. He'd grinned to himself when he saw her reaction to the room and was glad he'd picked out the best guest suite for her. He felt less happy when he caught her glancing at her suitcase and guessed her thoughts. He'd have to arrange for her to buy some new clothes. Maybe he could get a tailor to come up next week and take her measurements. As much as he was doing this to get his own back on Apollo, he was determined Ms Sawyer wouldn't suffer any more as a result of his actions. When she turned round and headed back to her suitcase, he quietly left to allow her the privacy she thought she already had.

THE NEXT MORNING Skye woke up early. Despite being in a new bed, she'd slept remarkably well and felt refreshed and ready to face whatever the day might bring. Determined to give her Mr Kamadeva a good first impression, she showered quickly then pulled on the smartest clothes she owned – a suit she'd bought from the high street at considerable expense for all the interviews she had mistakenly thought she'd be attending. Then she headed out.

The mansion was quiet and peaceful and nothing seemed to have been disturbed from the night before. Frowning, she wandered into the living room, but it was as empty as everywhere else. Seeing a set of stairs which she'd not noticed the evening before, she walked down, feeling distinctly nervous. Her heels clicked on the marble flooring, somehow making the whole place feel even emptier. There was a small door at the foot of the staircase so she reached forward and opened it, blinking as the morning sun immediately sprang into view. Realising she must be entering the pool area, she spotted a small table set up with a coffee pot, a jug of orange juice and various breakfast items. But there was still no sight of anyone else.

There was a small note folded up on one of the plates. Skye picked it up and read its contents.

Ms Sawyer,

Please enjoy your breakfast. When you are finished, there is a list of errands upstairs in the kitchen which I'd like you to run for me. The rest of the day is yours to do with as you see fit.

Kamadeva

Huh. So her mysterious employer still wasn't deigning to show his face. Maybe he was just a bit shy. She could certainly relate to that. Skye gulped down a croissant and quick coffee, then headed back upstairs, leaving the warm golden sunshine for another time.

There were five items scrawled in the same handwriting on a sheet of heavy cream paper, next to which sat a brand-spanking, new laptop. First on the list, she had to ensure the kitchen was fully stocked. A set of car keys had been left for her, along with instructions for how to get to the nearest town. There was nothing to suggest what Mr Kamadeva wanted the kitchen stocked with, so she'd just have to guess. Pulling out a drawer, she found a notepad and pen, then went round the kitchen methodically, opening every cupboard as well as the vast fridge freezer, and making a note of everything she saw there. She didn't find anything that suggested her employer was Indian – all the food and left-over items seemed to suit expensive European tastes. There were some oysters which, when she sniffed them, smelled decidedly off. Skye had never eaten oysters in her life but she was pretty sure they weren't supposed to reek of rotting flesh. The fridge also contained some squashed strawberries, over-ripe figs and dark chocolate. There was a particularly pungent cheese lurking at the back, too. Skye didn't recognise it and there wasn't a label, so she'd just have to do her best to source it.

She was halfway out the door when a thought occurred to her.

The note last night had said there was a snack prepared for her. Unless that had been a lump of dark chocolate and a glass of wine, there was nothing else she'd come across that was actually edible. And yet this morning she'd dined on fresh orange juice and a croissant which tasted as if it had just come out of the oven. So why was there no further evidence of real food like that in the kitchen? Puzzled, Skye scratched her head then decided she was over-thinking things. The orange juice and bread were probably all that was left in the house; if she'd had her pre-prepared snack the night before, that was probably what she'd have been eating.

Coop watched her go, grinning merrily to himself. He'd deliberately given her a list of things to do which would take her ages to complete. The shopping was the easiest, and even then he was fairly certain she'd spend the whole day trying to locate the cheese. The local market didn't tend to go in for such speciality items. But as long as little Skye Sawyer was busy, she wouldn't waste too much time worrying about her invisible employer. He'd have quite enjoyed tailing her to see how she got on but unfortunately his mother had already sent orders about three jobs he had to complete that day. It was annoying because he'd hoped to check on Apollo and see how he was doing now that his little lovebird had flown. It was probably just as well though. Coop doubted he'd be able to resist telling the god that Ms Sawyer was living with him; it would be more painful for Apollo to experience total loss and devastation before the searing hurt of jealousy.

'Love is a cruel mistress,' Coop said aloud, before smiling again and amending his statement to, 'Love is a cruel master.'

It took Skye ages to work out how to open the garage. She spent what seemed like forever hunting around in the darkness before she found the light switch, then she had to open the door so she could drive out. At least she located the nearest town easily enough but it took half an hour to find somewhere to park Mr Kamadeva's monstrosity of an SUV. He clearly wasn't someone who worried too much about the environment, she thought sniffily, when she finally found a space large enough.

Things didn't improve when she located the shops and the local market. She managed to get figs and strawberries easily enough, along with some orange juice, milk and coffee. But she couldn't find the sodding cheese for love nor money and, whenever she tried to ask anyone, they looked at her in alarm when they realised she didn't speak a word of Greek and backed away. Irritated with herself for not using the internet to find out what cheese was in Greek before she left the house, she eventually gave up and returned defeated to the car, only to find a motorcyclist had parked next to her and somehow managed to scrape its handlebars along the SUV's gleaming paintwork.

Wetting the edge of her sleeve with saliva, Skye tried to rub off the mark, but only seemed to make it worse. Her heart sinking at the thought of telling the boss she still hadn't met that she'd ruined what was probably his pride and joy, she clambered back into the car and drove off, momentarily forgetting she was supposed to drive on the other side of the road and almost taking out an elderly cyclist. Cheeks reddening in embarrassment as he gesticulated at her in a fashion which left absolutely no doubt as to its meaning, Skye felt utterly crushed.

By the time she found her way up the winding road and through the hills to Mr Kamadeva's house, her shoulders were slumped and she could feel a hard lump of tears building up inside her chest. Skye threw the keys back down onto the kitchen counter, where they landed with a clatter, and began to pull out the rotting food from the fridge to make way for the new stuff, cursing aloud all the time.

Coop, returning from the last of his mother's tasks, took one look at her dejected frame and reached out for her without thinking. He only just managed to draw back his hand in time before it connected with her cheek. The list he'd given her had been intended to occupy

EROS

her time and make her feel needed, not to upset her. He was so absorbed in watching her and wondering what he could do to make her feel better that he almost jumped out of his skin when the phone in his pocket began to ring.

Skye, hearing the ring from right behind her, jerked her head up and banged it painfully on the roof of the fridge. Yelling in pain, she twisted around, assuming that the mysterious Mr Kamadeva was there. But when she looked, the kitchen was empty and the ringing had stopped abruptly. An oddly appealing smell of earthy cedar lingered in the atmosphere.

'Mr Kamadeva?' she called out. 'Hello?'

There was a thump from another room. Skye followed the noise, her eyes narrowing. It wasn't possible that the billionaire had run away because she was about to turn around and see him, was it? Skye was shy – but even she wasn't as bad as that. Was anyone?

She felt an uncomfortable prickle across her shoulders and down her spine. Everything about this just felt wrong. Perhaps she'd made a huge mistake by coming here. She wandered through every room, peering into each one, until all that was left was the large door leading to the forbidden East Wing. Skye pressed her ear against it, but whatever – or rather whoever – had been making those noises and owned that phone had fallen completely silent.

Coop watched her warily, wondering what she was thinking. Her usually smooth forehead was furrowed and his hand itched to lean over and massage away the creases. Thank goodness he'd managed to turn the phone off before she'd turned around. After twenty-four hours, he didn't think Ms Sawyer was quite ready to believe she was living with an invisible god.

When she gave up, and walked back off to the kitchen, he quietly opened the door to the east wing, walked inside and pressed re-dial.

'Hey,' complained Hermes when he answered, 'what gives? You hung up on me!'

'I was with Skye,' Coop said.

'Who?'

He shook his head slightly. 'Sorry, Ms Sawyer. I was with Ms Sawyer. She heard the phone and obviously realised someone was there.'

'So she knows you're invisible?' asked Hermes, aghast.

'No, she was turned the other way,' Coop explained. 'Look, just don't call me in the future, okay? I'll call you.'

'Fine,' his friend said, with an obvious note of hurt in his voice.

'I just don't want her to think she's going crazy, that's all.'

'You know the easiest way to manage that would be for you not to live with her. She's going to catch on sooner or later, Coop.'

'How on earth is she going to do that? Who would believe they're living with the Invisible Man?'

Hermes sighed. 'I'm just saying I think this is a bad idea.'

'You've already said that,' Coop responded, 'several times. Anyway, what were you calling about?'

'I thought you'd want to know what was going on with Mr Sunshine.'

'Apollo?'

'Who else? He went round to your girl's house this morning and pretty much went crazy when she wasn't there. He's got half of his minions out looking for her. They'll trace her to that flight sooner or later.'

'Yeah, that doesn't mean he'll work out she's with me, though. I want him to enjoy the feeling of desperation that she might have disappeared before I move on to phase two.'

'Do I want to know what phase two is?'

'Probably not,' said Coop cheerfully. 'One more thing before you go, though, Herm.'

'What?'

'She's not my girl. She's just a means to an end.' And with that, Coop hung up.

CHAPTER

TEN

The next day, Skye prepared her own breakfast and sat eating it at the large kitchen table rather than taking it down to the pool. She was here to work, she told herself firmly, not enjoy the Greek weather and laze around as if she were on holiday. Mr Kamadeva had left her a new list of things to do, which she glanced over as she ate.

To begin with, there was a pile of yellowing handwritten letters in some incomprehensible language which he had asked her to type up. They sat on the table, at least an inch thick. Skye wasn't bad at touch-typing but it would take her at least the entire morning to complete the lot. After that, she was to bid for an ancient samurai sword which was going under the hammer at Sotheby's in England. Finally, she had to purchase a plot of land in Sicily.

Deciding to prioritise, Skye figured she could work on the typing at any time and that the auction wouldn't take place for at least another three hours, so the land purchase would probably be the best starting point. When she opened up her laptop and searched for it, however, she discovered it was an area of particular historical significance. There wasn't much visible on the land now, other than some very old stones marking out the site of an ancient temple, but the Italian government were trying to buy it themselves to preserve it for future generations.

She wrote out a note for her employer, detailing what she'd found out about the place and advised him that it might be worth reconsidering his purchase. Then she took the laptop into another room which was set up as a study and started on the typing.

A few hours later, her fingers starting to cramp, she took a break and returned to the kitchen to make a coffee. She saw immediately that her employer had written further instructions underneath her own note. Skye was confused. The study looked out onto the corridor which led from the east wing to the kitchen and she could have sworn there hadn't been so much as a shadow pass by. It was possible she'd been so engrossed in her work that he'd walked past and she'd not noticed but still...

Shrugging to herself, Skye read his latest words.

THE LAND IS *interesting to me. I think it would be a good site for a new resort to encourage more tourists into the area. This will help boost the local economy. Please proceed with the purchase.*

SHE FROWNED. Did he mean he was going to bulldoze what was left of the temple ruins in order to build a hotel? Unimpressed at his lack of social responsibility, she scribbled:

I AGREE *the land is interesting and the local area could do with some investment in order to boost the economy. However, as a site of historical significance, perhaps it would be best to find an alternative location for your plans.*

· · ·

BACK IN THE STUDY, she did some research and came up with a number of places ripe for development. They'd probably be better alternatives because they had improved transportation links and were more picturesque – and therefore more appealing to the tourist market. She wrote out a list and put it back in the kitchen.

When Coop came back and read her words, he grinned. He was only interested in buying the land because it used to house a temple which had been dedicated to his mother. Buying it would make her furious and he felt it was time he got a little of his own back on her for ganging up against him with Zeus. Not that being invisible was proving to be any hardship, of course. And he had to admit, he was slightly taken back that his apparently shy and mousy little house guest was taking him on and arguing the toss. Perhaps she wasn't as meek as he'd initially thought. Deciding to see how far he could push her, and have a little fun himself, he wrote down some more notes.

No. Much as I appreciate your research, this site is by far best suited to my plans. It will be an easy matter to have the old rocks pushed into the sea so that the land is cleared to build on. I think a casino would work well. We can create the Las Vegas of Europe!

SKYE WAS HORRIFIED when she read that last part. The Las Vegas of Europe? On that quiet, pretty little plot of land? Instead of the last remnants of an ancient building which had stood there for centuries? She didn't stop to think before she scrawled down her next words.

MONTE CARLO HAS that area covered already. You simply cannot destroy Italian heritage in that way. It's completely irresponsible. As a forward-thinking and respected businessman, you need to take a step back and consider the bigger picture.

. . .

WHEN SHE READ over what she'd written, she blushed. She'd only just started working for this man. She'd not even met him. And yet here she was, admonishing him as if he were a child. She considered scoring everything out and simply agreeing to his demands, but then decided the issue was important enough to make a stand. At least writing down her argument was easier than doing it in person, even if it did seem incredibly strange.

The next time she went back to see his response, all there was to read was a terse *Fine*. She gnawed at her lip, wondering whether she'd burnt all her boats and he'd decided she wasn't suitable as a personal assistant after all. Thinking about how strange the last forty-eight hours had been, Skye figured that wouldn't be a bad thing entirely, even if getting fired from two jobs in less than three days would have to be some kind of record. The elusive Mr Kamadeva, however, made no further reference to the altercation in any other missives.

It was later in the day, when she'd almost finished the typing, that the doorbell chimed, a long, loud sound that reverberated through the house. Skye scurried to open it. After not having spoken to anyone all day, it would almost be a relief to have another human being to talk to. When she managed to pull open the heavy wooden doors, she saw a slight man flanked by two younger women standing on the threshold.

'Ms Sawyer,' he said, bowing with a flourish. 'I have been sent here by a Mr Kamadeva to help you organise your wardrobe.'

Flummoxed, she gazed at him.

He explained further. 'We are to measure you up for some new outfits so that you can better meet the needs of your employer. He has suggested some lovely material which you may want to consider and a range of dresses that may suit you.'

The man waved a swatch of floaty, chiffon-like fabric in front of her. Skye gaped. 'I don't need any clothes,' she said.

He smiled at her patiently. 'Ms Sawyer, your employer wishes to help you become more,' he paused and looked her up and down, 'stylish. You should take advantage of this opportunity.'

Skye found her voice. 'Are you suggesting there's something wrong with what I'm wearing?' There was the slightest hint of a screech to her voice. She looked down at her functional black skirt and blouse. What the hell was wrong with what she was wearing?

'Absolutely not. Just that perhaps you might be more comfortable with more of a,' he licked his lips, 'range of clothing.'

Skye felt a flame of rage building up inside her. How dare he? There was nothing wrong with what she was wearing. She was damned if she was going to flounce around in something which not only wasn't appropriate to her position as a personal assistant but which was paid for by her boss. It made her feel like some kind of chattel. She firmly declined the man's offer, with as much politeness as she could possibly manage, then closed the door and marched off to her room.

Halfway there, she abruptly halted. Her eyes narrowed in suspicion. How did her employer know what she was wearing? They'd never met face to face. Skye glanced up at the high ceiling. Were there hidden cameras placed around the entire mansion? Were they in her room? The idea that she was constantly being watched sent trickles of fear down her spine. This was not good.

Coop's eyes followed her as she stomped off. The set of her back and the tight line around her mouth indicated that she wasn't best pleased. He was confused. All the women he'd had round before would have been thrilled to have a new wardrobe. Why she was so angry? She could wear whatever she pleased, but she looked uncomfortable in that cheap formal suit and he knew from the size of her suitcase that she'd not brought much with her. It was most curious. Eventually, deciding that the ways of women were a mystery, he let it go without pursuing it further. He didn't even mention it to Hermes when he phoned later on to find out what was going on with Apollo.

It was a private incident between him and Ms Sawyer, not one which should be aired to others.

'I do have work of my own to do, you know,' Hermes grumbled. 'I can't spend all day trailing around after the bloody God of Sun and Light. Sooner or later he's going to notice me. He's already in a foul enough mood as it is because he can't find the girl.'

'Come on, mate,' Coop had replied. 'I'm either out making more fools fall in love, or I'm making sure Ms Sawyer is being kept occupied. She zipped through all those tasks I left her yesterday so I had to come up with more today just to make it seem like I really need her around.'

'You mean Kamadeva needs her around. I can't believe you picked that as a name. What if she looks you up?'

'What if she does? She's hardly going to believe the truth, is she?'

'You're playing with fire, Coop. Anyway, how long is all this going to take? You can't keep her with you indefinitely.'

'It's only been two days. If I'm to make Apollo pay for being a prick, it's going to take a lot longer than that.'

'A week? Two weeks?'

Coop shrugged. 'Maybe a couple of months.'

'Months?' Hermes shrieked. 'You can't do that to her.'

'I'm not doing anything to her,' he answered calmly. 'She's got a job, she's happy, she gets to enjoy some sunshine for a change...'

'How do you know she's happy if you're not even speaking to her?'

There was a moment of silence then Coop changed the subject. 'Tell me what Apollo is doing.'

Hermes sighed. 'Oh, storming about and generally being a grumpy bastard. As I suspected, it took his guys all of about five minutes to work out she'd got on a plane to Greece. That's completely discombobulated him, you know, that she's wandered off to the motherland and he doesn't know where. I'm told he's barely slept since he found out she'd left. He even tore a strip off Helios for giving her the push from Nemesis. The man is well and truly head over heels and going completely nuts trying to track her down.'

An invisible smile of smug satisfaction crossed Coop's face. 'Excellent.'

CHAPTER
ELEVEN

Things did not improve for Skye over the next few days. She didn't catch either sight or sound of Mr Kamadeva but he left an increasing number of bizarre notes with ridiculous requests. She'd scribbled down an apology about the damage she'd unwittingly caused to his car and his response was to ask her to get him a new vehicle. The trouble was, the new car that he wanted was a 1954 Oldsmobile. There were only four of those bloody cars in the world and none of their owners were prepared to part with them at any cost. She'd relayed this back via a letter and received nothing more in return than 'Try harder'.

Her boss clearly believed that his money could buy him whatever he wanted. She wanted to scream that the world didn't always work like that; the trouble was there was nobody to scream to. Other than a few phone calls to her parents and one to Emma, Skye hadn't had a conversation with anyone who understood her for days. She'd always enjoyed her own company and not thought she was the type to feel lonely, but the strange emptiness of the mansion made her feel incredibly isolated. And there was that eerie feeling of being watched. She'd searched her own room for any sign of tiny cameras following her every move, but had found nothing. She'd done the same thing in the rooms that she frequented the most, and had still found nothing. But her fruitless search didn't dispel her sense of disquiet; after all, she was hardly a super spy who'd recognise a secret CCTV system when she saw one.

Taking the bull by the horns, she'd finally left a letter stating that she didn't feel comfortable living and working with someone whom she hadn't actually met; she didn't mention her suspicions about cameras because she didn't want to come across as ridiculously paranoid. Skye didn't like the idea of leaving an ultimatum, and she didn't want to give up on her new job quite so soon, but things were getting too weird. All she got in response was a note saying that Kamadeva would be away on business for the next week, and he'd talk to her when he returned. Balling her fists up in frustration, Skye swore she'd give him another seven days to present himself and then, if he still wouldn't come out and meet her face to face, she was packing her bags and going: job, crazy stalker and humiliation at home be damned.

She was tempted to try and catch her boss out and had even made a couple of half-hearted efforts at padding quietly along the corridor in the hope of catching him writing one of his little letters. Her efforts had been fruitless. If it wasn't for the fact she was living in rural Greece in the most luxurious house she'd ever seen, she'd think the last week was merely a daydream. Except there was no way her imagination would run to the level of luxury she was now getting used to. Through some internet research, she discovered that there was a genuine Picasso on one of the walls. She hated Picasso but having the real thing in front of her with its brash strokes and bold colours made her appreciate the painter in a way she never had before.

Of course Skye used Google to try to find out more about her employer. She ran a search on Kamadeva but, frustratingly, all that had popped up was that he was the Hindu God of Love. Right, she thought sarcastically, I've been given a job by Love and Associates to work for the God of Love who likes nothing more than to drive round in a gas-guzzling car, drink lots of wine and hide. She'd rolled her eyes and given up; clearly if he was as much of a recluse in the virtual world as he was in the real world, she'd never find out who he really was.

For Coop's part, he was enjoying having her around. She still dressed ridiculously formally and clicked around on the hard floors all day long in her silly high heels, but he had discovered he rather liked seeing her every day. Just the previous morning, he'd wandered into the kitchen to get a drink and she was dancing around and singing at the top of her voice at having finally located the cheese she'd been looking for in the market. She shook out her hair until it was all mussed up and was twirling around on her tiptoes, at one point almost careening straight into him as he leaned against the wall and watched her. He knew she was only acting with such abandon because she thought she was alone, and somehow that made the moment even sweeter.

She talked to herself all the time as well. She wandered from room to room murmuring comments, such as, 'He should be more environmentally friendly,' and, 'Maybe he was disfigured in a horrible accident.' He decided that he'd make her happy when he returned from the 'business trip' and tell her to buy a hybrid car instead of the Oldsmobile. Perhaps he could use the disfigurement story that she'd come up with and talk to her from behind a closed door to set her mind at ease. But then he wouldn't have the fun of watching her nose wrinkle and her lips purse when she read his notes to her.

At some point over the last few days he'd stopped thinking of her as 'Ms Sawyer'; now she was simply Skye. He told himself it was because he was getting so used to having her around. Considering that Zeus's missive had meant Aria had been summarily kicked out and no-one else was allowed to visit, he needed someone to provide a distraction.

On the fourth night of his supposed trip away, he was woken in the middle of the night by her calling out. Alarmed, he thrust his bedcovers aside and ran barefoot to her room. When he opened the door and saw her moaning, twisted up in a sheet on the middle of the bed, he didn't think twice. He went over and gently tried to shake her awake. She pulled away from him and thrashed out an arm. Coop grabbed her flailing limb and leaned over her body, this time gripping her shoulders and shaking her more vigorously to yank her out of whatever nightmare she was having.

Skye half-opened her eyes to find herself covered in a sheen of sweat and bathed in moonlight from the open window. Her arm tingled almost painfully and, when she glanced down, she saw that there were faint marks on her skin, which were already starting to fade away. A note of deep woody earthiness clung to the air. Part of her brain niggled at her as if in warning but, despite the vestiges of her bad dream, she felt incredibly – and oddly – safe. She closed her eyes and fell asleep again almost instantly.

The next morning the entire incident seemed as if it had been nothing more than a dream. Skye pulled on her black skirt and striped blouse, thrust her feet into her heels and wandered into the kitchen to make breakfast. Deciding it was simply too beautiful a morning to sit inside, she took it out with a tall glass of ice-filled juice and sat at the small table and chairs beside the swimming pool. She nibbled at a croissant and gazed out at the blue water, wishing yet again that she'd thought to bring a swimsuit. But how could she have known she'd have sole access to such a beautiful pool? She wondered whether she should have taken up the offer of a new wardrobe which Mr Kamadeva had offered. She doubted he'd have wanted to set her up so she could spend her days swimming, however. And if he had wanted to buy her a swimming costume or, heaven forbid, a bikini – well, that was just too creepy to consider.

A flash of bright plumage caught her peripheral vision and Skye turned abruptly to see what it was, inadvertently knocking the table and spilling the juice down her blouse. She yelped as the cold liquid soaked through the material and jumped to her feet, trying to wipe off the stain with the back of her hand.

Great, she thought ruefully, this is pretty much the only decent blouse that I've got and I've probably ruined it. Not that it particularly mattered when there was no-one around to ever see it. She had no idea why she bothered to keep dressing smartly; even when Mr Kamadeva was present, he didn't see her. Right now, he probably wasn't even in the same country and there certainly wasn't anyone else around to see that she was making an effort with her appearance. She glanced at the blue of the pool, then at the stain on her shirt and back again. What would Emma do right now? Skye smiled to herself. That was easy.

She unbuttoned her blouse and pulled it off. Then she unzipped her skirt and wiggled out of it, kicking her shoes to one side. She took off her underwear and threw the lacy scraps of material onto the pile of clothes, then stepped to the edge of the pool and dived straight in.

The initial shock of the cold water made her gasp but within seconds her body adjusted to the temperature. The feeling of the silky water against her bare skin had her closing her eyes in pleasure by the time she reached the other side of the pool. She pushed off with her feet, twisting round till she was on her back and floating, gazing up at the cloudless sky and wondering why she hadn't done this before. She stretched her arms out, starfish fashion, enjoying the buoyancy of the cool water, completely relaxed. An aeroplane was tracing its way across the sky and she remained there, watching its progress while she floated. Okay, she might be lonelier than she'd ever been in her life, but there was a lot to be said for being able to skinny dip in a private pool without any worry of being interrupted.

Coop, returning from an early morning assignment, walked into the kitchen expecting to see Skye perched where she normally was, perusing the latest list of strange things he'd asked her to do. Frowning when he realised she wasn't there, and concerned after the bad dream she'd had, he walked quietly round to her bedroom. The door was ajar and it was clearly empty. With an odd sense of disquiet, he went in, taking in the neatly made-up bed and the tidy surroundings. The sheer white curtain was flapping in the breeze from the open window so, without thinking, he walked over to tie it back. As he did so, he caught sight of Skye stretched out in the pool, her fingers gently moving through the water.

His mouth dried. The sun was glinting off the water as it rippled softly around her and her hair was spread out in a dark halo around her face. He took in the pale alabaster skin of her body and its curves. Even from this distance he could make out the full roundness of her breasts and the rosy pink of her nipples half submerged in the water. She was normally so prim and proper, it had never occurred to him to wonder what was underneath all those clothes. Now he wasn't sure he'd ever be able to forget. He watched as she turned over and began to swim with relaxed easy strokes and her lithe body cut through the water. For him, the swimming pool was usually nothing more than an ornament. He couldn't remember the last time he'd actually gone for a dip. Watching Skye made him want to dive right in alongside her.

His phone vibrated annoyingly in his pocket. He'd switched it to silent ever since the incident in the kitchen. He wasn't about to risk another near miss like that. There were others, apart from Hermes, who might call to see how he was doing with his new status as an invisible being: some out of solicitude and some out of glee. Without taking his eyes off Skye, he pulled it out and answered.

'The God of Love at your service,' he drawled into the speaker.

'Cupid, I need your help,' a sharp voice said.

Coop frowned slightly as he realised who it was. 'My little ray of sunshine. To what do I owe the pleasure?'

'You're good at finding people,' Apollo said without preamble. 'All that tracking down future lovers and shooting them thing that you do.'

'Mmm,' Coop said, as Skye reached the edge of the pool and twisted round to swim the other way.

'You will find someone for me.' It wasn't phrased as a request.

It was amazing how much her hair colour changed when it was wet, Coop mused. When it was dry, light bounced off its waves and there were red glints intertwined with darker highlights. Now it appeared a deep ebony colour, incongruent with the light blue of the water.

'Cupid!' Apollo roared.

'Oh, sorry,' Coop murmured, although he wasn't. 'What is it you want?'

'To find someone,' Apollo answered impatiently. 'An English woman. She was in London working at a club called Nemesis. Then last week she disappeared. I've had her traced to a flight to Greece but from Athens her trail vanishes. You will locate her for me.'

'Why would I do that?'

'I'll put in a good word for you with my father. Get him to change you back.'

'When has Zeus ever done what you've asked him?' The King of Heavens was not only notoriously fickle but he rarely took the advice of others, whether they were his own flesh and blood or not.

'I wouldn't ask if I wasn't desperate,' Apollo hissed. 'You really think I'd come to you for help unless I had no other option?'

'Well, with such flattery, I can't see how I could possibly refuse,' Coop commented sarcastically, hanging up the phone.

Skye swam over to the small ladder at the pool's edge and began to clamber out. Coop watched as her back turned to him while she scooped up her clothes and padded back inside, leaving a trail of perfectly formed footprints on the grey cement. Then he left her room and went back to his own chambers to have a very cold shower, completely forgetting about the Sun God.

CHAPTER

TWELVE

That night, Skye spent several hours tossing and turning before finally giving up on any semblance of sleep. She didn't know if it was the previous night's nightmare or her disquiet at feeling so alone in the great house, but she wasn't going to be drifting off into dreamland any time soon. Unable to continue lying in her bed staring at the ceiling, she got up and padded to the kitchen to get a drink of water, then wandered out to the garden to drink in the cool night air.

Skirting round the pool, she was about to sit at the water's edge when she caught sight of a small shape slinking off into the bushes. It was a cat, probably no older than six months. A smile curving her lips, she put the glass down and quietly walked after it, trying to coax it out. The animal backed into the undergrowth, large green eyes watching her balefully. It looked scrawny and skinny so Skye decided to try and crawl in to see if she could catch it. The least she could do was give the poor thing a decent meal.

She knelt down and wriggled forward, ignoring the damp earth against her nightgown. The cat remained where it was, staring at her unblinkingly. Skye pushed herself a little further in then, bit by bit, inched her hands forward, trying to avoid any sudden movements that would scare the kitten off.

After what seemed like an age, and when her fingers were barely an inch away from its fur, it stood up and stretched, then stepped forward and rubbed its head against her hand. Grinning in triumph, she grabbed it gently round its body and started backing out. When there was more room to move, Skye carefully turned herself around; the cat was starting to purr in her hands. Then, without warning, there was a splash from the swimming pool and the animal hissed in alarm, a growl building up in its throat. It pulled away from her and sped off into the night, nothing more than a streak of black against an already black night. Annoyed, Skye peered out at the pool to see what on earth had scared the cat, then sat back on her haunches in alarm.

The water was moving, small waves pulling away in opposite directions from the centre of the pool, all the way up one length, then back down again. It didn't make any sense. Skye blinked, watching the water and trying to work out what was going on. There wasn't any wind and she was pretty sure that if Mr Kamadeva had installed a wave machine she'd have noticed it by now. Fascinated by what she was seeing, Skye stayed where she was, staring out at the brilliantly illuminated pool from the gloom of the bushes. Then things got even stranger.

As she watched, the waves seemed to dissipate but the steel ladder suddenly creaked and she could have sworn she saw it move. Suddenly there was a light whipping sound and a spray of water landed with a spatter onto the hard cement surrounding the pool. Skye's mouth dropped open as first one wet footprint, then another, appeared out of nowhere, heading off in the direction of the house with short slapping thuds. For a moment, the magic footsteps seemed to stop right underneath her bedroom window and Skye's heart felt as if it were in her mouth. Then they continued onward. The small door leading up to the main house opened as if of its own accord and then closed again.

Skye remained where she was for several minutes, her brain unable to process what she had just witnessed. Eventually, she scrambled out from the undergrowth, walked over to the pool and stared down at the ground. She hadn't imagined it. There, drying on the concrete, was a trail of wet footprints. She knelt down and traced one gently with her finger. It was quite large, as if it belonged to a man. Skye sat down cross-legged next to it, watching it fade away as the water dried, and she tried to work out what she was seeing.

Several hours later, Skye was in the kitchen, flicking through various news items on the internet. She read through one then another, occasionally taking a bite of an apple and then reading some more. Taking care to breathe through her nose, she kept all her senses as alert as she could. When she thought she heard the floor creak and a light woody smell reached her nostrils, she stood up, walked to the fridge and pulled it open, looking inside. Then she swayed ever so slightly from side to side. She put her hand on the edge of the fridge door as if to steady herself, but it didn't work and her knees began to buckle underneath her. The ground rushed up to meet her and she landed with a heavy thump on the cold marble tiles.

Coop stared at her supine form in panic, not sure what had just happened. He rushed over to her and bent down, trying to lean in over her face to check her breathing. He could see Skye's chest was moving up and down but she was taking short shallow breaths as if she couldn't quite get enough air. Attempting to remember what little he knew about first aid, he moved his hands to her side to roll her over into the recovery position. And that was when she grabbed him.

As soon as Skye's hands connected with what felt like warm skin, a bizarre mix of exultation and fear rushed through her. The fact she'd been right, that she was living with the Invisible Man, didn't entirely make her feel better. Reacting quickly, she wrenched on the invisible limb, ignoring the deep grunt of pain she heard from her prey, and twisted round, hooking one of her legs round what she presumed was his torso and locking him into place on the cool marble floor. Then she stared down, realising how ridiculous she must look, hovering about half a foot in the air, even though she was actually straddling what felt like a very warm, very hard body.

'Why don't you tell me,' she said through gritted teeth, trying not to look as scared as she was feeling, 'exactly who you are and what the hell is going on?'

Coop gazed up at her in astonishment and with more than a tinge of admiration. He had no idea how she'd managed to work out he was there, or indeed that he was invisible, but he was rather impressed. He could easily escape from her tenuous 'capture', but he was enjoying the sensation of her thighs locked around his body. He relaxed and grinned.

'Bravo, Skye,' he purred softly.

At the sound of his voice, Skye stiffened and tightened her grip. 'What's the meaning of this?' she yelled, aware of the screech beginning to seep into her voice. 'Are you some kind of mad scientist?'

Coop chuckled. 'Hardly. Merely the victim of a rather undeserved punishment. Tell me, how did you work it out?'

Skye ignored him. 'Look, Mr Kamadeva,' she began.

'Coop,' he interrupted.

'Huh?'

'Coop. My name is Coop.'

'Whatever,' she dismissed. 'You need to tell me what is going on here – or else.'

'Or else what?'

Skye stared down at the blank floor underneath her. She had absolutely no idea. Now her suspicions were confirmed, she had no clue what to do next. Mr Kamadeva, or Coop, or whoever he was, didn't sound particularly upset or even worried that she'd caught him out. And if someone could genuinely be invisible, what else might they be capable of? She had a sudden vision of her body being fried and charred by lasers shooting out from a set of glowing eyes.

'Or else I'll call the police,' she said shakily. 'Let them decide what to do with you.'

'How will you get to a phone?' Coop asked, enjoying himself immensely.

Nonplussed, Skye rocked back for a moment. 'Er...'

'Let me help you.' And with one swift move, Skye felt the body underneath her twist. There was a pressure in the small of her back and, before she knew it, she was being flipped over until she was lying flat on the tiles and her imperceptible employer was sitting on top of her. She shrieked and tried to escape from beneath him, writhing in the iron-clad grip on her arms and thrashing her legs. She pulled one way then another, but no matter what she did, she couldn't budge an inch. Eventually, tiring herself out, she stopped.

'There now. Hold still, and I'll get you that phone,' murmured Coop, releasing one of her wrists and reaching into his pocket.

Skye watched, mouth dropping open, as from nowhere a mobile phone floated in the air. It moved down towards her.

'You need to dial 100 to reach the Greek police,' he added, placing the device in her free hand.

She stared at the phone, then stared up at where she presumed her captor's face was.

'Go on,' he urged. 'Tell them you're being held prisoner in a luxurious mansion by an invisible man. They'll rush straight over, I'm sure.'

Skye swallowed.

'Shall I dial for you?'

She watched disbelievingly as the buttons on the phone were pressed down and the number 100 appeared on the screen.

'All I need to do,' Coop said calmly, 'is press the little green button and you'll have a helpful operator to chat to. You can tell them everything. Just say the word, Skye.'

She gazed at the phone, realising the futility of such an action, then shook her head.

'Are you sure?'

Skye nodded. She was completely screwed. Nobody would ever believe her. She was being held by an invisible man with good taste in aftershave and soft furnishings. Her mutilated body would probably be found months from now, dumped in a Greek wasteland. She thought of her parents and how they'd react, and misery seeped through.

Coop watched the different emotions flit across her face. 'I'm not going to hurt you,' he said softly.

'You're invisible!' Skye scoffed.

He pulled himself off her body and stood up. 'Yes. I'm invisible. But it's only temporary and, believe me, Skye, I'm not a monster.'

As soon as his weight left hers, Skye sprang up and backed away. It was a long way to the front door and, even if she made it that far, he'd catch her before she took two steps outside. Wishing she'd thought this through more, she tried to inject some calm into her voice.

'So who are you really?'

Coop looked into her dark-brown eyes, realising that there were, along with the very obvious and palpable terror being displayed, little flecks of alluring green. He liked them, he decided.

'I told you,' he said, 'I'm Coop.'

'That doesn't tell me anything,' Skye hissed.

He walked towards her until he was right in front of her. She seemed to sense he was there because she immediately tried to sidle away. He grabbed one of her hands and squeezed it gently.

'Let's get a drink and I'll tell you.'

He pulled on her hand carefully, directing her towards one of the kitchen stools then, when she was seated, went to the fridge and pulled out a chilled bottle of wine. Skye watched from her perch as it was uncorked, then two long-stemmed glasses floated through the air and landed on the table in front of her.

'I don't want a drink,' she protested.

'It'll be a much more civilised way of explaining my story,' Coop murmured. 'Just two friends chatting over a glass of wine about the vagaries of life.'

'I'm not your friend. And it's not even ten o'clock in the morning!'

Coop poured the lightly fizzing liquid into first one glass, then another. 'So?'

Skye reached out and picked a glass up, lifted it to her lips and drained it. 'I don't want a damned drink.'

'Except you just had one,' he pointed out.

She stared at her empty glass. She'd not even registered her own action. What was wrong with her? Coop re-filled it then took a sip of his own.

'As I was saying,' he said, 'my name is Coop. But I'm also known as Cupid.'

Skye's brain felt fuzzy. 'Cupid?'

Coop nodded then remembered she couldn't see him. 'Yes,' he replied patiently.

'Like the cherub? The naked baby with wings and a bow and arrow?' The body she'd felt when they'd both been on the floor certainly hadn't been that of a child's.

Coop winced. 'Well, that's one interpretation. Personally I blame Michelangelo. I can assure you, I'm not a baby.'

Skye almost snorted. She could have told him that. She thought about what she'd read on the internet about the origins of the name Kamadeva. 'But you're still the God of Love?' she asked doubtfully.

He let out a bark of laughter. 'You're prepared to accept I'm invisible but not that I'm a god?'

'I'm not sure what I'm prepared to accept right now.'

'Fair enough. I can assure you, however, it's very true.'

Skye raised her glass to take another sip, realised what she was doing and placed it back down again. 'You said you're invisible because you're being punished?'

'My mother,' Coop answered caustically. 'She seems to think being isolated will encourage me to think more highly of love.'

'You're the God of Love and you don't like love?'

'"Love is not love which alters when it alteration finds, or bends with the remover to remove. "'

'"Oh no! It is an ever-fixed mark,"' Skye finished.

'Exactly.'

She frowned. 'I don't get it.'

'Neither did Shakespeare,' he commented drily. 'Don't worry, I'll show you later.'

This was getting stranger and stranger. 'So if you're Cupid, then your mother is...'

'Aphrodite, yes.' He watched her carefully. 'You still don't believe me.'

'No, I do, it's just...' Skye's shoulders sagged. 'Okay, you're right, I don't believe you.'

'Not to worry,' Coop said cheerfully. 'You will.'

Skye mulled everything over in silence for a few moments, chewing on her lip. Eventually, she tilted her head up. 'So why am I here?'

Coop looked into her face. He didn't want to tell her that he'd only brought her here to piss off Apollo. All of a sudden his actions seemed rather petty and he didn't want her to think badly of him.

'Well,' he prevaricated, 'Zeus ruled that no-one from Olympus is allowed to come and visit me. It's meant to make the isolation problem harder for me to deal with. Except he never said humans couldn't be here so I employed you.'

'Zeus? As in the Greek god? The one who's in charge of every-thing?' Skye couldn't keep the scepticism out of her voice.

'Hey,' he said, punching her lightly on the arm and making her jump. 'I'm a Greek god too.'

'This is so strange,' she said.

Coop eyed her. 'You don't believe just yet. Even with the evidence of my invisibility right in front of your eyes, you can't accept what I'm telling you.'

'Is that really surprising?'

'I'll prove it to you,' he said, jumping off his chair. He took her hand and pulled her gently in the direction of the front door.

'Where are we going?' Skye asked warily.

'To get some proof.'

Skye let herself be led. The feeling of his skin against hers was warm and the pressure on her hand was light. If he was taking her outside where she might have more chance of escaping, then he couldn't be entirely bad. But this was all still bloody strange.

CHAPTER
THIRTEEN

As soon as the door behind them closed, Skye realised something was very, very wrong. Instead of the leafy driveway, lined with orange trees and the sweet scent of honeysuckle in the air, they were standing in a large lobby. She felt a tug at her hand.

'Come on,' Coop urged.

Skye resisted, staring open-mouthed at her surroundings. Someone wearing a white coat pushed past her, clearly in a rush to get to wherever they were going.'

'What in hell?' she murmured.

'We're in a hospital,' Coop said with a trace of impatience.

'But...'

'It's a god thing,' he explained. 'I need to be here on orders of my mother, so I can transport just by stepping out my door.'

'Where's here?' she asked baffled.

'Malaysia,' he answered pulling on her hand again and this time succeeding in getting her feet to move in the right direction.

'Malaysia?' she squeaked.

A woman walked past her, giving her a very strange look. Skye snapped her mouth shut, and let herself be yanked into an elevator. As soon as she was sure they were alone, she spoke again. 'Malaysia?' she repeated. 'But that's on the other side of the world!'

'I told you, it's a god thing.'

Skye blinked rapidly. This could not be real. It simply couldn't.

'We need to hurry,' Coop murmured, when the elevator doors pinged open. 'There's not much time left.'

'Not much time for what?' Skye asked.

She didn't get an answer. Instead, she found herself jogging down a long sterile corridor, trying to keep up with the invisible force in front of her. They passed several rooms that she peered inside as they went. Each one appeared to be a ward, filled with beds and sick-looking people hooked up to all manner of machines.

'Ah, here it is,' Coop said finally, coming to one door which was only slightly open.

He entered, with Skye still clutching onto his hand. Inside there were eight beds, although only three were occupied. Coop ignored the first ones and headed straight down the room and towards a large window. Skye looked outside, gaping. There was a large car park – no surprise there – but beyond that she could see palm trees, bushes and exotic flowers. A sudden movement drew her eye and she realised there was a small monkey leaping from a branch down to the ground. It jumped along the car park to an overflowing rubbish bin, which it leapt onto.

'We really are in Malaysia,' she breathed.

'As I said,' Coop replied, giving her a gentle shove so that she was half obscured behind a curtain. 'Now, stay there and watch.'

'Watch what?'

'My job.'

'But I can't see you,' Skye protested.

'It's not me you need to be looking at.'

His hand left hers and she spotted a Chinese nurse walking in her direction. For a second, Skye stopped breathing, wondering how on earth she was going to explain herself and how she'd suddenly ended up hiding in a Malaysian hospital without any identification. Fortunately, the nurse paid her no attention; she didn't even notice her behind the curtain. Instead, she pulled across another curtain revealing a bed with a man on it. He had on a neck brace and his face was covered in scratches. One arm was hooked up to an IV line, while the other was swathed in bandages.

'Mr Tan?' the nurse asked, bending over the patient.

He murmured something.

'How are you feeling? It was a nasty car crash you had there. That road is particularly dangerous, you know. We get many patients coming in who've had accidents on it. You are one of the lucky ones, lah.'

Despite her banter, the nurse's tone was professional. As Skye watched, she busied herself around the bed, replacing the IV bag with a fresh one and checking the man's blood pressure and heart rate.

'It was raining,' he muttered. 'I lost control.' Then he switched to Chinese, saying something Skye couldn't quite understand.

Still not sure why she was there, Skye looked out of the window again. The monkey had disappeared. Disappointed, she returned her glance to the nurse – and her mouth dropped open. The nurse was sitting on the edge of the man's bed, holding his hand. Ignoring the pain, he had pushed himself up onto his elbows and was looking into her eyes.

'My name is Wei Li,' the nurse said softly. She reached down and brushed the man's cheek.

'I'm Jun,' he responded. His cheeks coloured. 'I know I look a mess right now but I promise you I'm actually a good-looking guy.'

She smiled at him. Except it wasn't the usual professional smile you'd expect to see a healthcare professional bestow on a patient; it was one which even Skye could recognise was filled with happy promise. 'I can tell. Because you are already handsome, even with those wounds.'

Skye felt Coop's hand slide into hers. He leaned in towards her, his breath hot on her cheek. 'Let's go,' he murmured.

Skye couldn't take her eyes away from the couple. 'But...'

'Now, Skye.' His tone was firm.

She let herself be led away. Coop kept hold of her hand so she knew where he was as they walked back down the corridor and into the elevator. Skye couldn't tear her mind away from what she'd just seen. One minute it was just a patient and a nurse, then the next it was as if... She blinked. That was unbelievable.

The pair of them emerged back into the hospital lobby and headed for the large glass doors. Before she knew it, she was back in the familiar surroundings of Coop's house, the front door closed again behind her.

'Well?' asked Coop's voice. 'Now do you believe me?'

'They fell in love,' she said wonderingly. 'Right in front of our eyes, they fell in love.'

'If you can call it that.'

Skye didn't hear the note of cynicism in his voice. 'What did you do?' she asked.

'I have a gun. It used to be a bow and arrow but they became rather cumbersome so I modernised. When that couple looked at each other, I shot them. And then they fell in love.'

'That's amazing. The look on their faces was so—' she paused, searching for the right word; unable to find it she settled on something more mundane, '—so happy.'

'Mmm.'

'Why them?'

'What do you mean?'

'Why those two? Do you just pick people at random and shoot them? Is it just luck they get chosen?'

Coop snorted. 'Oh no. My mother would have you believe it's written in the stars. That Fate decides they should be together.'

Skye's brow furrowed. 'So why do they need you?'

He laughed. 'I knew there was a reason I liked you. That's my point entirely. If they need me, they're not meant to be together. But according to my mother, some people need a nudge in the right direction.'

Skye sighed. 'It's beautiful. You're so lucky getting to do that. To make people happy has to be the best thing in the world to do.'

'But it's fake. I'm forcing them to feel something by shooting them in the heart. I'm taking away their free will.'

'They didn't look as if they were being forced into anything.'

'If love's not natural, then how can it really be love?'

'Coop, didn't you see the look on their faces? I've never witnessed anything so magical.'

'You quoted Shakespeare. That love is an ever-fixed mark. How can it be an ever-fixed mark if I create it in the first place?'

'But it will be ever-fixed now, won't it? They'll love each other for the rest of their lives. I could tell that just by looking at them.'

'"Love is not love which alters when it alteration finds,"' he quoted again.

'That's not what Shakespeare meant and you know it. Besides, you didn't alter love, you just helped encourage it along.' Skye wrapped her arms around her body. 'They're so lucky,' she whispered.

Coop's lip curled. 'That's what you want?'

'Isn't that what everyone wants? To fall in love? To be needed and desired and wanted by someone?'

'It's a house of cards, Skye. It's simply not real.'

'It looked real to me.'

He shook his head disgustedly. 'I thought you'd understand.'

He dropped her hand. Until that point, Skye hadn't realised he was still holding it.

'I've been doing this job for hundreds of years. You've seen it in action once, for a couple of minutes. Put yourself in my shoes and maybe you'll get it.'

'Your job is to change people's lives, Coop. Do you have any idea what I'd give to be able to do something like that? The only jobs I can get are bringing people drinks or tracking down stupid cars.' Skye realised what she'd just said and blushed.

Coop leaned in towards her and cupped her face in his hands, his thumbs brushing against her skin. He pressed the length of his hard body against hers, and Skye gasped. Then she felt his lips touch her own, feather light. He took one hand away from her face and trailed it down her body, cupping a breast.

'What are you doing?' she squeaked.

'Shhh,' he said softly, then kissed her again, but deeper this time.

His mouth became more insistent and Skye could feel her heart thudding in her chest. Her body relaxed and, without thinking, her arms reached around him. He has broad shoulders, she thought faintly, as her fingers traced the muscles on his back. Somehow the fact that she couldn't see him made her bolder, and she could feel herself pushing away from the wall and into him. His tongue flicked at her mouth, then his teeth nipped her lips. She moaned slightly, then suddenly he pulled away.

'Do you love me?' Coop asked with a casual tone.

'What?' Her senses were swirling and she struggled to make sense of the question.

'It's a simple question, Skye. You wanted to kiss me. You were enjoying kissing me. But do you love me?'

Befuddled, she searched for an answer. 'I . . . I hardly know you.'

She felt him take a step back.

'Exactly,' he said, sounding smug. 'You enjoyed the kiss and you desired me. But what you felt was lust, not love. You know why?' He didn't wait for an answer. 'Because love doesn't exist. Not real love.'

She reached out to slap him but misjudged where he was; her hand flailed through thin air.

'You're a bastard. That was a shitty thing to do.' She turned and stalked off, leaving Coop to watch her departure.

He raised his fingers to his lips as his eyes followed her. His heart was racing and he realised he'd been more affected by the kiss than he'd intended. He only felt that way because Aphrodite had pretty much curtailed any opportunity to satiate his more physical desires, of course. It might have been a shitty thing to do but Skye had needed to learn that lesson, even if it was a painful one. True love did not exist.

CHAPTER

FOURTEEN

T he next morning, Skye sat in the kitchen waiting for Coop. Judging by the empty bottles that stood on the side, it would probably be some time before he emerged. She'd been shaking with anger after his 'lesson' the day before, and it had taken her a long time to calm down. But she was feeling better now, and prepared to meet him. Just because she was quiet didn't mean she didn't have opinions of her own, she fumed. And just because she was quiet didn't give people like him carte-blanche to walk all over her.

Unfortunately for Coop, she'd also realised something else in the middle of the night. Suddenly everything was starting to slot into place and Skye was far from a happy girl.

It was almost midday when she heard a thud. She looked up from the article she'd been reading and saw one of the kitchen stools move slightly as Coop sat down on it.

'Get me a drink, would you, Skye?' he groaned.

She ignored his request. 'So you finally managed to get out of bed, did you? Exactly how much did you drink last night?'

Good grief, she sounded like his mother. 'I'm a big boy. If I want to drink, I'll drink.'

'Well, bully for you,' she said sarcastically. 'Because clearly your godly powers don't include being able to avoid hangovers.'

'Skye, this really isn't the time.'

'Oh, I think it's the perfect time. Because you're going to tell me all about a certain man, or should I say god, called Apollo.'

Coop felt his heart sink. 'Oh.'

'Did you really think I wouldn't put two and two together? You did that to him, didn't you? He hated me then all of a sudden decided I was his one true love. It was because of him I took this job! You screwed with him and you screwed with me!'

Coop sighed. 'It wasn't about you. He just needed taking down a peg or two.'

'Listen to yourself!' Skye snarled. 'All high and mighty about how you hate your job because you're forcing people to fall in love with each other. And then you go and force him to fall in love with me. To take him down a fucking peg or two.'

He blinked. 'You're angry.'

'You're goddamn right I'm angry. I had a good thing going. I had friends and a job and I was starting to have fun. By shooting your mate Apollo, you messed all that up for me. Why couldn't you pick on someone else?'

'You were,' Coop swallowed, 'convenient.'

'And you're a prick.'

He rubbed his forehead. 'I deserved that. But you didn't really have a good thing going, Skye. You shouldn't be working in a nightclub and serving drinks. You're better than that.'

'It wasn't your decision to make!'

'Which is my point about shooting people to make them fall in love,' he said tiredly.

'You do realise that makes it worse, not better? You hate forcing people into love and yet you did it to Apollo. You hate making life decisions for other people and yet you did it to me.'

'I didn't force you to take this job.'

'You didn't leave me with many other options.'

Coop felt as if the layers of his soul were being peeled away. Suddenly contrite, he looked up at Skye, wishing she could see his face and recognise the truth there. 'I'm sorry. I'm really sorry. It seemed like a good idea at the time and obviously it wasn't.'

'Obviously,' said Skye sarcastically.

He looked down, spotted her suitcase and looked back up again, alarmed.

'You're leaving?'

'Do you really expect me to stay?'

Coop stared at her, his eyes raking her face. 'I don't want you to go.'

'For once, this isn't about what you want. I've barely known you for twenty-four hours and all I've seen is someone completely self-centred. You treat people like garbage. You've treated *me* like garbage! I'm not your prisoner, Coop.'

'If this is about the kiss—' he began.

'It's about the lies,' she interrupted. 'All you've done is lie to me.'

'I won't do it again,' he said quietly. 'And I'll put things right with Apollo. I just need to get the two of you in a room together, that's all.'

'Oh, you'll put things right with Apollo,' Skye hissed. 'But I'm still leaving.'

Coop thought quickly. There had to be a way out of this. At the very least, he could buy himself some time to make her stay longer. He liked having her around and wasn't ready for her to go just yet.

'It will take me a few days to get Apollo to where I need him to be. I already said I need the two of you together to make things right.'

'So invite him here today and let's be done with it. I assume he has the same godly powers that you do and can transport himself here straightaway.'

'You remember the part I said yesterday about Zeus not letting anyone from Olympus come here? Apollo is Zeus's son. And, yes, he's a god with many godly powers. That means he's not allowed to come here. We need to arrange somewhere neutral and that may take time.'

'There is no "we" in this equation, Coop. There's only you. Arrange a time and a place and arrange it now.'

'Okay,' he said. 'There is just one thing though.'

'What?' she snapped.

'The girl I saw at Nemesis, the one I chose Apollo to fall in love with?'

'You mean me?'

'Yes, I mean you. That girl – that you – would never have stood up for yourself like this. So maybe being here is a good thing, Skye. For you and for me.'

Skye stared at him, suddenly without any answer.

He sighed heavily. 'I'll sort it out. Just give me a day or two, okay?'

'You've got forty-eight hours,' she snapped.

'Well, I'd better get a move on then, hadn't I?'

Skye sniffed in agreement, stood up, picked up her suitcase handle and trundled it back through to her bedroom. As soon as she was out of earshot, Coop reached inside his pocket and pulled out his phone.

'Herm?' he said, when his friend finally answered. 'I need some help.'

Hermes exhaled loudly. 'Why am I not surprised?'

HAVING AGREED with Hermes that his natural charm was the best way to win over Skye (at least, Coop had decided his natural charm would be the best way, Hermes had been less inclined to agree), he began with lunch. His head was still pounding from the wine he had drunk the night before but he managed to pull himself together enough to zip down to the nearest village and pick up a sumptuous lunch of olives, creamy soft cheese, crunchy bread and taramasalata. He laid everything out carefully on the kitchen table, adding a bunch of wild daisies and hyacinths as a centrepiece. Once he was satisfied with his efforts, he strode along the long corridor and knocked on Skye's bedroom door.

'What do you want?' she called out from where she lay on her bed, bemoaning the fact that she'd moved countries to avoid one male idiot and had ended up with an even bigger one.

Coop cleared his throat. 'I made lunch,' he shouted back.

There was a moment of silence.

'I'm not hungry,' Skye replied eventually.

'Come on, you need to eat.' Coop crossed his fingers tightly. 'I promise I'll be good.'

For a moment, he thought she was going to ignore him but then he heard her padding in his direction. She flung open the door with a surprising amount of force and stared out at him. She still looked pretty pissed off.

'How many times?' she snapped.

Not quite sure what she was referring to, Coop did his best to smile charmingly, hoping his tone of voice would reflect his expression. 'What do you mean?'

'How many times have you sneaked into my room? Have you been watching me all the time?'

Her eyes were narrowed in his direction, although she had slightly misjudged where his face was and was looking at his chest, which Coop found oddly off-putting. Nonetheless, the suspicion making the green flecks in her eyes more vivid was abundantly clear.

Coop blinked. 'I've not been watching you all the time, Skye. And I've not sneaked into your room.'

'I don't believe you.'

'Okay,' he demurred. 'I came in when you first arrived. But only to make sure you had everything you needed. I stayed for no longer than a minute or two. And I came in once when you had a nightmare. I tried to wake you up because you were crying out in your sleep.'

Shifting uncomfortably at the thought of him watching her sleep, Skye focused on her verbal attack. 'Those were the only times?' she demanded.

'Well, there was one other occasion when I didn't know where you'd gone so I came in to look for you. You weren't here.' He shrugged. 'So I left.'

She put her hands on her hips. 'When was this?'

Without thinking, Coop answered, 'Tuesday.'

Skye's face suffused with red. 'Tuesday? When...' she paused, 'when I was swimming?'

Uh-oh. Coop watched her carefully, trying to judge what the best answer here would be. 'Swimming?' he asked cautiously.

'Tell me the truth, Coop. You owe me that.'

He sighed. 'Maybe I walked out to the balcony to see if I could find you and I spotted you in the pool.'

Her face went even redder.

'Skye,' Coop began, 'I wasn't spying on you. I tried to give you as much privacy as I could and respect your space...'

The door slammed in his face. Shit. He remained there for a moment staring at it then walked back to the kitchen, a muscle throbbing in his cheek. That hadn't gone quite as well as he'd hoped.

Skye turned round and leaned with her back against the door. She couldn't believe he'd seen her swimming naked. She put her hands up to her hot cheeks and closed her eyes. She'd not thought things could get any worse. Now she'd have to spend the next two days with a man who'd seen every inch of her skin – and then some. She should have demanded he arrange to meet Apollo straightaway. Come to think of it, why didn't she just book into a hotel and get out of this place where she never knew whether she was being watched or not?

She sank down to the floor and hugged her knees. She didn't have an answer for that one. Skye wondered whether living with a genuine Greek god was attacking her subconscious and telling her to stay.

'A Greek god,' she whispered to herself. It sounded bloody ridiculous when she said it out loud. Of course that kiss would have meant nothing to him. Given the muscles she'd felt when his body was next to hers, he probably looked just like a Greek god was supposed to and could have his pick of women. She bit her lip. Hell, he'd probably been the inspiration for all those perfectly sculpted marble statues. . .

Her stomach rumbled, reminding her that she'd not eaten for several hours. Skye thought quickly. Perhaps it would be better to have lunch now when she knew where he was, rather than sneak into the kitchen later when she'd have no idea whether he was watching her or not. The thought of him hovering around, his eyes following her every move, was too creepy to think about. She wondered what else he might have seen her do, and the flush on her cheeks spread down to her neck and arms. Get a grip, Skye, she told herself. You can't let this man intimidate you, whether he's a god or not. Deciding that she wasn't going to spend the next two days cowering in her room – after all, she hadn't done anything wrong – she stood up, straightened her shoulders and went into the bathroom to splash cold water on her face. Then she went out to the kitchen to face him.

Coop, who'd been picking forlornly at the flowers and wondering what his next move could be, didn't hear her arrive. It wasn't until she spoke from behind him that he realised she was there.

'If I'm going to stay here for the next two days,' she said, hoping that he was actually in the room, 'we need to set some ground rules.'

He sprang up from his seat and turned to face her. There were a few tell-tale spots of red visible on her skin. It gave her a sexy, tousled look; Coop wondered what she looked like when she made love. He shook himself. Where had that thought come from? Trying to regain his composure, he answered her. 'Okay,' he said slowly, 'like what?'

'You need to wear a bell.'

He gaped at her. 'A ... what?'

'A bell, Coop,' Skye said impatiently. 'You know, ding-a-ling-a-ling?'

'You mean like a cat?'

She folded her arms. 'Exactly like a cat. That way I'll know where you are at all times.'

Good grief. If anyone ever heard about that, he'd be the laughing stock of Olympus.

'Fine,' he said stiffly. 'I'll wear a damn bell. Anything else?'

'You have to promise not to come into my room. Not ever.'

'Done.'

'And no lying.'

'The only reason I lied in the first place is because you weren't in a position to accept the truth,' he said.

'Coop,' she answered warningly.

'Okay, okay, no lying.'

'Fine, then. Now can I have some lunch?'

A grin spread across Coop's face. 'Of course,' he answered promptly. 'Then we can go out and buy your bell and meet a friend of mine at the same time.'

'A friend?' she asked suspiciously.

'Are you trying to insinuate that someone like me couldn't possibly have any friends?'

She blushed again. 'No. Just ... no.'

'Good. He's looking forward to meeting you.' Coop rubbed his hands in delight. He loved it when a plan came together.

CHAPTER
FIFTEEN

'Why do you have a car when you travel anywhere you want to in a blink of an eye?' Skye asked, as she parked next to a seaside café.

'I like driving,' Coop answered. 'There's an element of power and freedom I don't often get in the rest of my life.'

She scoffed, 'You're invisible. You can make people fall in love with each other. How can you say you don't have power?'

'First of all, I'm not invisible by choice, darling. Secondly, it's only people I'm told to target who I send my love bolts towards.'

'Love bolts? Really? Is that what you call them?'

'What name would you give them?'

Skye paused for a moment. 'I don't know. Something more romantic, I suppose.'

'Let me guess, you'd pick something like "heart flowers sent from heaven"?'

'No, don't be daft. I'd go for something catchier at least. Perhaps Byronesque,' she mused, '"immortal..."'

'Fire?' Coop finished.

Skye jerked slightly in surprise.

'What?' he asked with a sardonic edge. 'You think that just because I'm cynical about love, I don't read about it? Believe me, I spent many years trying to convince myself that what I was doing was a good thing, even in the face of overwhelming opposition.'

'What opposition?' Skye asked appalled.

'"Love goes by haps; some Cupid kills with arrows, some by traps". I think Shakespeare pretty much summed up what I do there.'

'Rubbish. "Love looks not with the eyes but with the mind, and therefore is winged Cupid painted blind". Also Shakespeare.'

'I'm not blind though,' Coop pointed out.

'But he's saying love is deeper than just liking someone because of the way they look. Therefore, love is true and good.'

'Yes, but "Cupid is a knavish lad, thus to make females mad." I think even you would agree with that one.'

Skye opened her mouth to argue further but she was interrupted by another voice. At least this one belonged to an actual, physical person.

'Really? Is this what you two do all day long? Argue about Shakespearean quotations?' said Hermes, appearing from round the side of the café.

'Hi Herm,' Coop said lazily. 'It's about time you showed up. This is Skye. Skye, Hermes.'

Suddenly feeling shy, Skye smiled slightly then looked down. Frowning at her, Coop moved, causing the bell which now hung round his neck to jangle.

Hermes blinked. 'What in Olympus's name is that?'

Coop snorted. 'A bell. She made me put it on.'

Hermes grinned at Skye. 'I guess there's no point asking who she is. Good work. It's about time this one was collared properly.'

Skye looked up, registering the open friendliness on Hermes' face and smiled back. 'It's kind of creepy,' she admitted, 'never knowing where he is.'

'I can imagine,' Hermes replied drily. 'Still, it's good to know you've taken him in hand.'

'I am still here, you know,' Coop interjected.

'Yes, but you're not staying. Your mother wants you to sort out some couples in Atlanta, doesn't she?'

Skye started. 'You're going?' As much as she had convinced herself she disliked the Love God, she had never met his friend until a minute ago. The last thing she wanted was to be babysat by some stranger.

Coop reached over and gave her arm a squeeze, bell ringing as he did so, although the unexpected action still made Skye jump.

'I won't be long. Don't miss me too much.'

'I'm not going to miss you,' she began. 'I could do with a break from your incessant complaining about your job.' Skye noticed Hermes grinning at her and realised it felt as if there was a hole by her side. 'He's gone, hasn't he?' she said.

Hermes winked at her and nodded. 'Never mind. Let's grab a drink and we can gossip behind his back.'

Before she could protest, Hermes took her hand and placed it on his arm, walking her towards one of the tables outside the café. He summoned a waiter and ordered two coffees, then fixed her with a serious gaze.

'So Coop tells me you're planning to leave.'

Squirming under his directness, Skye felt her cheeks warm up annoyingly. 'Yes. As soon as he's taken off this silly love compulsion from Apollo. And he's promised to do that by tomorrow.'

'Silly love compulsion?' he mused softly. 'You sound almost like him.'

'I'm nothing like him!' Skye protested. 'I would never manipulate people the way he does.'

Hermes watched her carefully. 'It's not entirely his fault, you know. His mother has him manipulating people all the time. It's hardly surprising that he's started doing it on his own.'

'But Fate...'

'Fate shmate. Do you really believe your destiny is written in the stars and you can't escape it?'

Skye looked away. 'No.'

'Why not?' Hermes prodded gently.

'Because I don't like the idea that I'm not in control of my own future. What's the point in doing anything if it's already going to happen no matter what I do?'

'Then perhaps you can understand a little of what he feels.'

'That still doesn't make what he's done to me any better.'

Hermes was silent for a second. 'No,' he said finally, 'it doesn't.'

The waiter arrived at their table and put down a pretty silver coffee pot and two cups. Skye smiled her thanks at him and he grinned back before walking back off to the kitchen.

'I'm sorry,' Hermes said, once the waiter had gone. 'I ordered for you. Perhaps you'd have preferred something stronger than coffee?'

Skye wrinkled her nose. 'Unlike your friend, I don't feel the need to down bottle upon bottle of alcohol to make myself feel better.'

Hermes sighed. 'He's in a bad place. He's been in a bad place for a long time. The drink, the women...' His voice tailed off.

'Women?' Skye felt a ripple of discomfort.

'He's a pretty boy,' Hermes answered. 'And if there's anything he knows about, it's the art of love. He has whoever he wants eating out of his hand.' He sent her an arch look. 'Apart from you, of course.'

She shook her head in disgust. Hermes reached over and took her hand. 'He's not a bad person, Skye. He's just been hurting for a very long time. There's almost no-one he trusts and can open up to. He needs someone to take him in hand and show him the right path.'

Her eyes narrowed. 'And you're trying to suggest that person should be me?'

'You don't have an ulterior motive,' Hermes pointed out. 'You're not trying to get into his mother's good books. You're not dazzled by his ridiculously handsome appearance and you're not trying to use him for anything.'

'No, I'm not. Because he's the one doing all the using.' She raised her eyes. 'You and he may have cooked up this little tête-a-tête to encourage me to stay, but it's not going to work. He needs to sort out Apollo so I can go home and get back to my life.'

'We didn't...'

'Don't insult my intelligence, Hermes,' she said quietly. 'I don't like playing games. And I'm not going to play the role of doormat for anyone.'

Skye stood up and pushed her chair back.

'Where are you going?'

'For a walk,' she answered. 'I need to clear my head. It'll be nice to know I don't have some invisible being trailing around with me at the same time.'

Hermes watched her departure then leaned over and poured himself a coffee. She certainly wasn't the kind of girl Coop normally hung around with, he thought, although he was starting to understand why his friend was so desperate to keep her around. The pair of them were probably better for each other than either of them realised.

There was a scrape as the chair to the left of him suddenly moved, groaned and shifted under an invisible weight.

'Where is she?' Coop's voice asked.

Hermes took a sip and carefully placed his cup back down. 'She's gone for a walk.'

'And? How did it go?'

He shrugged. 'As you'd expect. She's not about to suddenly change her mind about you based on a quick chat with someone she hardly knows.'

'Did you mention the drinking?'

Hermes sighed. 'Yes. And the women.'

'And she didn't bite?' The surprise in his friend's voice was palpable.

'No, funnily enough. I can't believe you really thought she would.'

'Bad boy syndrome,' Coop explained in frustration. 'Every woman secretly wants a bad boy to reform.'

'I don't think this one does.'

Coop cursed. Hermes eyed the apparently empty chair curiously. 'Why does it matter so much? Get another girl. I'm sure there are plenty of human women around who'd be happy to keep you company.'

'But Skye's efficient. She works hard and isn't afraid to stand up to me.'

'Is that the only reason?'

'Of course it is,' Coop answered, annoyed. 'What other reason could there be?'

Hermes shrugged and grinned. 'None that I can think of, mate,' he answered with a wink. 'Anyway, would you like a drink? I can get the waiter to bring over a Scotch.'

'Huh?' Coop asked, momentarily lost in a reverie about what he could possibly do to encourage Skye to stay. 'No, I'm fine. It's too early for alcohol. I'll have a coffee instead.'

Hermes' grin widened. 'Sure, Coop. Whatever you want.'

SKYE WANDERED along the pretty cypress-tree-lined boulevard, thinking about what Hermes had told her. Of course Coop would have a string of women at his beck and call. Why would she have presumed otherwise? He was the God of Love, after all. She wondered why it bothered her so much.

Her brow furrowed. It was probably because she felt sorry for him. All that time he'd spent making other people fall in love and he'd probably never experienced love first hand himself. He never would with his cynical attitude. Her frown deepened. And yet she could sympathise with his position. Perhaps it wasn't fair to all those people he shot his love bolts towards. But she remembered the look on the faces of the couple in Malaysia. How could that possibly be a bad thing?

She straightened her shoulders. No, she decided finally. He was just a petulant child who wanted everything his own way. Well, that wasn't going to wash with her. In less than thirty-six hours, when he'd solved the problem of Apollo, she would be free of him. She could forget she'd ever had the weirdness of working for an invisible love god. She pursed her lips. Easy.

CHAPTER
SIXTEEN

Coop kicked frustratedly at the wall, sending a cloud of red dust into the air. He had tried everything he could think of. He'd been nice to her. He'd offered her more money. He'd even worn the damn bell for the last two days at her behest. And Skye was still determined to leave. He was flat out of ideas. He watched her walk out of the bathroom wearing that stupid black skirt and prim and proper blouse and sighed. She'd tied her dark hair into a school-marmish bun. All it did was accentuate her cheekbones and give her a fragile, ethereal appearance.

'Where's Apollo, then?' she asked.

'You're in a rush to see him again,' he responded grumpily.

Skye jabbed a finger in the direction of his voice. 'Don't you dare, Coop. Don't you dare suggest this is because I want to see him. Let's not forget whose doing this was in the first place.'

'As if I could.' He grimaced. 'Let's get it over and done with. He's over there waiting by the pier.'

It had been almost too easy to get the God of Sun and Light to agree to come and meet them. Coop had rather hoped Apollo would put up more of a fight but as soon as he'd mentioned Skye's name, he had instantly agreed, champing at the bit to see her again. Coop had heard on the proverbial grapevine that Apollo had barely eaten or slept for the past week for worrying about where she was. Coop supposed he should be glad about that; instead he felt sad.

Skye peered off into the distance. The sky was already darkening into night but she thought she could make out a figure in the distance, leaning against the pier balustrade. She felt vaguely nauseous at seeing Apollo again. He'd been so horrible to her initially that she shivered at the thought of what might happen this time around. But it was clear there was no other way. If she wanted to be free of Coop, she had to do this.

Without waiting for Coop to say any more, she strode off in the direction of the lone figure. It wasn't long before the jangle of the bell signalled that Coop was following her. Admittedly he'd been very nice to her since the afternoon with Hermes, keeping his distance when she needed space but also chatting and joking with her when she felt a bit lonely. Part of her wanted to stay. Just a small part. She had a good job and, when he wasn't being a manipulative wanker, Coop was fun to be around. He made her laugh.

He's also an alcoholic womaniser, she told herself. He lied and cheated to get her to Greece, just so he could get some petty revenge. The quicker she was out of this situation, the better. She picked up her pace. By the sound of the bell behind her, Coop had slowed his. Typical, she huffed.

Stopping and turning around, she glared towards where she imagined he was. 'You're going to do this quickly, right? You'll shoot him as soon as we're together?'

'As my lady wishes.'

Skye's eyes narrowed. Was that a hint of sarcasm? Huffing again, she continued onto the pier. It was time to get this over and done with.

She was barely halfway along the wooden structure when the figure at the end turned round and spotted her approach. He immediately began jogging towards her. Skye felt her stomach sink ever so slightly.

'Skye!' Apollo called out. 'Where have you been?'

She rolled her eyes and stopped, waiting for him to reach her. The jangling bell behind her quieted as Coop halted to wait with her.

'Make this quick, alright?' she snapped, then immediately regretted her tone.

'He won't know what's hit him,' Coop murmured.

He reached inside his jacket pocket, pulling out his little golden box, flipped open the lid and began screwing the component parts together. His fingers trembled slightly and he cursed. Obviously he was nervous about what Apollo's reaction was going to be once the spell was lifted. But that was ridiculous: Apollo had deserved every inch of the misery he'd experienced.

Coop cast a quick look at Skye, whose back was ramrod straight as she watched Apollo's approach. She was right, though. She hadn't deserved any of this. He sighed inwardly and lifted his weapon towards the Sun God until his heart was in his sights.

Apollo ran up and caught Skye in a huge bear hug, wrapping his arms around her. 'I've been looking for you everywhere,' he said, pulling back slightly and looking into her eyes.

Skye shifted uncomfortably in his embrace. 'Well, you've found me now,' she said, wishing Coop would get a move on.

Apollo smiled, displaying white, even teeth. She'd forgotten how good-looking he was. Skye had the impression from Hermes that Coop was even more attractive. . .

Apollo leaned in, clearly aiming to kiss her. Skye moved her head to the side just in time and his lips landed on her cheek instead.

Coop's eyes narrowed. He sidestepped left and adjusted his aim.

'You're beautiful, Skye Sawyer,' Apollo breathed.

Coop's lip curled. Just because the Sun God thought he was in love with her didn't mean he had to slobber over her like that.

'Do it now.' Skye's voice was strained.

'Do what?' Apollo asked, confused.

Coop's hand twitched a millimetre to the left and he squeezed the trigger. He watched carefully as Apollo frowned, then abruptly took a step back. 'What...?' he asked, looking at Skye in confusion.

She stared at him, unblinking. He reached up and rubbed absent-mindedly at the spot where Coop had shot him.

'It's done,' Coop said quietly.

Apollo's face twisted and he stared behind Skye's shoulder at where Coop was standing. A look of comprehension crossed his face, and he snarled, 'Cupid. I might have guessed. This is all your doing.'

He shoved Skye out of the way and strode past her. 'Where are you, you bastard?'

'I'm here,' Coop answered, making no move to get out of the way and allowing the bell round his neck to ring so the Sun God knew where he was.

Apollo curled up his hand into a fist and lashed out, catching Coop on the chin and sending him reeling.

'You dared to do that to me? To shoot *me*?'

Wincing in pain, Coop straightened up. He was very aware of Skye watching the proceedings with fearful eyes. 'I'm sorry. It was a stupid thing to do.'

'Stupid? You have no idea, you little prick. I'm going to bury you for this.'

He punched out again, but this time Coop moved out of his reach.

'What? You can't face me like a man and fight?' Apollo sneered.

'You hit me,' Coop said tiredly. 'It hurt. So you can go back and tell all your minions how you beat me. Congratulations.'

'Oh, I'm just getting started. Come on, freak boy. Come and stand in front of me and I'll show you what I'm really capable of.'

'Apollo,' Skye began, taking a step forward.

'And you can shut the hell up as well. I bet you were in on the whole thing, weren't you?'

'She had nothing to do with this,' said Coop.

'Like I'll believe that,' Apollo said, scoffing. 'Well, fine, Cupid. If I can't see you to give you what you deserve, I'll just use her instead.'

Without further warning, Apollo spun round and grabbed Skye's arm, twisting it hard. She cried out in pain. Coop sprang forward, lunging at the Sun God.

'Leave her the fuck alone!' he yelled.

'Why?' Apollo twisted harder, a malicious smile spreading across his face.

Coop's fingers snatched hold of Apollo's arm. 'Let her go. She had nothing to do with this.'

Tears of pain were welling in Skye's eyes and she tried to pull away, but Apollo's grip was too strong.

'Let her go,' Coop repeated.

'You sound upset, Cupid,' Apollo grinned. 'Could it be you don't want your little human girl to get hurt?'

Coop snarled and, despite his best intentions to allow Apollo to rage until it was out of his system, he yanked hard on the Sun God's arm and balled his other fist up, slamming it into his face. Apollo let go of Skye and she crumpled to the side, clutching her arm.

'I think maybe I've touched a nerve,' he said. He glanced down at Skye. And with that he reached down, picked Skye up as if she were as light as a feather and threw her off the side of the pier. Her yell of surprise was suddenly muffled as she splashed heavily into the cold water. There was a shriek of pain from below.

Apollo smiled humourlessly. 'You get a lot of jellyfish in these waters at this time of year,' he commented.

Heart thudding with fear for Skye, Coop didn't think any further. He launched himself up and over the railing, landed in the water with a gasp and grabbed hold of her flailing body.

Apollo leaned over the edge and looked down at the pair of them. 'If you think I'm done,' he shouted, 'think again. I'm just getting started. You'll rue the day you crossed me, Cupid.'

'I'm already bloody ruing it,' Coop grunted from the water, as Apollo strode off.

Skye cried out again, and Coop shifted his body round to her back, one arm curving round her collar bone. 'Shh, it's okay, I've got you,' he reassured her.

'It hurts,' she whimpered.

'I know. We're not far from the shore though. Just stay with me.' He felt tentacles brush past his own skin and began to kick, pulling Skye with him.

'Kick for me, sweetheart,' he murmured in her ear.

Skye half nodded, sniffing, and did as he bade, even though her body was crying out in protest. Despite the warmth of his body against hers, she was already shivering and the searing pain of the jellyfish sting was seeping into her bones, making her muscles convulse and jerk in response. She gasped as a wave rose over her head, filling her mouth and nose with salt water. Coop tightened his grip round her body and kicked harder.

'It's okay, Skye, we're almost there,' he said, half closing his eyes. He should have taken steps to protect her from Apollo. He'd known the Sun God's fury would be thunderous but he'd not expected him to take it out on Skye. Coop's muscles tightened. He should have known.

After what seemed an age to Skye, her feet were finally dragging along the sand. Coop picked her up by her armpits and helped her wade the last few feet to the shore. Her teeth were chattering with cold but her skin felt as if it was on fire.

'It hurts,' she moaned.

'I know. Just hang in there and we'll get you home and treated.'

'Aren't you supposed to pee on me or something to make it better?'

Coop chuckled softly. 'It's not far to the house. Vinegar will work better, Skye. Unless you really want me to urinate on you, of course.'

She shuddered. 'It's okay, I think I can manage to wait that long.'

He grinned. 'I thought you'd say that.'

Coop reached down and scooped her up in his arms, cradling her shivering body in his arms.

'I'm too heavy!' Skye protested.

'No, you're not.' He walked carefully up the ramp to the waiting car, then bundled her inside, buckling her into the passenger seat.

'You can't drive,' she said as he got in and turned on the engine.

'Of course I can.'

'But what if someone sees you? Or doesn't see you rather? What will they think?'

'It's a short drive, Skye. Stop panicking.'

His voice was warm and gentle but it seemed to be coming from a very long distance. Skye felt very light-headed.

'He was so angry,' she murmured.

Coop's hands tightened on the steering wheel. 'Yes, he was.'

She said something else. Coop glanced over and realised her eyes were closing and her skin was very pale, apart from the livid red marks where the jellyfish had stung her. Alarmed, he speeded up.

'Don't fall asleep, Skye.'

She moaned. He took one hand off the wheel and shook her. 'Skye! Don't fall asleep!'

Her eyes half fluttered open. 'Not. Sleeping.'

'Good. Hang in there. We're almost home.'

The road curved round until finally the mansion was in view. Breathing a sigh of relief, Coop pulled into the driveway and stopped the car, then quickly got out and ran round to the passenger side. He flung open the door and reached in for Skye, picking her up again. He kicked open the front door, carried her into the living room and lay her gently down on the sofa. Then he sprinted into the kitchen, pulled out a bottle of vinegar and a clean cloth and rushed back.

He put some of the vinegar onto the cloth and began dabbing at the painful red marks. Skye stiffened in protest.

'It's okay,' he hushed her. 'Just stay still.'

Carefully pouring more vinegar onto the cloth, he continued to dab at the welts. She moaned again.

'Skye, I'm going to need to take off your blouse.'

'No,' she shook her head.

'I have to,' he said gently. 'I need to get to all the stings. You can trust me, I promise.'

Skye looked in the direction of his face and gave a small nod. He smiled down at her, brushed away the wet tendrils of hair from her face and began to unfasten the buttons on her blouse. He sucked in his breath when he saw the extent of the marks on her body. He'd bloody well kill Apollo the next time he saw him. Making sure every red welt was covered in vinegar, he laid the cloth to one side and picked her up again.

'What are you doing?' she protested.

'You need to rest,' Coop said, shifting his weight so she was secure against his chest.

He began to walk carefully down the corridor, passing her bedroom.

'Wait!'

'I promised you I wouldn't go into your room, remember? Just relax, Skye. Don't worry, I'll look after you.'

Everything seemed rather hazy. Being carried by the invisible Coop was quite possibly the oddest sensation in the world. If she kept her eyes open, it appeared that she was floating in mid air through the house. It made more sense to close her eyes than to let her brain struggle with what was happening. And her eyes were so heavy anyway, it was a struggle to keep them open.

'That's it,' he said softly from above. 'Just rest.'

She gave in to the darkness and succumbed to sleep.

CHAPTER

SEVENTEEN

When Skye woke the next morning and stretched out her limbs, the first thing that assailed her was the smell. It was as if she just walked out of a fish and chip shop after liberally dousing herself in vinegar. Her skin felt tingly and tight and there was a heavy weight curved round her waist. Opening her eyes, she took in her surroundings. She was in a bedroom and it wasn't her own.

The bedsheets half covering her body were white, contrasting against the heavy mahogany of the bed frame. The room seemed similar to her own, but there was something more masculine about it. The warm weight against her skin tightened and pulled her closer.

Coop.

'You're awake,' he murmured in her ear. 'How do you feel?'

Trying to force herself to relax, she pulled away and sat up. Realising all she was wearing was her underwear, she snatched up the sheet to cover herself, blushing as she did so.

'Uh, fine,' Skye answered. 'Fine. The stings don't hurt so much now.'

She heard the bed creak as Coop sat up. He had to resist the urge to reach out and smooth away her hair from her face. He could feel himself hardening and moved further away to try to avoid alarming her.

He cleared his throat, hoping his voice sounded normal. 'That's good. I'll nip down to the village and get some antibiotic ointment though. You were hurt pretty badly.'

Skye drew her knees into her chest. 'Thank you,' she said quietly.

'For what?'

'Helping me. You didn't have to.'

'You didn't think I'd just leave you there, did you?'

Skye half-shrugged, a little embarrassed.

Coop watched her carefully. 'I'm going to make him pay for what he did,' he said finally.

She blinked. 'You mean Apollo?'

'Who else?' There was a grim note to his voice.

'Coop, you can't,' she said flatly.

'Of course I can.'

'No, you can't. Unless you put a stop to this, it'll never end. You shot him so he threw me into the sea. Now you'll do something else, then he'll do something else and it'll just escalate until someone gets hurt.'

'Someone already got hurt,' he growled.

'I'm fine.'

'There was no reason for him to pick on you, Skye.'

'He thought I was in on the plan,' she pointed out.

'I told him...'

'Coop,' she interrupted, 'just leave it. Please?'

He stared at her. The green flecks in her eyes were pleading with him. Sighing heavily, he acquiesced. 'Fine.'

She smiled softly. 'Thank you.'

Coop looked down and traced a shape on the smooth sheet. 'You know, it might be best for you to stay here for a while. Until we're sure the jellyfish stings have gone away.'

Skye looked down at her body. The marks were already starting to fade. Last night seemed like nothing more than a bad dream.

'You're right,' she found herself saying. 'Maybe I should wait. It would be best to make sure they've completely healed before I travel.'

Coop tried to keep the smile out of his voice. 'I'll go and see if the pharmacist is open. The ointment will probably help with the pain.'

Skye nodded slightly, listening as he sprang up, bell ringing as he did so. Then the bedroom door opened and closed and she heard him padding off into the distance. She hugged her knees closer to her chest. Why had she done that? There was nothing to stop her from leaving now. It was hardly a long flight back to the wet grey skies of England, so using the stings as an excuse didn't really wash. And yet she didn't want to leave. She'd be going back to yet another jobless existence. Here it was sunny, and she had a job that she rather enjoyed, despite Coop's many strange requests. And there was Coop.

She chewed on her lip. He'd done everything she'd asked of him. He'd reversed the love spell on Apollo and he'd not lied to her since she'd confronted him. And last night... She sighed. He'd been so gentle and tender and made her feel so safe. Then there was the way his arm had felt when it had tightened round her and pulled her closer to him. She clenched her teeth and told herself off. He wasn't interested in her. The kiss he'd faked on her had proven that. Plus, there was the part about him being able to have any woman he wanted. He'd hardly pick her, would he?

Skye extricated herself from Coop's sheets and out of the bed. It would be at least an hour before he returned. That gave her more than enough time to get back to her room and shower off the stink of vinegar. Then she'd call Emma. Her old friend would be able to give her some sound advice.

HALF AN HOUR LATER, Skye was curled up on her enormous bed, finally wearing clean clothes and feeling ten times better. Emma, who'd been delighted to hear from her, had been regaling her with stories about life back in London. It sounded as if she was having a whale of a time. Strangely, however, Skye had realised she didn't miss it at all.

'So what's the gossip with you? How's life in Greece?'

'It's good,' Skye answered slowly.

'Well that doesn't tell me anything! What's your mysterious boss like?'

Skye took a deep breath. 'He's really nice.'

'Nice?' Emma screeched into the phone. 'Is that all you can say?'

'Okay, he's more than nice. I, um, fell into the sea last night and he rescued me.'

'You fell into the sea? How in the hell did you manage that?'

'It's a long story. The thing is, Emma,' Skye began.

'Is that you've fallen for him, haven't you?'

Skye didn't answer.

'I knew it. I could hear it in your voice. Skye, it's never a good idea to get involved with your employer.'

'I'm not involved with him,' she said. 'He's not interested in me. He's unbelievably good looking.' Or so I've been told anyway, she thought. 'He's wealthy, charming, funny. He can have his pick of any girl.'

Emma bristled on her behalf. 'Hold on, don't put yourself down, Skye. Any guy would be lucky to have you. Have you met any other girls?'

'No,' she admitted.

'Well then! He's free, you're free. I've changed my mind. Screw the employer part. You need to go for it, girl.'

'It's not that easy,' Skye said. 'I told him I wanted to leave.'

'Why would you do that?'

She sighed. 'It's complicated.'

'Skye Sawyer. You're an intelligent, beautiful woman. If he doesn't want you, then it's his loss. But if you don't try, if you don't tell him how you feel, then you'll never know what could be. Regret the things you do...'

'Not the things you don't,' Skye finished. 'You're right, Emma. It's just easier said than done, that's all.'

'Rubbish. You've got nothing to lose.'

She was probably right, Skye figured, hanging up the phone. Because judging from the way she felt at the moment, she'd already lost everything she had to lose. Her heart. She hadn't realised it until this very moment. She barely knew him. He was invisible, for goodness' sake! And yet somehow, the way he'd looked after her last night had shown her what she'd been feeling all along. What a mess.

The door to the mansion banged open and she heard Coop calling out her name. Feeling suddenly awkward, she got to her feet and went to meet him, realising from the sounds he was making that he was in the kitchen.

As soon as she entered, he spoke, a surprised and not entirely happy note in his voice. 'You're up and dressed,' he commented.

'Yes,' she replied, 'and feeling a lot better.'

Coop had been hoping he'd find her still wrapped up warm in his own bed. 'That's good,' he murmured. 'I got you that ointment and some food.'

'Thank you.' Skye shifted her weight. What on earth was she going to say now? She racked her brains. Damn it.

Coop gazed at her. She still looked drawn and the welts were still painfully visible on her soft skin, but she seemed well. More than well. The last thing he needed was for her to decide she was well enough to travel back to England after all.

'Will you take me with you today?' she asked suddenly.

He started. 'Um...'

'When you go out to do your job? You know,' she cocked her fingers into the shape of a gun and aimed it towards him.

He blinked. That was good. If she was with him, then she wouldn't be thinking about leaving. 'Certainly,' he responded. 'I've got three to do today, so it may take some time.'

She smiled, her face lighting up. 'Brilliant. I want to know more about what you do.'

'You should go and put on the ointment first.' His voice was gruffer than he'd intended. 'It'll help with the healing.'

Skye nodded. That was twice he'd spoken and sounded annoyed. She wondered whether he was starting to wish she'd just make her mind up and leave. Biting her lip, she grabbed the jar of antibiotic cream from the counter. 'I'll be back soon.'

He nodded back at her then remembered she still couldn't see him. Bugger it.

'Great,' he said. He almost added that he could help her put on the cream but then recalled the way his body had responded to her that morning. It was probably safest to leave her to it.

By the time she returned, he had made her a light breakfast and left it on the counter. Her cheeks coloured when he referred to it, as if she were embarrassed that he'd bothered to make her a meal. He scowled. He preferred it when she was arguing with him. At least then he knew where he stood.

When she had finished eating, he reached out and took her hand. She jumped, making him wish he hadn't.

'We should get going,' he said softly.

'Okay, great. Where to?'

'New York.'

Skye's eyes widened. Coop grinned. 'Have you been before?'

She shook her head.

'Well, maybe we can squeeze in a bit of sightseeing along the way.' He pulled her gently towards the door. 'Are you ready?'

'Yes.'

'Then let's do this.'

He opened the door. The pair of them stepped through and Skye found herself blinking to adjust to the sudden change in light. 'It's night time,' she said surprised.

Coop laughed. 'Of course it is. There's a seven hour time difference.'

Skye could have smacked herself on the forehead. She had sounded like some kind of naïve little girl. Why hadn't she thought of the time difference before she spoke?

'"Time",' he quoted softly, '"on whose arbitrary wing the varying hours must flag or fly."'

Time certainly flew when she was with Coop, Skye thought.

'You know your Byron,' she said aloud.

'Did you ever doubt it?'

She smiled in answer and looked around. 'So where are we exactly?'

'MoMA. The Museum of Modern Art.'

'It's 3 am though. Surely it's closed.'

'It may be closed but some people are working late.' He moved behind Skye, holding her by the waist and gently moving her so she faced a small glass door set in the side of the building. 'Watch.'

Fully aware of his proximity, Skye tried to remember to breathe. Before long the door opened and a small figure wearing a long coat and a rather precarious-looking hat emerged. Whoever it was waved to someone inside, probably a security guard, and then began to make their way down the steps to the pavement. A sudden gust of wind blew through the street, whipping off the hat and sending it tumbling down.

'Her name is Alice,' Coop said into Skye's ear, as he pulled out his gun. 'And there, to your left, is Frank.'

Skye turned to see a man walking towards them, hands stuffed in his pocket. She watched, her heart in her mouth at what she knew she was about to witness. Alice's hat was still scuffing its way along the street towards the man called Frank. He bent down to pick it up, while she ran towards it.

Coop, feeling oddly bereft now that his hands had left Skye's warm body, quickly assembled his weapon. He might not believe wholeheartedly in what he was doing, but it seemed that she did. If doing this impressed her, then that was good enough reason for him. Coop aimed quickly and fired. And frowned. He stared at the couple, then down at his gun before flicking a glance at Skye who was still watching the pair of them, unaware that anything was amiss. Shit. He'd missed. He never missed. Trying not to panic, he aimed again, breathing a silent sigh of relief as his second shot found its mark. Then he quickly turned to the man and squeezed the trigger in his direction.

Skye watched as Frank scooped up the hat and presented it to Alice with a bow and a flourish. She took it, putting her hands up to her face and seeming to giggle.

'That's amazing,' Skye whispered.

Coop barely noticed. He was still trying to work out what had gone wrong. If his mother found out, she'd be furious. He looked again at Skye.

'Doesn't anyone ever see you?' she asked. 'I mean, you'd think someone would notice a man pulling out a golden gun in the middle of a city. Even at this time of the morning.'

'People only see what they want to,' Coop answered, focusing on her rather than his failure. 'Olympus is the same. We have a large complex near Litochoro. If you don't expect it to be there, you won't see it. It's all to do with belief or something.'

Skye shook her head. 'Wow.'

Coop turned to watch the couple standing together under the dark sky. Even from this distance he could see the look of surprised adoration with which Alice was looking at Frank. If only Skye would look at him that way, he thought idly, then caught himself. Where in the hell had that thought come from? Besides anything, she couldn't even see him.

'Come on,' he said. 'We have a bit of time before the next one. How do you fancy standing on top of the Empire State Building?'

'Isn't it closed?'

'Shut your eyes,' he whispered in her ear, 'and you'll find out.'

She did as he bade, opening them only when he instructed her to do so. When she did, she was almost completely bowled over.

'Oh my God,' Skye breathed. 'This is unbelievable.'

The whole of New York lay before them, twinkling lights stretching across the sweeping dark purple night sky. She could make out the silhouettes of famous landmarks she'd only ever seen in films. It was utterly breathtaking.

'Can you see that?' she asked Coop, pointing towards the glittering river.

He smiled, watching her face glowing. 'Yes.'

'It's magnificent.'

Coop moved up behind her and gently held her shoulders. Skye, feeling the pressure of his hands, held her breath then slowly turned towards him. With her heart thudding in her chest, she seized the moment and reached out with one extended palm, feeling it connect first with his broad chest, then upwards to the rough hair where his shirt opened and over the stubble of his chin. She rested her hand on his cheek and, for the first time, it seemed to Coop that she was gazing into his eyes.

He leaned forward and kissed her, his arms reaching round her back and pulling her in towards him. His tongue ran over her bottom lip and his teeth nipped at the soft flesh there, then he deepened the kiss, entwining his fingers in her long hair. She tasted of toothpaste and freshness and Coop was drowning in her scent.

Without warning, Skye pulled away. Her face was flushed and her breathing quick, but there was a wary, troubled expression on her face. 'Is this another lesson?'

Coop stared at her, not sure at first what she was referring to. Then dull comprehension seeped through.

'No. By Olympus, Skye, no. I...' He stepped back and raked a hand through his hair. 'I want you. More than I've ever wanted anyone.' As soon as he said the words, he realised they were true. He took both her hands in his and fixed his eyes on hers. 'Do you...?' he swallowed. 'Do you want this?'

She nodded mutely and he felt cascading relief and joy flood through him.

'I've still got two more jobs to do,' he said, struggling to focus on anything other than her.

Skye looked confused for a moment, then her face cleared. 'Are they close by?'

'Not exactly.'

She licked her lips and his eyes followed her small pink tongue. 'Well, let's hurry up and get them over so we can get back home.'

He pulled her to him and planted a long hard kiss on her lips, and whispered in her ear, 'Yes, let's.'

BY THE TIME they made it back to the mansion, Skye felt more nervous than ever. Coop's attitude towards his final two jobs had been perfunctory to say the least; even her continued amazement at what he could achieve with a single shot was dampened by the anticipation and trembling excitement she felt in the pit of her stomach. He'd taken every opportunity to brush lightly against her, making her shiver. They certainly hadn't gone on any more side trips to do some sightseeing.

As soon as the door closed behind them, she felt him move in front of her and press her against its sturdy wooden frame. Regardless of whether she could see him or not, she could certainly feel every inch of him. With his hot breath on her cheek, she reached up and traced her fingers over his biceps, marvelling at the rippling strength she felt there. Then his breath moved down her face until she could feel it at the base of her neck. He moved his arms, pinning her against the door so that she was trapped.

If this is what it's like to be the prisoner of a love god, then give me more, Skye thought, before his lips pressed against her skin and all thought fled from her mind.

'Don't move,' he whispered and began trailing kisses up her neck, pausing to nibble gently with his teeth at a place near her ear.

Skye sucked in her breath and closed her eyes while Coop

continued upward, his kisses becoming more gentle as he reached her mouth. The hot, hard length of his erection pressed insistently against her and she moaned under his lips. As if in answer, he began to move his mouth back down her neck again, his kisses searing into her skin. This time, however, he didn't pause at the base of her neck but continued downwards until she could feel his breath warming her through the light fabric of her blouse.

'You have no idea,' he murmured, 'how much I hate this piece of clothing. I think I've wanted to rip it off you since the first time I saw you in it.'

Skye opened her mouth to protest but, before she could say anything, he shifted his weight slightly, still keeping her in place against the door while he pulled hard at the top of her blouse. Buttons flew off and spun across the marble floor, leaving her top half exposed.

Coop returned his mouth to her skin, kissing her collar-bone and the softer flesh below. He paused briefly at the lacy edge of her bra, then his tongue moved down to the bare skin at the valley between her breasts and back up again. Skye shuddered.

Gently, he reached up to one bra strap and pulled it down her shoulder before doing the same to the other. Then he peeled the lacy cups down, exposing her breasts. Skye felt him take a momentary half step backwards. A hot flush suffused her skin.

'You shouldn't be embarrassed,' he said softly. 'You're beautiful.'

As if to emphasise his point, he leaned in and kissed her on the lips, then used his right hand to cup her breast. She felt his finger and thumb take her nipple tenderly and she gasped.

Now that she had some more freedom to move, Skye reached out to find Coop's own shirt. He caught her hand, however, and gently pushed it back against the door.

'You're a goddess, Skye,' he said. 'I want to pay homage to you. Let me do this.'

Swallowing hard, Skye let her arm relax. Then Coop's mouth found her breast. His tongue circled her nipple then he began to suck while his hands reached down around her back to the waist of her skirt. Before she could move to allow him easier access, he had unfastened the button and the zip and her skirt pooled in a black circle on the floor.

His lips left her breast and she started to utter a muffled protest but they immediately scorched a trail down her midriff. Skye's hands involuntarily reached down until she realised they were clutching at what had to be Coop's hair. Part of her registered that it felt softer and slightly longer than she'd imagined, but it was a half-formed thought as Coop's tongue found her belly button, rimming round it gently until she was gasping. As his head lowered even further, she removed her hands from the down of his hair and pressed her palms against the warm wood of the door, her back arching. He pulled back slightly, although she could still feel the fire of his breath against her skin and, with one finger, he traced along the edge of her pants. Then his tongue followed the path his finger had taken.

Coop moved back again and rolled down the edge of lace barely an inch, tracing over the newly-exposed skin again with his finger. His tongue followed. Skye moaned and moved her own hands to pull off the fabric between them, but he took her hands again and returned them to the door. Then Coop himself gently peeled her underpants over the curve of her hips and down past her legs to join her skirt on the floor. For a heartbeat, he seemed to hang there, doing nothing. Not being able to see him was incredibly erotic and yet so unbelievably frustrating at the same time. Fortunately he didn't keep her waiting for long, gently inserting one hand between her legs to coax them open before his mouth pressed into her, flicking at her clitoris. Skye cried aloud in pure, uncontrolled pleasure.

Once her body had stopped its orgasmic shuddering, Coop stood up. He took her hand and guided it to his chest, directing her fingers to unfasten each button and expose the smooth hard flesh under-neath. Once he had shrugged off the shirt, he took her palm and pressed it against his heart, not saying anything but allowing her to feel how fast his pulse was racing. He left her hand there while he undid his trousers and pushed them down over his hips, kicking them quickly away. Then he grasped her hand in his and gently pulled it down until she could feel the rough hair underneath his belly and the hot, hard rigidness of his erection. Her fingers circled his girth and, finally, it was Coop's turn to moan aloud.

Skye closed her eyes in delight at his reaction, lightly moving her fingers up his length and marvelling at his size and smoothness. Coop leaned in towards her.

'Enough now,' he murmured in her ear.

He positioned his weight against her and thrust inside her wet warmth, completely filling her body and soul. Skye curved her arms around his back and the pair of them moved together in unison, hips rising to meet each other's while their breath quickened. Her skin slick with sweat, Skye felt herself tipping over the edge.

'Coop,' she moaned.

His lips found hers for one prolonged kiss, then he whispered in her ear. 'Skye.'

Coop slammed into her for one final tumultuous thrust and the pair of them exploded in a tingling, shuddering, shivering wave.

CHAPTER

EIGHTEEN

Coop's phone buzzed annoyingly. He ignored it and pulled Skye's sleeping frame closer to his, hooking one leg round hers as if to hold her in place and prevent her from ever leaving. She murmured something and reached behind her, her hand seeking the warmth of his skin.

The phone buzzed again. Skye shifted slightly, the sound finally penetrating her sleep, and her eyes fluttered open.

'Your phone,' she muttered.

Coop propped himself up on one elbow and gazed down at her. 'I can't hear anything,' he said softly.

The corners of her mouth curved upwards. 'Nothing?' she teased.

'Not a thing,' he asserted, pressing his lips against her temple. 'Other than my heart, which is probably thudding loudly enough to wake the dead. It must be the excitement of waking up next to you.'

Skye turned towards him, wishing she could see his face and look into his eyes to read the expression there.

'I'm pretty excited too,' she whispered.

Coop trailed one finger down the curve of her waist and she shivered. Then the phone buzzed yet again.

'You should probably get it,' Skye said.

'I should probably throw the damn thing into the pool,' he grumbled, reaching over her to scoop it up from the bedside table and answer it.

'Love God speaking,' he purred into the receiver while lazily caressing Skye's bottom lip with his thumb.

'Where in the hell have you been?'

'Hello, Mother.'

Skye abruptly sat up and pulled away from him, her eyes wide.

'I simply do not have time for your flippant, devil-may-care attitude. Why didn't you answer your phone before now?'

'I was busy. You should be happy, mother,' he said, keeping a careful watch on Skye. 'I've done what you thought I never would.'

'And what's that exactly?' Aphrodite snapped.

'Fallen in love.' The tone of Coop's voice was soft but, nonetheless, Skye's entire body tensed and her mouth dropped open.

There was a moment of engulfing silence. Coop reached out and squeezed Skye's hand, barely registering the fact his mother was no longer speaking. His concern was the woman in his bed.

It wasn't long, however, before Aphrodite found her voice. 'Interesting,' she said, in a tone which conveyed entirely the opposite. 'And would this be the reason why I've just discovered you missed a target yesterday?'

Coop frowned. How in the hell did she manage to find these things out? He shrugged. 'I suppose so,' he answered eventually. 'It wasn't a problem though. I corrected it immediately. Besides,' he chided, 'you should be happy for me. I've finally discovered the meaning of love. True love. It turns out it does exist, after all.'

Aphrodite failed to notice the sincerity in her son's voice. 'I have had enough of your cynicism and antipathy towards everything our family stands for,' she said. 'You have an hour to present yourself at Olympus.'

Coop opened his mouth to retort, but she had already hung up. He sighed heavily.

'What's wrong?' Skye asked anxiously.

'It's my mother,' he answered. 'She insists I show my face at Olympus within the next sixty minutes. Frankly, I'm tired of being at her beck and call.' He leaned over and kissed her. 'I've got you, Skye. Why would I ever need anyone else?'

She pulled back. 'You're going to go, though?'

'And leave this "hallowed temple, this soft bed"? No way.'

Skye wasn't going to be distracted, even by the poetry of John Donne.

'She's your mother.'

'I'm not a little boy. And she can't treat me like I'm her servant.'

Skye was silent for a moment, then she took a deep breath and spoke. 'Coop, do you think maybe she treats you that way because you've been acting like a little boy?'

He stiffened.

'I'm not trying to be hurtful,' Skye interjected, reaching out one hand towards him. 'It sounds crazy but I think I'm in love with you too. I never thought...' Her voice trailed off for a second.

'You think I'm a little boy?' he asked flatly.

'I know you're not. But,' Skye looked down, 'you have been a bit, um, self-centred sometimes.'

Coop moved back, pulling himself out of bed.

'Don't be annoyed. I'm sorry, Coop, I shouldn't have said anything.' Skye hugged her knees to her chest, dismayed that she was already screwing things up.

'No,' he answered, sounding distant. 'You're right. I have been acting like a petulant, spoilt brat. The way I treated you proves that.'

'Coop...'

'Shh,' he said, opening his vast wardrobe to hunt down something suitable to wear. 'You need to say what you really think, Skye. *I* need you to say what you really think. Because being with you makes me want to be a better person. A more mature person. You deserve the best and you shouldn't be afraid to tell me what you think. I'm going to go to my mother and prove to her that I've changed.' He licked his lips. 'Or at the very least that I'm changing.'

Skye blinked, at a sudden loss for words.

'Get dressed,' he instructed.

'What?'

His voice was gentle. 'You heard me. You need to come with me to Olympus so my mother can meet you for herself. Then she'll understand.'

'I can't come to Olympus!' Skye squeaked.

'Of course you can. I want you to meet her. I want to show you Olympus and where everything really happens. I want you to know everything there is to know about me, Skye.'

She bit her lip. 'She sounds a bit scary.'

'My mother? She's a bloody dragon of a woman.' He bent over and kissed her forehead. 'But she'll also love you as much as I do. "Come away, O human child",' he quoted, '"To the waters and the wild. "'

'Well if W. B. Yeats thinks it's alright, then I suppose I can't argue,' she answered, smiling up at him and trying to ignore the whirlpool of trepidation building up in the pit of her stomach.

'It'll all be fine.'

Skye had never seen anything like it. The golden gates which led into Olympus were vast. They swung open noiselessly as she approached hand in hand with Coop, revealing an even grander courtyard within. Standing next to the gates was a motionless guard, clad from head to toe in shiny armour. Even his face was obscured by a helmet. Intricate eyeholes were carved into the bronze, but all Skye could see through them were dark shadows. She shivered.

'Oh my God,' she whispered.

'Oh my gods,' Coop corrected with a laugh.

She dragged her gaze away from the sinister guard and looked around. The guard didn't move a muscle, allowing the pair of them to walk through. 'Everything's so pristine and perfect.'

'Believe me, it gets rather tiresome after a while,' Coop said as they passed a gigantic statue of Zeus glaring down at them with a thunderbolt clenched in his frozen fist. 'All this white marble and gold opulence. Spend too long here and you'll find yourself longing for something more mundane and down-to-earth.'

'Is that why you don't live here?'

'It gets a bit stifling,' he admitted.

Skye stared around her. 'I can even see my reflection in the stone. Who on earth does the cleaning?'

Coop pursed his lips. It had never occurred to him to wonder. The pair of them turned left down a sweeping corridor. Several giggling girls dressed in swathes of white fabric passed by, giving Skye curious glances.

'You're still invisible,' she commented. 'They can't see you either.'

'No, they can't.' He squeezed her fingers gently. 'It's only temporary, Skye. Does it bother you?'

'I'd like to know what you look like,' she said softly. 'To look into your eyes.'

'You've got little green chips.'

'Eh?'

He smiled. 'In your eyes. You've got flecks of green. They become brighter when you're angry. Or happy. Last night, when we were together, they were the brightest I'd ever seen. You know, when you...'

Skye went bright red. 'Okay, you don't need to spell it out.'

Coop laughed. 'Don't be embarrassed. I'm going to need to make sure I do a lot of things to make them stand out that much again. Lots and lots and lots of things.'

Skye went even redder.

Coop tugged at her hand. 'Come on,' he said. 'I'll give you the guided tour later. After I've made your eyes go greener and after we've faced my mother. She's just down this way.'

Swallowing hard, and praying the flush in her cheeks was going to die down quickly, Skye nodded and let Coop lead her down the next corridor, past open gardens with elaborate fountains and grand-looking rooms which she only caught brief glimpses of. She could have sworn that in one she spotted a man who looked as if he had the top half of a muscular man and the bottom half of a goat. She shook herself. This was certainly all a far cry from life at home. Unfortunately their short walk was over far too quickly and they were soon standing in front of an unassuming door, which was engraved simply with a single rose.

'Her quarters are in here,' Coop said.

'Okay.'

'Don't be afraid, Skye.'

'Okay.'

'I mean it. I won't let anything happen to you.'

She nodded. 'Okay.'

He squeezed her hand once more and pushed open the door. What was revealed within was extraordinary. Skye gaped up at the high ceiling adorned with a painted landscape of cherubs and clouds dancing across a blue sky. The walls were, surprisingly, not the marble white of the corridors but instead a soft rosy pink. In the centre of the room there was a gilt table with ornate legs and a huge display of exotic flowers. And standing next to the table was the most beautiful woman Skye had ever seen. Her face was unlined, although she had a maturity about her that suggested years of wisdom and experience. Long golden hair flowed down her back, almost reaching to the floor, and her hands were clasped in front of her. She was staring at Skye with an icy blue expression in her eyes.

'Mother,' said Coop.

'You're late.'

'I got here as quickly as I could. You didn't give me much time to get myself and Skye ready.'

Aphrodite's lip curled ever so slightly. 'I didn't ask you to bring your latest girlfriend. I asked for you.'

Skye stiffened. Latest girlfriend?

'She's not my latest girlfriend,' Coop said, with a dangerous edge to his voice. 'She's my soulmate.'

Aphrodite folded her arms. 'I'm not in the mood for your jokes, Cupid.'

'And I'm not joking.'

Skye felt a tremor run through her. Coop's goddess mother wasn't scary; she was absolutely terrifying.

'Well, she'll need to wait out here. You and I are going to have some words together first.'

'Anything you say to me, you can say to Skye also.'

Aphrodite glared. 'We're going to do this alone.'

Skye let go of Coop's hand. 'It's okay,' she said, giving the invisible shape beside her a small nudge. 'I'll wait here.'

Coop would have continued to protest to the contrary, but there was a flicker of fear in Skye's eyes which made him relent.

'Fine then,' he snapped to his mother, softening his tone when he spoke to Skye. 'I won't be long.'

He leaned towards her, his lips gently brushing against hers. Despite her surroundings and Aphrodite's glare, Skye still felt a shiver of pleasure run through her.

'I won't go anywhere,' she promised.

Aphrodite sniffed, and turned her back on them, her sandals slapping against the cool floor. A door ahead of her opened and she entered. Coop brushed Skye's cheek with the back of his thumb then followed his mother in. The door closed firmly behind them. Skye exhaled audibly and leaned against the wall. Coop's mother was certainly nothing like her own warm and friendly parents. Part of her was starting to understand his relentless need to kick back against Aphrodite's authority.

Skye shook her head to herself. This was probably going to be even more complicated than she had realised.

As soon as the door closed with a dull thud behind him, and Coop registered who else was in the room, a snarl escaped him. 'What in the hell is he doing here?'

Apollo grinned lazily. 'Your mother is concerned about you, Cupid. I suggested I might be able to help out.'

Flickers of hot anger ran through Coop. 'This is ridiculous. I'm not about to let this jumped-up prick of a god give me a scolding.'

Aphrodite's answer was cold. 'You'll do as I damn well say. Apollo's been kind enough to offer us his time. You'd do well to show some gratitude.'

The scowl on Coop's face grew. It was probably just as well he was invisible; at least it meant he didn't have to mask what was written all over his face. His bloody mother had always had a soft spot where Apollo was concerned. If only she'd see him for what he really was, then she wouldn't be so quick to admit him into her inner sanctum. But Coop still had Skye's admonishment about his self-centred nature ringing in his ears. No matter what it cost him, he was going to act like someone she could be proud of. He straightened his shoulders. How hard could it be to play nice?

'I apologise,' he said stiffly. 'It is very kind of you to interrupt your busy schedule to offer some counselling.'

A shadow of surprise crossed Apollo's face, affording Coop at least some satisfaction. Perhaps this wouldn't be so bad after all.

'I fully understand,' said the Sun God suavely. 'It's not easy to accept advice from others.'

'And I'm sure your advice will be golden,' interjected Coop.

Apollo's eyes narrowed for a heartbeat then his features smoothed over.

Aphrodite clapped her hands. 'Excellent. Now that's out of the way, explain to me exactly what happened yesterday.'

The missed shot. Coop shrugged and decided the truth was his best option. 'Skye was with me. I suppose I was trying to impress her. Or perhaps I was a bit distracted by her presence.' His voice grew earnest. 'I really am in love with her, Mother. It's just crept up on me. I get it now. I've never felt so,' he paused, 'so contented before. I want to make her happy. I want her to be by my side forever. I even want others to experience what I'm experiencing. If I can do that by shooting them, then I will damn well shoot them. Because nothing feels like this. It's indescribable.'

Aphrodite studied her son. 'You're telling the truth.'

He looked her in the eyes. 'Yes,' he said, 'I am.'

'So how long have you known this Skye girl, Cupid?' interrupted Apollo.

'My name is Coop,' he answered through gritted teeth.

'Coop then. But you've still not answered my question.'

Apollo knew full well just how long he'd known Skye; he could hardly bring up that fact in front of his mother, though. He rolled his eyes in exasperation instead.

'A couple of weeks. What of it?'

Apollo rubbed his chin with his thumb, looking troubled. 'Oh.'

'What is it? This is good news, Apollo. This is all I've ever wanted for him.' There was a glint of happiness in Aphrodite's eyes.

'You're right,' he said slowly. 'It's good news. Of course it is. It's just...'

'What?'

Apollo shrugged. 'It's really not my place to say, you know. You should celebrate your good fortune.'

'Apollo,' Aphrodite said with a hint of steel.

He pasted on a look of embarrassment, while Coop glared at him suspiciously. Clearly Apollo was out for revenge; Coop just had to work out what he was planning so he could stop him in his tracks.

'We don't want to embarrass him further, Mother. Why don't we let Apollo get back to his busy lifestyle and you can come out and meet Skye properly?'

Aphrodite, however, wasn't paying attention. 'Come on. Speak up,' she insisted.

The Sun God shrugged. 'It's just, well, we know that Cupid – sorry, Coop,' he corrected, 'has made a few mistakes lately.'

Coop growled. 'What of it?'

'Well, if I'm not mistaken, true love on its own needs time to develop. Isn't that right, Aphrodite? Obviously you are far more of an expert on the subject than I am.'

'You are right,' she answered slowly. 'There are exceptions but without an arrow or bullet from Coop, it does usually take time. Sometimes a long time.'

Apollo gave her an innocent smile. Her eyes widened and she gasped. 'Coop, you didn't!'

'Didn't what?' he said, not entirely sure where Apollo was heading.

'You shot yourself!'

His mouth dropped open. 'No. Absolutely not.'

'How did it happen?'

'Mother, I did not bloody well shoot myself!'

Apollo shook his head. 'There's no harm in admitting your mistakes, Cupid. You've been under a lot of pressure lately. But with the fact you shot the wrong person a couple of weeks ago, then missed someone entirely yesterday...'

Coop couldn't help himself. He lunged towards Apollo, launching a tightly clenched fist in the direction of his face. Even though the Sun God must have known it was coming, he didn't attempt to get out of the way.

'Cupid!' exclaimed Aphrodite.

'I'm sorry,' said Apollo. 'Clearly the passion he feels is strong. It can only mean it's not real.'

'It's bloody real, you wanker!' Coop thought quickly and switched tactics. 'And do you know what? Even if it's not what you call real, it doesn't matter. You keep telling me, Mother, that the love bolts are meant to be. That they create true love. Well then, here you go. True love. What does it matter either way?'

Aphrodite looked troubled. 'Yes, but Fate decrees...'

'Not for gods,' he interrupted. 'We make our own fate.'

'That's true,' said Apollo. 'And there is, of course, another way to find out whether this is meant to be or not.'

'What's that, genius?' snarled Coop.

He smiled. 'The girl.'

Coop's stomach dropped. The last thing he wanted was for Skye to have to deal with Apollo any more than she already had.

'You're right,' Aphrodite said. 'Has she told you she loves you?'

'Of course she has!'

'Are you sure?' asked Apollo. 'What were her exact words?'

Coop thought back, then cursed inwardly. Damn it to hell. 'She said she thought she loved me this morning.'

'Thought?' There was an unpleasant gleam in Apollo's eyes.

He sighed. 'Yes. But I know she does. She's shy. She wouldn't have wanted to say it outright. She was prevaricating and thinking out loud...'

'I don't like this,' said Aphrodite.

'No,' Apollo added. 'Neither do I. And she is human, as well.'

'What the fuck does that mean?'

'Coop! Language!'

Apollo shrugged. 'Humans have been known to twist the truth from time to time to get close to us and the seat of power. To obtain immortality. They can be very manipulative.'

The rage inside Coop boiled over. 'She is not like that!'

Apollo met Aphrodite's eyes; she nodded back at him, concerned.

'There are many humans who would do almost anything to avoid the fleeting nature of their lives. The prospect of immortality is a desirable one.'

'You can't believe this idiot, Mother!' Coop yelled. 'Skye is the kindest, most trustworthy person I've ever met. She's not after sodding eternal life!'

Aphrodite tapped her mouth thoughtfully. 'Far be it from me to stop the course of true love. Especially when that love involves my son.'

Coop breathed a sigh of relief. Thank goodness.

'But,' she continued, 'we need to be sure she is genuine. That this love is genuine. There have been too many mistakes lately, Coop. I don't need to spend any more time picking up the pieces after you. And I don't want to see you get hurt.'

Stung, Coop took a step back and folded his arms. Let his mother and bloody Apollo do whatever they wished. All they'd discover was that he and Skye were in love. He tried to push away the tiny voice of doubt that was whispering inside his skull. She did love him; she had to.

'So what do you propose?'

Aphrodite paused. 'Has she ever seen you? I mean, you met her after Zeus put on the invisibility spell, right?'

'Right,' Coop said tiredly. 'She doesn't know what I look like.'

'Well then, we use that. I'll lift the invisibility for the next three nights between the hours of dusk and dawn only. If she can avoid sneaking in to catch a glimpse of you, then we'll know it's true love. It'll mean she trusts you completely and you can trust her.'

'She'll have to know the spell is lifted,' said Apollo sternly. 'And most definitely not realise that this is a test.'

Aphrodite nodded. 'Yes, you're right, Apollo,' she said.

Fuck off, Apollo, thought Coop. 'This is ridiculous,' he said aloud. 'It will prove nothing.'

'No, I think it'll prove a lot. If she can overcome her fallible human nature, I think we can safely say her love is real.'

'And if she fails the test,' Apollo interjected, 'you'll have to agree to leave her to live out the remainder of her human life without you.'

A twist of pain wrenched at Coop's heart. 'What's to stop me from leaving right now, taking her with me and never returning?'

'You're a god, Cupid,' Aphrodite said softly. 'You've got responsibilities. You know things don't work that way. Sooner or later you'd be forced to return. And things wouldn't be pretty for either you or your girlfriend. Zeus would see to that.'

Coop clenched his teeth, avoiding the expression of smug self-satisfaction on Apollo's face. 'Fine.'

'Give me your word.'

'Do you really need me to say it? By Olympus, you have my sodding word. But in three days' time, you'll be sorry you ever made this happen.'

Aphrodite sighed. 'I hope so. For your sake, I really hope so.'

NINETEEN

When the door finally re-opened, Skye was dismayed to see Apollo striding out. She had no idea what he'd been doing with Coop's mother but considering how angry he'd been when Coop had lifted the love spell, she was pretty sure that whatever he'd been up to, it wouldn't be in either her or Coop's best interests. He walked right up to her with a smile plastered on his handsome face. Skye pressed herself against the wall and wished she were as invisible as Coop.

'Ms Sawyer,' he purred, taking both her hands in his. 'What a pleasure to see you again.'

A hot flush began at the base of Skye's neck and started to spread upwards. She'd not been expecting this level of congeniality; antagonism would probably be easier to deal with.

She inclined her neck stiffly. 'Mr Apollo.'

He laughed. 'Oh, I'm hardly a "mister". Dear me, I dread to think what darling Cupid is telling you about our little world if you're addressing me as such.' He paused for a moment and eyed her curiously. 'Isn't it strange that you can't see him?'

Skye eyed him nervously. 'I'm used to it now,' she said finally.

'But how can you possibly trust someone you can't see? They say the eyes are the window to the soul, don't they? If you can't ever see what's in his eyes, I don't understand how you can stand to be around him. He could be rolling them to the heavens whenever you speak. Or making faces behind your back.'

'I don't need to see his eyes to know that he's trustworthy,' Skye spat back. 'Unlike you. I can see your eyes perfectly well and I don't trust you an inch.'

Apollo threw back his head and laughed again. She had the distinct feeling that he was laughing at her, rather than merely her words.

'He's terribly good looking, you know,' he murmured, leaning in to speak closer to her ear. 'I wonder if he's too handsome for you. I mean, you're pretty in a human kind of way, I suppose, but if you saw him you might start to wonder whether you're really good enough for him.' He reached out and touched her shoulder. 'Perhaps you're right and it's better that he stays invisible, after all.'

Skye wasn't sure whether she was being insulted or Coop was but, before she could reply, the Sun God had released her shoulder and was smoothly walking away.

Coop emerged from Aphrodite's chambers after staying behind to inform her just how little he thought of her efforts to test Skye. He caught sight of Apollo leaning into Skye's taut frame, his eyes travelled to the hand that was resting lightly on her shoulder and he scowled in annoyance. He stalked up to the pair of them, reaching them just as Apollo took his grubby paw off her and left.

'What did he want?' he snapped.

Skye jumped. 'I wish you'd put the bell back on. I never know where you are.' She sighed and tugged at her hair. 'I think Apollo was trying to wind me up. Knowing that doesn't make it easier though. He still succeeded in completely riling me.'

Coop felt immediately guilty. 'I'm sorry. He's an arse.' And a scheming, manipulative prick, he added silently to himself.

Skye glanced over at the open doorway. 'Is your mother coming back out?'

Coop gritted his teeth angrily on Skye's behalf. Aphrodite had stated in no uncertain terms that until Skye passed – or failed – the test, she would have nothing to do with her.

'I'm sorry. She's,' he paused, unwilling to tell a lie, 'being difficult.'

Skye winced. That didn't sound good. The note of worry and underlying rage in Coop's voice meant she had to make sure he was okay, though. 'It's alright,' she reassured him. 'Mums are often protective of their sons. Just give her a bit of time. Besides,' she said, trying not to fish too hard for information, 'how many other girls have you brought to meet her?'

Coop barely registered her words. 'She just doesn't understand!' he burst out. 'She'll put absolutely no credence in the way I feel. She'd rather believe Apollo and his lies than listen to what I have to say.'

Skye reached out gingerly, her fingers brushing against his cheek. 'Oh, Coop,' she murmured, unsure of what to say. 'I'm sorry.'

You've got absolutely nothing to be sorry about. It's the rest of us who should feel sorry about what we're doing, Coop thought, his anger continuing to grow.

He took Skye's hand and gently squeezed it. 'Come on,' he said. 'Let's just go home.'

Feeling ridiculously relieved, Skye nodded vigorously. Thank goodness. She'd had quite enough of Olympus and its machinations and marble. If she never came back here again, it would probably be too soon.

Coop kept hold of Skye's hand as they walked back through the airy, impressive halls of Olympus. Even now, back in his own home, he seemed reluctant to let go. Skye was enjoying feeling protected by him, although she finally extricated her fingers from his when they entered the kitchen. For some reason the visit to Olympus had made her absolutely ravenous. It must be a reaction to all that stress, she mused.

'I'm going to fix a sandwich,' she announced. 'Would you like anything?'

I'd like us to run away together and never deal with any of this crap ever again, Coop thought miserably.

'That would be nice,' he said aloud.

Registering the unhappiness in his voice, Skye paused and looked in his direction. Now that they were away from the confines of Olympus, Aphrodite and her concerns seemed very far away.

'What's really wrong, Coop?'

'Nothing,' he grunted, immediately regretting his terse reply when he saw a hurt expression flit across her face. 'It's just...' He sighed, and watched her carefully. 'My mother is going to lift the invisibility spell every night between dusk and dawn.'

Skye's eyes widened. 'That's brilliant! I'll be able to see you! We'll be able to...' her voice trailed off and her cheeks coloured at the thought of the new carnal delights offered by actually being able to see Coop. Not to mention the fact she'd feel closer to him when she knew what he really looked like.

Coop sat heavily down on a nearby stool. 'We also have to stay apart from each other during those hours.'

Skye blinked. 'What? Why?'

He ran his hands through his hair. 'We just do. I can't explain it right now, Skye. I just need you to promise to stay away from my rooms during those hours.'

Skye stared at the space occupied by his voice. 'I don't understand,' she said in a small voice.

Coop could see why. But considering the restraints placed on him by Apollo and his mother, there was little he could do to explain. Inwardly cursing the pair of them, he reached out and drew Skye to him. 'It's only for three days,' he murmured in her ear. 'Then we'll be free to be together. Just trust me.'

Clouds of suspicion floated through Skye. 'You mean we're not free to be together now? Even though we're here together now?'

'As I said, my mother is being difficult.'

Skye frowned, trying to sort things out in her head. She'd heard of men who were tied to their mother's apron strings, but she'd never imagined Coop would be one of them. Maybe it was a good thing, she mused. If he was respectful of Aphrodite, it showed how important family ties were to him. And that could only be positive, right?

'Okay,' she answered slowly.

'Really?'

'I don't really have much choice in the matter, do I?'

Coop swallowed and moved back slightly so he could look into her face. Despite what he'd just told her, the trust in her eyes made his blood sing. He didn't deserve her, but he was damned if he was going to ever let her go. A sudden thought hit him and he grinned. Nobody had said she had to stay with him over these three days. If she was out of country then there would be no chance of her slipping into his rooms during those hours when he was visible. He trusted her implicitly but he was still concerned about what Apollo might do to force the issue. He wouldn't put it past the Sun God to do something sneaky to have things work out in his favour. This way, there would be no chance of that happening.

'Actually, Skye, why don't you take this opportunity to go back home? See your parents and your friends? Because I'm not sure I'll be willing to let you out of my sight after these three days are over.'

There was the slightest edge of glee to Coop's voice which made Skye pause. She wanted to yell about the fact that he was never in her sight so this was hardly fair. But it would be good to see her family and catch up with Emma and the girls. She just wished she understood more about what was happening; there was definitely something else going on and Skye didn't like being kept out of the loop. Didn't Coop trust her? She gnawed on her lip then made a decision. If this was what he needed her to do right now, she'd do it.

'Okay,' she said, 'I'll go back home until the end of the week. After that...'

'After that, I'm going to tie you to my side so you never leave again,' he whispered in her ear, before his lips moved down her neck and began planting little kisses along her nape.

Skye shivered. She hoped this was some weird thing he had going on with his mother and not a convoluted way to get rid of her and get back to all his other girlfriends. Then Coop's mouth found hers and she stopped thinking entirely.

CHAPTER

TWENTY

L ater that day, when Skye stepped out of the airport and
realised just how cold and wet and grey the weather was
back in Britain, she was too focused on keeping her head
down to avoid the freezing rain to spot Apollo's golden head on the
other side of the road, watching her and smiling unpleasantly to
himself at Coop's predictability.

The Sun God knew that, without Coop in tow, it would take the
girl several hours to get back to her parents' house. That gave him
plenty of time to put his own plans into action. If there was a flicker
of guilt inside him, then he squashed it quickly. Both the girl and the
stupid cherub had conspired to humiliate him in front of all of his
friends. He'd made a complete fool of himself and there was no way
he was going to let that slide. Coop and Skye were going to pay for
what they'd done to him.

Less than an hour later, he caught sight of Skye's mother
entering the small local supermarket. Following her in, but moving
quickly across a couple of aisles to wait for her to catch him up, he
began perusing the wine section, selecting a bottle at random to pick

up and study. It was cheap plonk but it would serve his requirements.

Fortunately, the woman was a fast shopper and it didn't take long before she was wheeling her trolley past him. He cleared his throat and aimed for a congenial tone.

'Excuse me?' he said.

Skye's mother looked surprised and turned to face him. 'Yes?'

'I was wondering if you could help me. I'm cooking dinner tonight for a friend. A special friend. I want to get some nice wine to go with it but I don't really drink myself. Could you help me out?'

Her eyes crinkled at the edges. 'I can try. Does your, erm, friend, like red or white?'

'I have no idea,' Apollo said, looking stricken. 'Does it make a difference?'

'Why certainly!' she laughed. 'But if you don't know, perhaps it would be wise to go in between and try a rosé instead.'

Aiming for baffled, Apollo shrugged helplessly. 'What's a rosé?'

She smiled. 'You really don't drink, do you? Here, I'll show you.' She pointed towards the left, picking up one bottle and holding it out to him. 'This is a rosé wine. You'll need to chill it before you serve it but it's not too expensive and it tastes quite nice. I'm sure your friend will enjoy it.'

'Thank you so much!' Apollo beamed. Before she could leave, he spoke again. 'I just want to make sure everything goes right. I really want to make her happy. I've only known her for a couple of weeks but I can just tell that it's meant to be.'

'Oh, young love,' Skye's mother said warmly. 'There's nothing quite like it.'

'Indeed,' he agreed. 'This happens to me all the time, to be honest. When I fall, I fall hard. I'm always in love for the first couple of weeks.' He paused and looked earnest. 'Sometimes even months. It's important to keep them happy to begin with. Then when the sheen wears off and I'm bored with them, at least they've had a good time and have some pleasant memories to remember me by. I find that being in love is only fun during the initial period. I like the excitement and the nervous fluttering feeling you get. Once that rubs off, well, it's time to move on.'

The flicker of distaste which flashed in her eyes told Apollo he'd found his mark. Trying not to grin, he continued. 'Thank you for your help. I'm sure she'll enjoy this wine.'

Skye's mother pasted on a smile and pushed her trolley forward again. 'You're welcome.'

Apollo watched her go, amused at the straight line of her back which indicated her disapproval. As soon as she had disappeared from view, he put the nasty looking wine back on the shelf and checked his watch. Nemesis would be open in a few hours and Helios had already agreed to let him in early to have a chat to the girl's friends. This was going to be easier than taking candy from a baby.

When Skye finally pushed open the door to her parents' house, feeling distinctly damp and very tired, she felt a rush of warmth at the familiar sights and smells. With Coop to distract her, she'd not had time to think about missing home; now she was thrilled to be seeing her parents in person rather than talking to them on the phone. Both of them immediately appeared in the small hallway, huge smiles stretching across their faces.

Her father stepped over and reached out to envelop her in a huge bear hug. 'We've missed you!' He pulled back and looked her up and down. 'You're looking good, Skye. You're looking happy.'

Skye glanced over at her mother and saw the equally approving expression on her face.

'That's because I am,' she said softly. 'I've got so much to tell the pair of you.'

'It's great to have you home,' her mum said. 'Let me put the kettle on while you go upstairs and have a shower and change into some dry clothes. Then you can tell us all about it. Greece sounds wonderful.'

Skye's eyes shone. 'It is, Mum, it really is.'

Half an hour later, all three were in the living room. The rain outside had picked up tempo and was drumming against the window but inside the house was warm and cosy. Skye curled her legs up underneath her and sighed happily.

'Even though it's only a short visit, it's great to be back.'

'Are you sure you can't stay for longer?'

Skye nodded. 'I promised Emma I'd go and visit her on my last night. I've only got three days. I need to be back in Greece by Friday.'

Her father frowned. 'He doesn't give you much time off, this boss of yours.'

Skye's eyes lit up. 'He's not really my boss,' she said. 'Not any longer.'

Alarm showed on both her parents' faces.

'Has he fired you?' her mum demanded. 'Just like that awful Helios man? I've still got half a mind to go down to London and tell him just what I think of the way he treats his employees. Honestly, giving you the sack when all you were doing was standing up for yourself.' She shook her head. 'It's not on, Skye. You've still got rights, you know.'

Skye smiled at her vehemence. 'It's okay. It all worked out for the best,' she reassured her. 'And I've not been fired by my new boss. It's more like our relationship has, um, changed.'

Her mum looked confused for a moment then her expression cleared. 'Oh. Oh! You mean...'

Skye grinned. 'Yes. He's wonderful, Mum. I've never met anyone like him before. His name's Coop and he's thoughtful and kind. He loves literature and he's forever quoting it to me. I'm in love. Really, genuinely in love.' Skye's cheeks reddened at the truth of the words but her heart felt full to bursting.

'But he's your employer,' her mum said, looking troubled. 'Are you sure he's not taking advantage of you and the situation?'

Surprised that her mother wasn't happier for her, Skye answered, 'No! Definitely not. He's told me he loves me and I believe him. We just fit together. He's not perfect by any means but his faults make him even more endearing. You'll meet him soon and you'll see.'

'I'll look forward to that,' her dad said gruffly. At least he seemed pleased for her.

'You've barely known him a month, Skye,' her mum interjected. 'How can you know you're in love?'

'I just know,' Skye said quietly.

'What does he do, this Coop?'

Skye was prepared for this. As much as she loved her parents, she didn't think they'd quite be prepared to listen to the fact that Coop was an invisible love god. 'He runs a dating agency,' she said smoothly.

The corners of her mum's mouth turned down. 'Does he, indeed?'

'Mum! What's that supposed to mean?'

'Someone who runs a dating agency sounds like someone who knows a lot about the mechanics of love. Who knows how to give the impression of being in love.'

'You've not even met him and you're already doubting him.'

'I'm sorry, sweetheart,' her mum answered. 'It's just I met this awful man today who...'

'I don't care about some man you met today, Mum! Coop isn't some stranger I met on the streets. If you knew what he'd done for me and the way he treats me, you'd think differently. We really are in love.'

'It seems so fast. So sudden.'

'That doesn't make it wrong.'

Her mum sighed. 'You're right. Just tell me this, does he do it often?'

Skye was puzzled. 'Do what often?'

'Fall in love. Some men are like that, you know. Serial monogamists who always have a new girl on their arm.'

'This is ridiculous! You should trust me and trust my judgment.' Skye pushed away the little voice in her head that reminded her of Hermes' words about all the women Coop had been with in the past. She also tried to forget that Coop hadn't answered her question about how many times he'd taken girls to meet his mother. She didn't believe he was lying when he told her how he felt. The emotion in his voice was too clear. Besides, why *would* he lie? He had nothing to gain from it.

'Marj,' her father chided, 'Skye's looked into his eyes and seen the truth there. She's not some airhead who lurches from man to man. We should be happy for her.'

Her mum shook herself. 'You're right. I'm so sorry, Skye. It's just because of this man in the supermarket. He seemed to think it was okay to fall in love at the drop of a hat and then move on a heartbeat later.'

'Only you could get into a conversation about love in the supermarket, Mum. Coop's not like that. He didn't even believe in love until a couple of weeks ago.'

'Then I'm happy for you,' her mum said, standing up and moving over to give her a big hug. 'I shouldn't have questioned him. Perhaps you'll bring him with you next time?'

Skye smiled and nodded. Only if he's not still invisible, she thought, biting her lip. He sent you away, the little voice inside her whispered. You've not looked into his eyes and seen the truth there at all. Skye swallowed. No, she had to trust him. She *did* trust him. He felt the same way about her as she did about him.

Two days later Skye met Emma in the heart of Covent Garden. Her friend bounded up to her with a face wreathed in smiles.

'You look amazing!' she yelled. 'How the bloody hell are you?'

Skye smiled. 'I'm good, Emma, really good.'

'It's so great to see you! I've got loads to tell you.'

Emma pulled on her arm and led her to a nearby coffee shop. They ordered a pot of tea and sat down together.

'So how are Joy and Chrissie?' Skye asked, once they were settled.

'Oh, they're the same as ever. They say hello and to tell you they're missing your baking.'

Skye grimaced. She'd avoided ovens and anything like cupcakes since her disaster at Nemesis. 'Tell them I said hi.'

'I will, I will,' beamed Emma. 'But let's get down to more important things.' Her face turned serious. 'Your boss and the crush you've got on him.'

'It's not a crush,' Skye said quietly. 'I'm in love. You should meet him, Emma. He's just perfect. I can't believe how lucky I am.'

The shadow on her friend's face was unmistakable.

'What is it?' Skye asked.

'I shouldn't say anything.'

'But you will,' Skye said. She knew Emma too well to expect her to stay quiet when she had something to say.

Emma cut straight to the chase. 'You told me he was handsome.'

Skye's tongue stuck to the roof of her mouth and she nodded mutely.

'You've never set eyes on him, have you?' Her friend eyed her unhappily.

Skye started. 'How the hell do you know that?'

'It's true then.' Emma's shoulders sank. 'I had hoped it wasn't. Skye, how can you be in love with someone when you don't even know what they look like?'

'You don't fall in love with someone because of their looks. It's personality and what's inside that counts. You can't tell me you think otherwise.'

'Not entirely, no, but...'

'But what?'

'Think of a painting. You buy a painting because you like the way it looks. Most people don't understand the craftsmanship or skills or thought that goes into it. You need to have a baseline attraction from the start.'

'I'm not in love with a painting.'

'No,' Emma agreed. 'You're in love with someone who could walk past us right this very moment and you wouldn't know if it was him or not. That's crazy, Skye.' She pointed to a dreadlocked man strolling past. 'It could be him.'

'It's not him.' Skye said flatly.

'How do you know? It's creepy, hon, not knowing who he really is.'

'I do know who he really is,' Skye burst out. 'How do *you* know I can't see him?' she repeated.

Emma shifted uncomfortably. 'I promised I wouldn't say.'

Skye stared at her. 'That's not fair. You're meant to be my friend.'

'And what kind of friend would I be if I broke my word to someone else? What kind of friend would I be if I didn't speak up when I'm worried you're making a big mistake?'

'I can't believe you're trying to tell me that appearance is more important than personality.'

'I'm not. But you can't deny that appearance counts. What if you finally see him for what he is and realise you're not attracted to him?'

'That's ridiculous.'

'No, it's not. You can bluster and pretend all you like, Skye, but physical attraction is important.'

'Not that important,' Skye said stubbornly.

'Okay, then, what about trust?'

'What do you mean?'

'How can you trust someone when they won't show you their face?'

Skye looked down. 'I trust him.'

'Do you? It doesn't sound like you do.'

'Emma...'

Her friend put her hands up in mock surrender. 'Okay, fine. I won't say any more. Just think about it. For me? If you get the opportunity to see him in person you should take it. What's the worst thing that can happen?'

A ripple of unease ran through Skye. 'I don't know.'

Emma sat back. 'See? At least you'll know then who he really is. It's not about being shallow, Skye.' She dropped her voice to a whisper. 'It was a guy called Hermes who told me.'

Skye blinked. Hermes? But he was Coop's friend. Why would he be running around talking to Emma behind Coop's back?

'He made me promise not to tell you who he was,' Emma confided. 'I think he likes you and doesn't want to see you get hurt.'

'Did he tell you what Coop is?' she asked cautiously.

'The god part? Yeah. That's freaking weird, hon. But I'd always had a few suspicions regarding Helios, you know. Once I went into his office and the place was bathed in light. It was so freaking bright, I thought my eyeballs were going to be seared off. But it wasn't the electric light that was causing it. And then this one time I thought I saw...' Emma's voice trailed off. 'It doesn't matter.'

'You're taking that part remarkably in your stride.'

She shrugged. 'Hey, I'm an open-minded kind of gal. But not so open-minded as to think you can have a genuine relationship with someone when you don't know what they look like.'

'It's not his fault he's invisible.'

'So he says,' said Emma. 'Hermes suggested there was more to it. That he'd deliberately made himself invisible.'

Skye's brow furrowed. That just didn't make sense. Why would he do that?

'Look, let's forget it. Your room is all ready for you and I've got the night off. Let's have fun tonight and you can decide what to do tomorrow when you get back to Greece.'

Skye clenched her teeth. No. This was ridiculous. First her mother thought her relationship with Coop was doomed, now her best friend seemed to think they couldn't possibly have a real relationship together. Neither of them understood. And what on earth

Hermes had been doing, she had no idea. Despite having only been away from him for two days, she missed Coop desperately. She needed her friends and family to see how wonderful he was. But they'd not even met him yet and already they were against him. Skye was going to prove otherwise. Lion, not mouse, she told herself. Instead of waiting for things to happen to her, she was damned well going to make them happen herself. She stood up and pushed her chair back.

'Actually, Emma, I'm not staying after all. I'm going back home.'

'To your parents?'

'No,' she said firmly, dropping some money on the table. 'To Greece.'

THERE WAS no driver to pick her up from the airport this time. Coop wasn't expecting her back for another day. She'd been lucky to get on the last flight to Athens as it was; by the time she reached the mansion, he'd probably be fast asleep. But that was okay. She'd wake up his visible self and they could look into each other's eyes properly. He'd understand. If it meant the other people she cared about were more inclined to love and trust him, it was worth it. Digging into her bag, she had just enough cash to pay for a taxi through the winding hills.

Unable to relax, she fobbed off the taxi driver's attempts at conversation and stared out of the window. The moon was covered by clouds and even the lights of the city seemed dull. Trepidation and excitement bubbled in the pit of her stomach. Occasionally she felt a flicker of doubt and worried whether she was doing the wrong thing, but then she put those thoughts aside. Coop had asked her to promise not to try to see him while he was visible but she'd not said the words, so there was no promise to break. Besides, if he'd missed her as much as she'd missed him, this was going to be a hell of a hello.

The truth was that Coop *had* missed her desperately. He'd spent the previous two days moping around the mansion, listlessly wandering from room to room. Skye's scent was still lingering in the air and everywhere he went there were traces of her presence. The only thing he'd found to take his mind off her had been his job; somehow going out and helping others to find love made him feel better. He made a mental note to tell that to his mother. She'd been on at him for years to appreciate his job more; now he had Skye, he did.

After tossing and turning for two nights, barely able to sleep, today he'd gone for a long swim so he felt tired when he clambered in between the cool sheets of his bed. Unfortunately that meant he fell asleep almost instantly, failing to hear the sound of the taxi – and Skye – pulling up outside.

After paying the driver, and with her heart in her mouth, Skye walked up to the front door of the mansion and carefully opened it. The house was dark and quiet. Skye grinned to herself. He'd be surprised to see her but – she hoped –happy too. She kicked off her shoes and padded through the house to the wing where his bedroom was.

At the door, Skye put her hand on the knob and began to twist it, then paused suddenly and pulled back. Doubt filled her: was this the right thing to do? Coop had seemed adamant she mustn't see him while the invisibility spell was off. She thought of Apollo's caustic comments about how handsome Coop was. Was that because he wasn't good looking at all? Was he actually some kind of monster with horns and scaly skin?

But she'd felt his skin. It was smooth. And there certainly weren't any horns on his head. She'd run her hands all the way through his soft hair. Even if he wasn't as good looking as she'd been led to expect, it hardly mattered. Appearance wasn't important, no matter what Emma said. In fact part of her hoped he didn't look like a love god should –then she wouldn't feel inferior next to him.

She stood there, staring at the barrier of the door. This might be her only chance to know what he looked like. His mother might decide to keep the invisibility spell on indefinitely. Skye straightened her shoulders. She spent far too much time doing what she was supposed to, instead of what she wanted to. Seeing him would put the naysayers in their place. Even if Coop was angry, he'd get over it. She smiled to herself. She'd make sure of that.

This time she placed her hand on the doorknob and didn't hesitate, turning it and stepping decisively into his bedroom. The lump in the centre of the bed indicated he was there sleeping. Skye's heart was pounding. She took a step towards him. Then another. At that moment, the wind shifted and the clouds covering the shining brilliance of the moon shifted. A shaft of light hit the bed through the open window and Skye gasped.

He was unlike anyone she'd ever seen. She'd thought Apollo, for all his faults, had been handsome but nothing prepared her for the sight of Coop. He was naked, with half a sheet twisted round his body, revealing sculpted muscles. Muscles she'd only felt with her fingers and now could see with her eyes. His arms were covered in sweeping dark tattoos, similar to traditional Maori or Celtic ones she'd seen in pictures, but those hadn't been so elegant or intricate. In repose his face was angelic and somehow hard at the same time. The golden curls on top of his head would appear feminine on anyone else but on Coop they somehow added to his masculinity. She reached out to brush one away from his cheek and, as she did so, his eyes opened.

For a moment the sleepy violet of his irises took her in, warm delight filling them to their depths, then suddenly they clouded over and he sprang up and stared at her in dismay.

'Skye,' he whispered.

She smiled at him. 'Coop. I'm sorry. I know you said to stay away but I had to see you. I had to know what you look like. You understand that, right?'

A muscle clenched in his cheek and it appeared as if a great rage was filling him. His body shook and he clenched his fists at his sides.

Then he sprang forward without warning and pulled her to him, his mouth curving down towards hers.

Skye opened herself up to him, locking her arms round his neck and leaning into his hard body. As erotic as it had been making love to him without being able to see him, this was far, far better. He deepened the kiss until her senses were drowning and then, abruptly, pulled away. Skye moved towards him and he held up his hands as if to ward her off. He shook his head sadly, an angry fire still within him, although it didn't seem to be directed at her.

'Doubting Skye,' he said softly, reaching one hand out to cup her cheek. Then he blinked and two enormous white wings appeared at his back as if from nowhere.

Skye stared open-mouthed. Before she could react, he turned and leapt into the air. He flew out of the window, silhouetted for a heart-beat against the orb of the moon as he turned to look at her one last time. Then he was gone.

PART TWO

'Cupid being more and more in love with Psyche, and fearing the displeasure of his Mother, did pearce into the heavens, and arrived before Jupiter to declare his cause.'

Source: Apuleus (translated by William Adlington)

CHAPTER
TWENTY-ONE

Three days later, Skye stepped off the train at Litochoro station. It didn't take her long to realise that she was in the middle of nowhere. The few other passengers who had got off with her had already vanished and there was no-one else in sight. A distant rumble of thunder made her jump and a few drops of heavy rain began to fall from the overcast sky.

Her heart sank further. Three days. Three nights. Interminable nights. Since the moment Coop had flown out of the window with those magnificent snow-white wings, there had been no sign of him. She'd spent the first few hours staring out into the night sky, expecting him to return. Then, when he didn't, she had started to panic. The realisation of just how badly she had screwed up sunk in, along with the overwhelming sense of loneliness which suddenly pervaded the once warm and welcoming mansion.

It wasn't until the following evening that she finally appreciated he wasn't coming back. Skye had virtually ransacked the place searching through drawers and cupboards for a contact list. Coop had a mobile phone; surely Hermes would have one too. He would know how she could find him. But she'd come up empty. Even if

Hermes was in a position to help her, she had no way of getting in touch with him. She had no way of getting in touch with anyone, apart from her own friends and family, and she knew that they would be unable to help her. She had created this situation herself; now she had to find a way to resolve it. Coop had asked for her promise to stay away from him while he was visible; she had broken his trust. She could only hope she could persuade him to give her a second chance.

Turning up the collar of her thin jacket and starting to trudge down a winding road, which she hoped led to the small town, Skye felt numb with weariness. The gates of Olympus were the only place she could think of to try but, without the magic of Coop's godly powers, she was forced to find a way to reach them on her own. Unfortunately she had very little to go on. She knew from what Coop had told her that Olympus was somewhere near Litochoro, but she had no idea how to find it. Skye had spent several hours researching, and looking for some – any – kind of guidance. Nothing she had come across helped. She was banking on the thought that someone who lived in Litochoro would be able to guide her. Otherwise, all would be lost.

The looming mountain, which she presumed was Olympus itself, was shrouded in heavy fog. The wind had started to pick up but, instead of helpfully blowing away the clouds and clearing the sky, all it did was blow around her with increasing ferocity. Her eyes were starting to smart from the rain that was blowing into her face and her teeth were chattering. Skye was so lost in her own well of misery that she didn't hear the car coming up from behind her until it was almost too late.

Half turning then registering the headlights that were beaming down on her, Skye's heart leapt. Without thinking, she stuck out her thumb in the universal signal of a hitchhiker. Unfortunately, the driver either didn't see her or chose to ignore her and didn't slow down. The wheels splashed into a large puddle on the road, sending a wave of water in her direction. Skye tried to jump out of the way but it was to no avail and the cold, dirty water drenched her from head to foot. Rubbing at her face and eyes with the grubby sleeve of her jacket, she blinked after the car as it disappeared; yet again, she was alone on the miserable, grey road.

It was some time later, when Skye felt as if she'd been walking for hours, that a dim shape appeared on the horizon. Blinking at it and trying to work out what on earth it actually was, she picked up her pace. At this particular point in time, any form of shelter would be welcome. She wasn't sure when she'd ever felt so cold. Surely Greece was supposed to be warm and sunny? It was if the gods themselves were against her. Coop's unhappy eyes, with their unbanked fires of rage, flashed into her mind. Maybe they were. Maybe the gods of Olympus were going to do everything they could to prevent her from reaching Coop.

Instead of weakening her, however, that thought strengthened her resolve. Skye was going to confront the fact that she'd screwed up head-on and do whatever she could to make amends. She couldn't imagine a life without him and she was damned if anyone was going to stop her. Until she saw Coop for herself and he said he wanted nothing to do with her, she wasn't going to give up.

The poor visibility on the winding road was such that she was less than twenty metres away when a shape up ahead began to take form. It was a ramshackle stone building with one wall crumbling down on the north side and a wooden door hanging precariously off its hinges at the front. It didn't matter. Shelter was shelter, and Skye ran inside, ducking her head and scooting into the dark interior. There was a strong smell of manure but at least it was fairly clean. She kicked away rotting wood and debris from one corner and slumped down against the wall, hugging her knees to her chest. Outside, the wind howled as if in rage that she was no longer out in the open and the rain slammed down onto the tin roof, creating a thunderous racket. But she was safe and under cover. She'd just have to hope that Coop was somewhere nearby.

THE TRUTH WAS that Coop was barely five miles away, hammering on the door to his mother's chambers. He'd spent the last three days trying to gain an audience with her. All he'd received in return were messages stating that she was too busy to deal with him but that in light of his recent actions, the invisibility spell was being lifted for good. He had the impression that she thought he should be grateful. As if.

'Mother!' he yelled through the massive doors. 'You can't ignore me forever!'

He kicked the door in frustration. If he could just speak to her, he'd have a better shot at persuading her this wasn't Skye's fault. He could hardly blame Skye for wanting to see him in person. Although he'd felt a wave of crushing disappointment to begin with, and a deep feeling of disquiet that she'd not trusted him, he realised she really did love him as much as he loved her back. She wouldn't have left her friends and family to come back early to him if she hadn't. He just had to keep remembering that. They'd been so close to the deadline. If only she'd hung on for a few more hours, everything would have been alright.

Not for the first time he cursed himself for falling asleep and not hearing her come back to the mansion. She was going to be punished for the vagaries of the gods and it just wasn't fair. He replayed the look on her face when he had left over and over again. She'd been stunned when his wings unfurled but that expression had quickly turned to horror as he'd flown out of the window. She deserved a second chance. *They* deserved a second chance.

He began thumping on the door again.

'Mother! Open the goddamn door!'

'You do realise half the palace can hear your bloody caterwauling?'

Coop stiffened at the familiar voice and turned round slowly to confront the smarmy grin on Apollo's face. 'Yeah?' he said challengingly. 'Well, if you want me to shut up then tell her to come and talk to me.'

'She's your mother. It's not as if I'd have any sway with her.' Apollo smirked.

Coop bunched his hands into fists and took a deep breath. 'Of course you don't,' he said sarcastically.

The God of Light widened his eyes dramatically and clutched his chest. 'Dear me! Are you trying to insinuate that this sorry mess you've found yourself in is my fault? I'm horrified.'

Coop began to turn away, disgusted, but Apollo wasn't going to let him off that easily.

'You know those humans are amazingly easy to manipulate. It took me barely a minute to, shall we say, encourage her mother to see you as a danger to her daughter. And the friend! Well, she was even more persuadable.'

Coop froze and spun back, taking a threatening step towards Apollo. 'It was you!' he spat. 'I thought as much.'

Apollo grinned. 'I watched her going back to see you. She looked so happy. It was as if she couldn't wait to burst in and see you for the first time in person.'

Every muscle in Coop's body bunched up. Unfortunately Apollo still wasn't finished.

'You know,' he mused, 'she actually looked rather pretty. All glowing and in love.' He raised his eyebrows pointedly. 'Now that she's free I may have to seek her out for myself. Considering, after all, that it was me she was initially interested in.'

Coop didn't wait any longer. He sprang towards Apollo, fists flying in all directions, swiping at him with every ounce of energy he could muster. The Sun God dodged him, but Coop didn't give up and barrelled into him, knocking him to the floor. He drew back one fist and slammed into Apollo's face, enjoying the sickening crack as he broke his nose. Then he pulled back for another shot. Before he could launch his fist forward, however, an iron-clad hand gripped it, preventing him from moving.

Coop twisted his face upwards, wincing in pain as his fingers were crushed, determined to see who had dared to prevent him from smashing Apollo's face. As soon as he registered who was interrupting their fight, however, Coop's body went limp. Damn it all to hell, Hades and the Underworld.

'Father,' coughed Apollo.

There was a visible curl of distaste on Zeus's lips. He tightened his grip on Coop's hand, making him groan involuntarily. 'What exactly is going on here?'

'As you can see,' said Apollo, clambering to his feet and ignoring the blood flowing freely from his nose, 'the little cherub here has decided to go postal on me.'

Coop snarled, finally wrenching his fist free from Zeus, and sprang upwards.

Zeus's face remained emotionless. 'The little cherub? The God of Love? You allowed him to hit you?'

Two high spots of colour lit Apollo's cheekbones. 'He came at me from nowhere!' he protested.

'You little shit!' spat Coop. 'You wanted me to punch you. You were fucking asking for it.'

'Be quiet,' Zeus commanded. Although he barely raised his voice above normal speaking level, his authority and tone brooked no argument. He gestured towards Apollo. 'Did you goad him?'

Apollo looked down at the floor and mumbled something. Zeus took a step towards him. 'What was that?'

'He started it.'

Zeus's eyebrows shot up for a second before his face shuttered again. 'He started it?'

'He shot me with one of his damned bullets. He made me think I was in love with some stupid girl!'

'She's not some stupid girl!' yelled Coop, unable to keep quiet.

'Shut up!' roared Zeus. 'The pair of you are gods, for Olympus's sake! And yet here you are behaving like a pair of three year olds. You,' he jabbed his thumb at Apollo, 'you are meant to be my son.

You're meant to hold yourself at a higher standard. And the best explanation you can come up with is "he started it"?'

Coop couldn't help smirking, but Zeus turned on him too. 'And you! You've been given the right to change people's lives for the better. But instead of being proud to hold that honour, you've grumped and whined about it for years. And now you're treating it as some kind of prank. What were you thinking, shooting him?'

Coop's head drooped. 'You're right, I just…'

'I know I'm goddamned right, you idiot!'

'I messed up,' Coop said honestly. 'I realise that now. I'm not the person I was three weeks ago. I've changed.' He raised his eyes and stared at the King of the Heavens, unblinkingly. 'You need to believe me.'

'You've changed. After the years your mother has spent agonising over your childish behaviour, now you've changed. And it's only taken three weeks.' The sarcastic edge to Zeus's voice was clearly audible.

Coop took a deep breath. 'I fell in love. I am in love. She's the most perfect person in the world.'

'Except she can't be trusted for even three days not to spy on you,' interjected Apollo sneeringly.

Coop rounded on the Sun God. 'You made that happen! And she wasn't spying. She thought she was doing the right thing.'

'Oh yeah? How do you know? She only thinks she loves you. Anyway, she's human; she'll have changed her mind by next week and moved on to someone else.'

Zeus reached out to Coop and placed a restraining hand on his arm to prevent him from going after Apollo yet again. 'I know a little something about human women,' he said gruffly. 'Who is this one?'

Coop had to bite his tongue to prevent himself from retorting that the only reason Zeus knew a little about human women was because he'd spent half his life shagging as many as he could lay his hands on.

'Her name is Skye,' he said quietly.

'And you should know, Father, that she colluded with Cupid to bloody shoot me so I'd fall in love with her.'

'That's not true!'

The tiniest frown marred Zeus's forehead. 'Let me get this straight. You,' he pointed at Coop, 'shot my son so he would fall in love with a human girl. Then you fell in love with her yourself.'

Coop nodded.

Zeus continued. 'Then you,' he pointed at Apollo, 'did something to prevent this Skye from being with him.'

'I didn't...'

'Be quiet, Apollo. I know what you're like and I know what you're capable of doing. Sooner or later you are going to need to learn some respect for others.'

'None of this is her fault,' Coop said desperately. 'I've behaved like a world-class fool. I know that. I deserve to be punished. Just ... just don't punish her as well.'

'You made the deal, Cupid. Three days. If she could have managed to avoid sneaking in to see you for three short days, then you'd have won. But she couldn't. If she really loved you, she wouldn't have done that, no matter how much I meddled.'

Coop ran his hands through his hair. 'It's not about winning any more, Apollo. Don't you see that? This isn't a competition. It's my life. My happiness. Her happiness. We're meant to be together. Just because she made one mistake doesn't mean she should be punished for the rest of her life too. She had nothing to do with me shooting you. She was just in the wrong place at the wrong time.'

Zeus pursed his lips thoughtfully. 'Does she love you?'

The door to Aphrodite's quarters slammed open and she appeared in the doorframe looking somewhat tired. 'She failed the test, Coop. She's only human. You'll end up getting hurt, sooner or later.'

Coop faced her. 'I'm not a little boy any more, Mother. You have to let me make my own mistakes and stop interfering. Besides, this isn't a mistake and she does love me.'

'How do you know? You weren't so sure before.'

'Because if she doesn't then I've got no reason to live,' he said simply.

Zeus met Aphrodite's eyes and a look passed between them. Apollo was staring at Coop, his mouth half open.

'It does sound as if there's an easy way out of this,' Zeus began.

'No.' Apollo shook his head fervently. 'He gave his word. Either she passed the test and they could be together, or she failed and he never saw her again. And she failed. End of story.'

A growl rumbled in Coop's chest and he pulled his shoulders back. A flicker of agreement crossed Aphrodite's face. 'It's true,' she admitted. 'That was the deal.'

'But...' Coop began to protest.

Zeus held up a heavy finger in warning. 'Then my hands are tied. The deal is done.'

'You'll get over her,' Aphrodite said. 'There are lots of human girls around. And lots of minor goddesses who would be far more suitable for you. Any of them would be thrilled to have you as their consort. Not to mention that you'll know they have no ulterior motives in wanting to be with you.'

'I will not get over her,' Coop forced out. 'Don't you get it?'

Apollo's eyes were lit from within with a malicious gleam. 'It's merely an immature infatuation, Cupid. You'll feel better in a hundred years or so.'

Coop snarled. His mother shook her head. 'You still have a lot of growing up to do, darling.'

Coop tightened his hands into two hard fists and tried to force down the painful knot that was gathering in his chest.

'Don't let me see you two fighting again,' Zeus ordered. 'Or the consequences will be dire.'

'Of course, Father,' stated Apollo, shooting a nasty sideways look at Coop.

Aphrodite turned and walked back into her rooms, closing the door softly behind her. Zeus raised his eyebrows meaningfully at

Coop and strode off, Apollo trotting dutifully at his heels. Coop scowled after the pair of them, doing everything he could to quell the rage and hurt inside him, and forced himself not to run after them and throw himself at them in a suicidal attack. Instead he remained where he was, frozen, barely registering Hermes pad up to stand next to him.

'So,' his friend said, 'neither Zeus nor your mother will listen?'

Coop grunted in response. Hermes looked at him worriedly. 'You're not planning on doing anything stupid, are you, Coop?'

A tiny muscle throbbed in Coop's cheek. 'No. That's what they're expecting. At least that's what Apollo's expecting. I could run out of here and find Skye and we could elope together. We could find somewhere to live out the rest of our days. Except I'm immortal and she's not. And she deserves a better existence than one that means cowering against the retribution of Olympus for the rest of her life. No,' he repeated, shaking his head. 'There's a way out of this where I can get both Zeus and my mother to see past what I was like before and recognise that what Skye and I have is real. A way where they'll let her in, let us be and see that I've changed – as incredible as that may seem.'

Hermes clapped his hands together. 'Great! What's the way?'

'I don't know,' Coop responded glumly. 'I haven't worked that out yet.'

CHAPTER
TWENTY-TWO

S kye couldn't remember a time when she'd felt this cold before. It was as if the wind was piercing through her very skin and attacking her bones. She had a fleeting vision of her bone marrow gradually turning into ice and frozen stalactites hanging off her heart. She wasn't going to give up though. Not without seeing Coop and trying to explain what she'd done. If she could just talk to him and beg his forgiveness, maybe everything would be alright.

She pushed away the terrifying thoughts of hypothermia and focused instead on imagining Coop's arms around her, hugging her to his warm body and keeping her safe. Outside the wind continued to howl but the rain that had been hammering down upon her meagre shelter was starting to dissipate. Skye bit her lip. She could stay where she was, and hope the rickety roof and crumbling walls would shelter her until morning, or she could make a break for it. Falling asleep where she was could end up being a bad thing.

She remembered a story she'd heard once about a young woman making her way home from a New Year's Eve party, who curled up to sleep in a field when she lost her way and never woke up again. Skye was determined that wasn't going to happen to her. At least if the rain had lessened its onslaught, it would be easier to continue her hike towards Litochoro. Perhaps there she'd be able to find a cheap hostel where she could get a hot shower.

Making a decision, she pulled herself to her feet and grabbed her small bag. She was shivering uncontrollably. She gritted her teeth and forced her stiff and protesting muscles to move out back to the road. She could do this. She had to do this. It couldn't be much further.

The wind whipped her hair about her face, and her eyes stung. Glancing down the road and seeing nothing ahead other than darkness, she took a deep breath and shouldered her bag. If nothing else, jogging in what she hoped was the right direction would help to keep her warm. With one last quick glance at the shambling ruins of the house, she turned left and made a move.

The truth was that Skye wasn't as far away from Litochoro as she imagined. Neither was she as alone as she had assumed. Overhead, Zephyr, the God of Wind, was making his way back to Olympus. He'd been amusing himself out on the Pacific Ocean, tweaking the trade winds here and there to cause havoc to the human sailors participating in the Transpacific Yacht Race. He was a bit of a gambler and, with a considerable amount of cash on an Australian team to win, he had decided to help his cause along. It wasn't that he needed the money or that he really cared who won. He simply enjoyed reminding the humans who was really in charge. He'd have stayed for longer, ensuring his gamble paid off, but the breaking waves on the horizon suggested that Poseidon had caught wind, so to speak, of his antics and was on his way to interfere.

As much as he hated to admit it, Zephyr was fully aware Poseidon's power was far greater than his own. Poseidon disliked any of the gods interfering with the humans. The pair of them had almost come to blows several years back when Zephyr had attempted to help out a small fishing boat which was in trouble off the coast of Indonesia. The results hadn't been pretty. Zephyr still had nightmares about that day and Zeus himself had been so livid that he almost stripped both of them of their remaining powers. It was only the fact that no-one else could take on the enormity of working with Mother Nature that had saved them both.

Zephyr snorted to himself. He didn't understand what Poseidon's problem was. Just because he'd had that problem back in the nineteenth century, when he tried to help the *Mary Celeste* and it had all gone pear-shaped, didn't mean that he should object to ever coming to the aid of humans again. The Sea God had suggested that with the advent of lighthouses, and then satellite navigational equipment, the humans no longer required his services. When Zephyr had brought up the tragedy of the *Titanic* as a counter-argument, Poseidon had remained markedly unamused. It was probably just as well he omitted any mention of the Bermuda Triangle, he thought ruefully. Poseidon did not enjoy being reminded of his mistakes.

Zephyr was so deep in his ruminations that he almost missed her. In fact he would have, were it not for a sudden flash of lightning which lit up the area and highlighted her figure as she jogged slowly along the road. Wheeling round, he went back for a closer look, blinking in surprise when his second glance confirmed what he thought he'd seen.

It was rare to catch a human out in this weather in this day and age. Mechanised transport meant they were normally safely wrapped inside metal shells. Zephyr occasionally wondered whether they had forgotten there was joy to be had in being outside and enjoying the power of the elements screaming around them. But to see a human woman out on her own and braving this weather reminded him that some humans were more brave – or more foolhardy – than others.

He swooped down. She was a pathetic, bedraggled figure. It seemed curious that she was so close to Olympus and unlikely that it was a coincidence that she was out here. The inhabitants of Litochoro enjoyed their creature comforts and would do what they could to avoid being outside during such a storm. And it was hardly tourist season.

Zephyr watched her for a moment or two. If he were Poseidon, he'd just sweep past her and leave her to her fate, whatever that may be. But she looked so small and forlorn. Zephyr grinned. This woman, whoever she was, was fortunate indeed that he had come past at this exact moment. Closing his eyes for a heartbeat, he made a few small changes to the howling atmosphere before continuing on his way.

Below him, Skye was almost at the point of collapsing when the wind suddenly did something different. It shrieked around her, practically lifting her off her feet, and then abruptly changed. Where she had been battling against it, feeling as if she were pushing through it, now it was at her back and gusting in the direction she wanted to go. Its force was so strong and so powerful, it felt as if she were flying down the small road. She was moving at twice the speed. Skye had the oddest feeling that if she stopped her legs from moving, the wind would continue to push her forwards and lift her up towards her destination. She found herself sprinting easily along the curving road until, all of a sudden, a cluster of twinkling lights finally signalled that Litochoro was just ahead.

Gasping with relief and praising her good fortune, Skye allowed the wind to carry her forward and down. The town was larger than she'd imagined but, even in the darkness of the evening, the terracotta roofs and whitewashed walls were welcoming. She could just make out the glimmer of the nearby ocean.

As soon as she passed the first buildings on the outskirts of the town, the wind faltered and began to die down. It was still bitterly cold, to the point where she wouldn't have been surprised if it began to snow, but she had made it. Now all she had to do was find some real shelter for the night before beginning her search for Olympus the following morning.

For the first time in what felt like days, Skye smiled.

Back within the walls of Olympus, Zephyr headed through the marbled hallways. He paused when he caught sight of Coop and Hermes up ahead, debating whether to join the pair of them for a moment. The three gods often swapped stories about the humans they came across, and Zephyr was sure Coop would be interested in hearing about what he'd done that day to piss off Poseidon.

Snippets of their conversation floated over to him about the whereabouts of some girl who was no longer in Coop's house, nor with her friends or her family. With an irascible edge to his voice, Coop was demanding Hermes work harder to find her. Hermes, in return, was saying it didn't matter where she was, Coop wasn't allowed to see her or talk to her. Deciding to leave them to it, a faint grin crossed Zephyr's face. Coop was ever the ladies' man; his latest conquest had no doubt realised this and was refusing to see him. Zephyr had heard enough of Coop's moans on the subject of love not to want to listen to any more right now. He strolled off to seek out more good-humoured entertainment.

CHAPTER

TWENTY-THREE

The skies were clear and sunny the following morning, as if the storm had been a figment of her imagination. It was still cold, but the air was crisp and clean. Skye checked out of the small pension where she'd found a cheap room and went in search of both breakfast and information.

After purchasing a deliciously flaky pastry from a small bakery, she eyed the man behind the counter thoughtfully. He had a friendly face, she decided, so she swallowed hard and asked him, 'Um, do you speak English?'

His eyes twinkled at her. 'Can't afford not to. Not these days. This is a tourist town, after all.'

A mixture of relief and nervousness squirmed through her. Skye could feel her cheeks warming at the ridiculousness of her next question, but she quashed her embarrassment and took a deep breath. 'I don't suppose you could tell me where Olympus is?'

He let out a deep belly laugh, its rumble filling the small warm shop. 'Step outside and look up! You can't miss it.'

Skye scratched her head awkwardly. 'Not the mountain. The, um, palace. With the gods in.'

He suddenly stopped laughing, his face closing up. He half turned away, as if fascinated by rearranging some loaves of bread. 'You've been reading too many fairy stories,' he grunted.

Skye stared desperately at his back. He obviously knew something but he was unwilling to talk about it. 'But...' she began.

He looked over his shoulder. 'Sorry. Can't help you.'

Damn it. It was clear he wasn't going to say anything further. Skye sighed and left. She'd just have to find someone else to help her. This would be a whole lot easier if Coop hadn't taken her to Olympus using his godly teleportation skills. At least then she'd have a chance of retracing their steps to find it on her own.

The thing was, there were people who knew of the existence of Olympus as the lap of the gods – and who knew how to get there. Coop had told her that worshippers and supplicants who still followed the old ways sometimes gathered at the mountain. Emma had found it remarkably easy to believe in the sudden revelation of the gods' existence; even though most of the world lived in total ignorance of the fact that the ancient Greek myths weren't actually just myths, it wasn't a complete secret either. All Skye had to do was find someone to point her in the right direction.

Casting around, she spotted an elderly woman on the other side of the street, carrying a bag of heavy shopping.

Skye jogged over. 'Can I help you with that?'

The woman turned and smiled at her, answering with a stream of incomprehensible Greek. Clearly, even if she knew about Olympus and where it was, Skye wouldn't be able to understand her. It served her right for not spending more time learning the language. Once she sorted out this mess with Coop, she promised herself she'd make more of an effort. *If* she sorted out the mess with Coop, she amended.

Gesturing towards the woman's bag, she mimed the action of helping to carry it. The woman grinned more broadly and held the bag out towards her. Skye took it, hoping they didn't have far to walk. Resting one hand on Skye's free arm, the old woman began speaking again in Greek. Skye smiled in return and shrugged to indicate she didn't understand. The woman laughed and continued to chatter. At least with the sun finally shining again, it was a pleasant stroll.

They made their way down the street, eventually turning into a cobbled road. The woman pointed ahead of her, seeming to indicate her house was just up ahead. Skye returned her shopping bag and cocked her head, not holding out much hope but figuring it was worth a try anyway.

'Olympus?' she asked, her eyes scanning the woman's face.

The woman threw back her head and laughed, patting Skye on the arm and turning away. Skye's mouth twisted ruefully. It had been a long shot at best.

The next person she tried was a younger man who she spotted close to the beach. Not only was there a better chance that someone younger would speak English, but perhaps someone closer to her own age would be more sympathetic to her cause. This particular man didn't look like a tourist although neither did he look like he was in a rush to get anywhere or do anything. Straightening her shoulders, Skye walked up to him and smiled.

'Excuse me,' she said, keeping her fingers tightly crossed, 'but I'm trying to find Olympus.'

He looked at her, dark eyes glittering and grabbed her arm, twisting it almost painfully. His face loomed down towards hers. 'They won't help you, you know. They won't help anyone,' he hissed, a cloud of stale breath hitting Skye as he spoke.

Alarmed, she tried to wrench her arm away, but he tightened his grip. 'Let me go,' she said, sounding considerably calmer than she felt.

'They don't care about you,' he half sang.

'Sir, please let go of my arm.'

'They don't care about me,' he trilled, 'or the fish in the sea.' A half mad expression crossed his eyes. 'But why bother with the sea when they already have enough water for tea!' He frowned and shook his head. 'No, no, no. Enough water for me. No. Enough water for glee. Gleeee!'

He dropped her arm abruptly and wandered a few steps away from her, still muttering to himself. Skye backed off until she was sure he'd forgotten about her, then walked quickly in the opposite direction, rubbing her arm and grimacing. Perhaps walking round the quiet streets of Litochoro and asking random strangers for help wasn't the brightest idea she'd ever had.

She sat down on a wall beside the seafront, her shoulders slumping, and gazed up at the mountains encircling the houses. Mount Olympus stood proudly over them all, snow-capped and majestic. Skye could see why the gods chose this area to live in: it was stunning. Between the sapphire sea, the jade green of the surrounding forests and the backdrop of the mountains, the place was picture perfect.

Skye cast her eyes over the entire vista, wishing she'd paid more attention to what was around the palace of Olympus rather than the palace itself. She had a vague memory of some trees and that was about it. But between the town and the mountain were acres of trees. It could be almost anywhere. Chewing her bottom lip, she tried to think. There had to be a way to find it. Unwilling to ask anyone else for help after her last encounter, she was running out of options. Skye scowled. There had to be a map or a sign or something. Anything.

She froze. Maybe there *was* something. Pulling out her phone, she turned it on and scanned through its contents until she found what she was looking for. She might be able to go one better than a map. The internet connection was weak but eventually the familiar screen of Google Earth popped up. She'd downloaded it months ago, simply out of curiosity. Skye had been particularly amused to see her father had been captured in his scruffiest clothes in front of their house. He'd been crouching down as if inspecting the wheels of his car and was revealing more skin than her mother would have liked. However, silly voyeurism aside, the app did have its uses.

Skye quickly typed in Litochoro, bringing up the town and locating the spot she was in. The photos must have been taken in the height of summer because the pretty seafront looked considerably busier than it was now. Zooming out and scanning the area, Skye searched for any clues as to the whereabouts of the gods' palace. There were no buildings that looked remotely like the marble mono-lith Coop had taken her to, but she did find a small road leading away from the town and winding through the surrounding forest. Previous visitors had taken photos of different spots but the majority of them were of trees with varying degrees of sunlight filtering through their leaves or shots of the mountain itself.

Frustrated, she ran a hand through her hair. Maybe she could find the road that led through the trees and follow it in the hope of seeing something. It seemed like a stab in the dark. She frowned. According to the satellite imagery, there was a waterfall called Agios Dionisis, which looked pretty; she could aim for it. The guy who'd grabbed her arm had been babbling about water. What was it he'd said? They have enough water for tea? Whatever it was, it hadn't made much sense. Then her eyes widened. Coop had quoted Yeats' description of a waterfall before they'd left for Olympus.

"'The water and the wild",' she whispered softly to herself, springing up.

The waterfall had to be involved; it was too much of a coinci-dence otherwise. Spurred on, she looked at the map and estimated it would take her little more than a couple of hours to reach it. If it didn't work out, she'd have more than enough time to get back to the town before dark and get a room again for another night. But it would work out. It had to.

Skye arrived at the waterfall faster than she had thought she would. The winter chill made her move quickly and it was an easy trek to the well-signposted beauty spot. The roar of water, swollen as it was from the previous night's storm, reached her ears long before she caught sight of the water itself, gushing down into a sharp ravine etched on either side with slate-grey rock.

She peered over the edge. The place seemed deserted. It had been too much to hope that she'd reach the water's edge and, all of a sudden, the glory of Olympus would reveal itself to her. That didn't prevent her feeling disappointed, though. Sighing audibly, she picked her way down to the pool at the bottom. After coming all this way, it would be churlish to not see it properly.

Once she reached it, she gasped in awe. The pool was a stunning limpid green colour, and the waterfall was truly astounding. Kneeling down, she trailed her fingers in the water and drank in the peace. Mist was sweeping in down from the high sides of the tree-lined gorge. It was truly magical.

Skye considered her options. She could travel out from the waterfall in concentric circles. Then at least she'd know for certain that the palace was nowhere in the vicinity. She wasn't leaving until she'd found the damned place and spoken to Coop; she wasn't about to give up on what felt like her one true shot at happiness without a fight.

She glanced up at the sky. It wouldn't be long before it started to get dark; considering how close she'd come to dying of hypothermia the night before … it would probably be wise to head back to Lito-choro and try again tomorrow.

With that thought in mind, she stood up – and almost jumped a foot in the air when she registered the two figures staring silently at her. How had they clambered down to the pool without making a sound? Skye blinked rapidly several times then took a step towards them.

'Hello.'

Standing by the water's edge hand in hand, they stared at her. Neither seemed to be wearing much clothing. The woman was draped in green, but her arms and most of her legs were bare. The man, who was what could only be described as classically beautiful, with alabaster skin, high sculpted cheekbones and dark hair, was wearing an artfully draped scarlet sheet. For a moment, Skye wondered if she'd interrupted a lovers' interlude; maybe they'd been swimming in the pool when she came along. That was ridiculous though. The temperature had to be close to freezing.

Without a word, the man let go of his girlfriend's hand and gracefully moved towards the water. The girl panicked, attempting to recapture his palm, but he brushed her off. She looked so hurt at his dismissive action that Skye felt sorry for her. Her boyfriend was clearly an arse.

Trying again, Skye offered the girl a small smile. 'I'm Skye. Are you from around here?'

The girl blinked slowly. 'Around here?'

Skye nodded. 'Yes. I'm actually not here for the waterfall. I was looking for Olympus.' She laughed slightly nervously. 'Not the mountain. The, er, the palace.'

Smiling back at her, the girl replied. 'The, er, the palace.'

Heat flooded Skye's cheeks. Was she being made fun of? She glanced at the man, who seemed to be kneeling down over the water's edge and staring intently into it. What he was looking at, she had no idea. Feeling like an idiot, she called over to him. 'Do you know where Olympus is?'

He ignored her. Skye's chest was getting tight. She looked back at the girl who was watching her with an expression of extraordinary sadness.

'Olympus is?' she said softly.

Something in Skye snapped. 'There's no need to be bloody rude! Since arriving here, I've almost been blown away by a thunderstorm, died from hypothermia, been laughed at by an old woman, attacked by a young man and now you two are treating me like I'm some kind of freak!' Her voice was rising with every word, bouncing off the ravine walls and echoing around. 'All I sodding want to do is to find Olympus so I can tell the man I love that I made a mistake and beg him to forgive me.'

The girl looked away. 'Beg him to forgive me.'

'Jesus Christ!' Skye shrieked. 'What is wrong with you?'

'You?'

'Dion,' said the man.

Skye stared at him. He was still gazing dreamily into the water. She stomped over to him. 'What did you say?'

He reached up to his hair and twisted a curl round his finger, half smiling. Skye realised he wasn't smiling at her; he was barely aware of her presence. Instead, he was looking at his own reflection in the water. She almost kicked him.

'What did you say?' she said, forcing herself to keep her tone even.

'Dion,' the girl whispered.

Skye put her hands on her hips and stared hard from one to the other. Then she pulled out her phone and furiously jabbed 'Dion' into it. Almost immediately, several results sprang up. Skye's mouth dried. Apparently, Dion was an ancient ruined city that had been built at the foot of Mount Olympus to honour Zeus, the King of the Heavens. And it was less than ten minutes' walk from the top of the waterfall.

Her heart thudding in her chest, she turned on her heel and ran back to the path leading up the ravine's sides.

'Thank you!' she squeezed out.

'You,' said the girl.

The man didn't reply. Skye didn't care. This had to be it. This had to be Olympus.

CHAPTER

TWENTY-FOUR

As Skye marched along the narrow path leading to Dion, she scanned through various websites on her phone to find out more information about the place. It had been used as a religious sanctuary since the fifth century BC and had an altar to Zeus, and a temple for his daughters, the Muses. Skye could have kicked herself for not taking note of its existence before. She just had to hope that the strange couple at the waterfall weren't leading her on a wild goose chase.

Everything she was doing was surreal. Having been confronted by Coop's invisibility had made it easy not to question his existence and that of Olympus and the other gods. The idea that she was now travelling to an ancient temple where she would find Zeus himself was nuts. She couldn't care less about Zeus, though. All she cared about was finding Coop and persuading him to give her a second chance. She might come across as a stalker; maybe all she'd been to him was nothing more than a one-night stand. But the thought of him made her soul sing so she had to try. He had told her he loved her. That had to be worth something. Skye tried to ignore that he'd also told her emphatically that he didn't believe in love. Right now, she didn't have much choice.

It didn't take her long to find the site. When she emerged from under the canopy of trees and gazed out across the fallen stones and sweeping grassy walkways, however, she scowled and cursed aloud. There was nothing there except a collection of ancient rubble. Pretty impressive ancient rubble, but rubble nonetheless. Skye yelled aloud in frustration then picked up a small stone and threw it with all her might. Goddamn it all to hell.

'I think that's rather uncalled for, don't you?' said a male voice from behind her.

Skye turned round slowly. A tired looking man was standing in front of her, his head cocked as he warily watched her hands which were still bunched into tight fists. Loosening her fingers, she forced herself to relax, ignoring the embarrassment she felt at her momentary tantrum.

'Hi,' she said awkwardly.

'Hey.' He brushed past her and began walking down one of the paths which led to the centre of the ruins and what appeared to be a large open area. Skye thought briefly of the man who'd grabbed her arm in Litochoro that morning and that she was now in the middle of nowhere with a strange man who could potentially be a serial killer. Then she rolled her eyes. She couldn't treat every stranger as if they were dangerous; besides, this guy couldn't have looked less interested in her if he'd tried.

'Excuse me?' Her voice was more of a squeak than a yell.

Either he didn't hear her or didn't care. Determined not to let the opportunity slide by her, she caught up to him and tried again. 'Excuse me,' she repeated, this time more loudly.

He turned towards her, his expression showing that he was trying to be polite but desperately wished she would go away and leave him alone. Skye realised there was something strangely familiar about him, as if she'd met him in another life. He certainly looked as if he'd seen better days. Heavy bags lay under his eyes and his clothes and hair were rumpled and unkempt.

'What can I help you with?'

Skye answered him with a question. 'Where are you going?'

His face closed up. 'None of your business.' He turned again to go.

A ripple of something akin to excitement ran through her. There was nowhere else to go here other than the collection of old stones and half-forgotten ruins. If that was all he was interested in, why would he try to hide it? There was more to this guy than met the eye.

Skye took a deep breath. 'You're going to Olympus, aren't you?'

He gestured at the air in front of him. 'As you see.'

Her stomach dropped. 'Where...?' She licked her lips. 'Where is it?'

'Apparently all you have to do is believe.' He smiled sadly. 'I'm sorry, I have to go.'

'I believe,' she whispered to his back. 'I've been there before.'

Almost as soon as she finished speaking, there was a ripple in the air, some kind of vague shimmer like you see on hot days. This had nothing to do with the weather, however. When Skye blinked and peered more closely, the shimmer solidified and hardened into the familiar outline of Olympus, with its towering marble walls and gigantic wrought gates. Her knees buckled and she stumbled. It was here, after all. Had her belief been stronger when she was with Coop himself? Was that why she was only seeing the palace now? She thought of the last words he'd said to her: 'Doubting Skye'. She shook herself. It didn't matter. She was here now. In a matter of moments she could be facing Coop again.

Running forward until she was just behind the man, she felt her heart thudding painfully in her chest. He stopped at the gates and spoke to the guard, seemingly unfazed by the armour and the dark shadows which represented his eyes.

'Oz,' the man said. 'My name is Oz.'

Skye suddenly realised where she'd seen him before. He was the lead singer of Orpheus, the band that had played at Nemesis the evening she'd met Apollo for the first time. What was he doing here?

'Purpose of business?' the guard asked robotically, in a voice that sent shivers down Skye's spine.

'I'm here to petition Hades,' Oz answered, his voice laden with pain.

'Hades isn't here.' The guard took a step forward, but the singer stood his ground.

'Then let me see another god. I don't care which one.' He shook himself slightly. 'No, I do care which one. Let me see Hera.'

Skye watched as the guard bowed his head and stepped aside. 'Access granted.'

She grinned. At least entering Olympus on her own was going to be fairly easy. As soon as Oz had passed through the gates, she stepped forward.

'Name?'

'Skye,' she said firmly. 'Skye Sawyer.'

The dark holes in the guard's helmet where his eyes were supposed to be bored into her. She had to force herself not to take a step back.

'Purpose of business?'

Here goes. 'I'm here to see Coop. Cupid,' adding helpfully, 'the God of Love.'

The guard stood still. Skye tried to smile.

'Let me in please,' she said in a small voice.

'Access denied.'

Skye gaped at him. 'What?'

He didn't answer.

'No!' she shouted. 'You can't do that! You let *him* in. Why won't you let me in?'

The guard still didn't answer. Enraged, Skye sidestepped left, leapt through the open space next to him and began running. Unfortunately, she'd barely gone three steps when she was dragged backwards and thrown back out.

'Access denied.'

'Fuck you!'

She threw herself at the guard and began pummelling his chest with her fists. 'Let me past!'

'Access denied.'

'Why? Did Coop tell you not to let me in?'

'Access denied.'

'Give me a reason, damn you!'

'Access denied.'

She tried to get past him again but this time he was ready for her, and she barely put a toe inside the gates before she was picked up by her collar and tossed back out. Landing with a painful thud, tears of frustration pricked at her eyelids. Coop really didn't want to see her. It had been over the moment she'd walked into his bedroom; she'd just been too stupid to see it.

'Skye? Is that you?'

Scrambling to her feet at the familiar voice, Skye felt rage filling every pore. If Hermes hadn't sought out Emma and told her about Coop, then Skye would probably never have returned early to Greece. This was all his fault.

She launched herself at Hermes and slapped him across the face. It was the first time in her life that she'd ever hit anyone and it was surprisingly satisfying to see the shock reflected in his eyes.

'You prick!' she shouted. 'Why did you have to get involved?'

He took a step back and held up his hands to shield his face. 'Whoa! What are you talking about? I only did what Coop asked me to.'

Time froze around her as Hermes' words sank in.

'He...' The sick feeling in her stomach intensified but she managed to find her voice. 'He asked you to do this?'

Hermes nodded earnestly, his eyes scanning her face. 'We didn't know where you went, Skye. I've been searching all over for you. I don't think Coop ever dreamed you'd come here.'

All the pieces were starting to fit into place. The hard knot of pain which had been in her chest since Coop had flown out of the window intensified. Of course he didn't think she'd come here, Skye thought dully. Because turning up at the gates of Olympus would cause problems for him when he clearly considered her as nothing more than an irritant. Despite all his fine words and what she'd assumed were heartfelt kisses, she was nothing to him. He'd sent his best friend to Emma. He and Hermes had probably cooked up the whole thing as a way to get rid of her without Coop having to dump her personally. Tell the silly human girl not to go and see him and manipulate her friend to encourage her to do just the opposite...

It had all been a game to him, just like the stupid thing he had going on with Apollo. Another 'lesson' to prove that true love didn't really exist. Skye felt as if she was going to vomit all over Hermes' shiny wingtips. How could she have been so stupid? The whole invisibility thing had probably been a ruse as well.

Apparently oblivious to her soul-destroying epiphany, Hermes grinned at her. 'I need to tell him you're here. You have no idea how he'll react when he finds out.'

Skye thought that she had a pretty clear understanding about how Coop would feel about her sudden appearance. 'Great,' she answered flatly. 'You go do that.'

Hermes threw his hands up in the air. 'Don't be daft! You can come in with me and show him yourself.'

'They won't let me in.'

Hermes looked momentarily nonplussed. 'Oh,' he said. 'That kind of makes sense. Never mind. I'll go and find Coop and bring him out here.'

Skye clenched her teeth. No doubt this was so that Coop could humiliate her completely. *Look at what reality is like*, she imagined him taunting while the other gods and the stupid fuckwit of a guard looked on. *How could I love you? You're just a pathetic human who can't even come into Olympus without my say-so.* She let out a small moan of despair.

Hermes looked alarmed. 'Are you alright?'

She lifted up her head and looked him directly in the eyes. 'I'm fine,' she said. 'I can't wait to see Coop. I'll stay right here while you go and get him.'

'Fabulous! Just hang on, this won't take long.' He moved past her and walked through the enormous gates, the guard not even registering his entry.

Skye watched as he was swallowed up by the marble interior. She was damned if she was going to wait around here for Coop to treat her like she was a speck of dirt marring the perfection of his snowy white wings. Screw that. But she wasn't going to let him get away with this scot-free, either. If he thought he could humiliate her, she'd find a way to humiliate him right back. She had truly believed he was her one shot at happiness; right now the only thing preventing the pain in her heart from consuming her was the rage she felt at his casual manipulation.

'Lion, not mouse,' she said aloud. Coop had enjoyed quoting Shakespeare. He'd appreciate this quotation. '"If you prick us, do we not bleed? If you tickle us, do we not laugh? If you poison us, do we not die? And if you wrong us, shall we not revenge?"'

Her voice was soft but the guard still turned his head and stared at her. Skye dropped a melodramatic curtsey, then spun on her heel and left.

LESS THAN FIVE MINUTES LATER, Coop came flying out of the gates, his heart hammering with excitement.

'She came here!' he shouted to Hermes, who was falling behind. 'My mother and Zeus can hardly stop me from seeing her now. It would be bad manners to ignore her and, Olympus knows, my bloody mother is all about manners.'

He came to a skidding halt when he realised the area in front of the palace was empty. 'Where has she gone?'

Hermes, panting, came up beside him. 'Er ... she was right here.'

Coop slowly turned around and walked up to the guard. 'Where did she go?' The emotion in his voice was barely under control.

The guard didn't answer.

'Where did she fucking go?' he yelled, pulling back a fist and slamming it into the shiny helmet. 'Did someone take her? Was she attacked?'

The guard didn't so much as flinch.

'Where is she?'

'Coop,' Hermes began.

Sick with worry, Coop looked at his friend in utter anguish. 'Find her, Herm.'

Hermes nodded and sprang up into the air. Skye couldn't have gone far.

CHAPTER

TWENTY-FIVE

I t was true that Skye hadn't gone far – but she hadn't gone in the direction that anyone would have expected. Rather than sticking to the trail, she had skirted the trees which lined the steep hills around Olympus and the ruins of Dion and begun doubling back. There was more than one way to skin a cat, she thought grimly, keeping a close eye on the palace walls for any weaknesses or gaps. The marble grandeur stretched back for what seemed like miles. It didn't matter, she wasn't in a rush. Not now.

As she made her way carefully along the tree-lined path, she replayed all the things Coop had said to her.

'I've finally discovered the meaning of true love,' she mimicked. 'You deserve the best, Skye.' What. A. Prick.

She was so caught up in her revenge fantasies that she almost missed the flicker of white by the towering palace wall.

'Pssst!'

Alarmed, she peered through the leaves to get a better look. Her brow furrowed when she saw who was trying to get her attention: it was the old woman from Litochoro whose shopping she'd helped carry.

Skye warily stepped out from the trees and walked towards her. The woman grinned manically, immediately bursting into a long babble of Greek. Bemused, Skye shook her head to indicate that her inability to speak or understand Greek hadn't miraculously changed since that morning. The elderly woman ignored her and continued to chatter while tugging on Skye's sleeve. Still baffled by her sudden appearance, Skye let herself be led. The woman took her right up to the very edge of the palace walls and pointed at them.

Skye shrugged helplessly. 'I don't know what you mean,' she said.

Without pausing for breath, the woman continued to speak, pointing first at the wall and then at Skye.

'I'm sorry,' Skye began.

Letting out an exasperated sigh, the woman took hold of Skye's hand and pushed it onto the surface of the wall. It was cool and very, very smooth. The elderly woman mimed climbing up it.

Skye shook her head. 'It's too tall and too perfect. There's nothing I can grip on to.'

The woman nodded vigorously and began speaking more quickly. She gesticulated fiercely, her hands waving down the length of the wall and then moving round in a circle. Comprehension dawned.

'You're saying it's like this all the way round, aren't you? That the only way is past the guard.' Skye's posture deflated. 'You're saying I won't find a way in.'

The woman beamed at her. Skye realised that, despite her age, she was still a strikingly attractive woman. She had no idea why the woman had come here; it appeared she was trying to help her out. At least there were still some nice people left in the world, Skye thought sadly.

She pursed her lips. There were other ways to get revenge than confronting Coop in person. She could cut up all his clothes back at the mansion, or throw paint over his car. But that would only hurt him materially and Skye doubted it would make much difference to him, considering how wealthy he was. No. She needed to see him really hurting, the way that she was right now.

Her thoughts were interrupted by another stream of Greek from the woman. Skye waited till she finished talking and then took her hand. 'Thank you,' she said. 'I don't know why you've helped me, but I appreciate it. I just need to find another way to confront him.'

The woman cocked her head and fixed Skye with a steely gaze. 'Eros,' she said simply.

Skye stared at her. That meant love, didn't it? She snorted. 'Not any more.' Her heart wrenched in pain.

The woman tsked and pulled out something from the bag at her feet. Skye stared at it then looked at the woman's face.

'A grappling hook?' she said disbelievingly.

She received a wide grin in return. The woman mimed throwing it up the wall and using the rope to clamber up. Skye's eyes drifted to the wall, to the hook then back up to the wall again.

'Why do you have a grappling hook with you?' She glanced at the old woman. 'Never mind. Let's give it a shot. How hard can it be to use this? I've seen a few ninja movies in my time.'

The woman's eyes widened for a moment then she handed over the implement and took a step backwards. Skye's eyes travelled up the expanse of the wall. It really was very high, at least thirty feet tall. She glanced doubtfully at the hook in her hands. It was a lot heavier than she'd expected. The last time she'd tried to throw anything like this had probably been the javelin during her high school days. After she'd sent it flying off course and almost impaled her PE teacher in the process, she'd avoided anything similar.

Taking a deep breath, Skye tried to focus and aim. She was attempting to breach the walls of Olympus, where the Greek gods lived, with the help of a crazy pensioner who was apparently a cat burglar in her spare time. Good grief. Then Coop's face flashed into her mind and her resolve hardened. She adjusted her arm slightly and threw the hook up with every ounce of energy she could muster.

The metal clanged noisily against the marble barely a few feet up the wall and fell back down, narrowly missing Skye's head. It thudded down uselessly to the ground.

'Shit.' She picked it up and tried again.

This time she managed to get it higher but it was still nowhere near the top. This was never going to work. She was no ninja after all. Skye looked back at the old woman and gave her a look of resignation. The woman grinned in return and held up a single finger. Puzzled, Skye was about to ask in English what she meant when a sudden crack rent the air around her. As if from nowhere, the large figure of a man appeared, replete with flowing white locks. Skye gaped.

The man's startlingly blue eyes slid in her direction then snapped to the woman, who was still there, grinning.

'Pandora!' he roared.

The old woman dipped slightly, before straightening up and blinking innocently.

The man let forth a torrent of angry Greek. Pandora merely smiled back before calmly answering while pointing occasionally to Skye. When she finished speaking, the man bent down and scooped up the grappling hook. He turned to Skye and thrust it in her direction.

'She met you this morning,' he said.

It wasn't a question but Skye nodded quickly anyway. She was absolutely terrified. As the man spoke, he seemed to grow in stature. His white hair suggested old age but there was nothing elderly about him. Skye had the horrible feeling she knew exactly who he was.

'She was rather impressed at your determination,' the man continued. He waved the hook close to her face. 'You were never going to get into Olympus with this toy, however. It seems to be my lot to be plagued by foolish humans today.' He appeared more exasperated than angry. 'So you're the girl who's finally caught Cupid's heart?'

Colour lit Skye's cheeks. 'Actually, no,' she said. 'I'm the girl who he treated like an idiot. He thought he could play me for a fool! He thought he could pretend to be in love with me just for kicks! Well,' she blustered, 'he can't!'

The man pulled the hook back and absent-mindedly scratched his chin with it. 'Interesting,' he murmured.

'Interesting?' shrieked Skye. 'Interesting? This is my life he's been playing with! You lot might be gods but you've got no right to treat us as if we're you're playthings!'

The man raised his eyebrows. 'I'd been led to believe you were quiet and shy.'

Skye blinked. 'Coop's been talking about me? To you? But aren't you...?'

He nodded. 'Zeus. King of the Heavens to you.'

'Oh.' Skye's voice returned to a squeak.

'I can see why he likes you,' Zeus mused. 'It's almost a shame he's forbidden from ever seeing you again.'

'Forbidden? But...'

'You broke your promise,' Zeus said gently. 'You were not to attempt to see him in his corporeal form. By doing so, you revealed your human fallibility.' He shrugged. '*Que sera sera.*'

'What?' There was a high note to Skye's voice. 'Was this your idea? Or his?'

'I think it was my son's.'

'Apollo,' Skye breathed.

'Just so. Now tell me, why do you not believe Cupid loves you?'

'He doesn't like being called that,' she snapped. 'His name is Coop.'

Zeus smiled faintly. Skye realised she'd just scolded the most powerful god on Earth and swallowed, focusing on answering his question instead.

'I thought he'd contrived everything,' she explained. 'To get me out of his life. That's why Hermes went to my friend and told her about Coop. So I'd want to prove her wrong and would return to Greece to see him before I was supposed to.'

'Hermes did that?' Zeus snapped his fingers together and, almost immediately, the messenger's figure appeared.

'Your Majesty,' he bowed, 'I am yours to command. I just wonder if perhaps you could give me a bit of time first. You see, there's a girl...' Hermes' voice trailed off when he saw Skye and his mouth dropped open. 'You're here?'

She scowled at him. 'As you see.'

Zeus ignored her. 'Hermes, did you speak to this girl's friend last week?'

'What?' He looked surprised. 'No. I don't know what you're talking about.'

'But Emma said...' Skye began, before faltering. Then her eyes narrowed. 'Emma said it was Hermes. It could actually have easily been someone *pretending* to be Hermes. Someone like your son.'

'You mean Apollo.'

Skye nodded miserably. At every opportunity she'd had to trust Coop, she'd failed. He'd not been trying to get rid of her after all.

Zeus seemed to read her thoughts. 'You doubt him a lot.'

'I...' she hung her head. 'Yes, I do.'

Zeus made to turn away. 'And that was your downfall.'

'Wait!' Skye cried. 'If your son hadn't got involved, then I wouldn't have gone to see Coop.'

'You have no proof Apollo did this.' Zeus frowned. 'Although I wouldn't be surprised if he did.'

'So? You're the King! Give us another chance!'

He shook his head. 'I can't.'

Pandora said something. Hermes leaned in to Skye. 'She's saying that Zeus forgave her once for being too curious. Therefore he should forgive you too.'

Skye shot the old woman a grateful look. So she really was *that* Pandora then.

'That was a long time ago,' answered Zeus in English.

Making one last-ditch attempt, Skye wrung her hands. 'I didn't promise!'

'Hmmm?'

'I didn't promise I wouldn't see Coop. I never said the words.'

'But it was implied.'

'I didn't promise,' she repeated stubbornly.

Zeus's eyes bored into her, as if searing her soul. Skye held her breath. Please, she prayed inwardly. Oh, please.

'Wait here,' he said gruffly. Then, as quickly as he had appeared, he vanished.

Skye turned to Hermes. 'I'm sorry,' she said guiltily. 'I thought...'

He put a hand on her shoulder. 'It's okay. I understand.'

'Do you think Zeus will let me see Coop?'

Pandora shook her head.

'No,' agreed Hermes. 'He can't. The deal was done and Zeus cannot change it.' He squeezed her shoulder. 'There's still hope though.'

'What do you mean?'

'He may just manage to get you a little wiggle room. He is the King of the Heavens, after all.'

'Nothing's changed,' said Aphrodite. 'Even if the girl didn't promise, she still revealed her weak human nature when she sneaked in to see him.'

'One might argue she was provoked into that action,' said Zeus mildly.

'He's my son. Nothing would make me happier than to see him in love. But I want to see him with someone worthy of his attention.'

'By trying to scale the walls of Olympus, she has perhaps proved her worth. It was a bold move.'

'It was a foolish and impetuous move. I need Coop to be with someone who will encourage him to mature. Not someone who will allow his adolescent behaviour to continue.'

'He loves her.'

'He *says* he loves her. He'll change his mind next week.'

'I don't think he will. Aphrodite...'

'Fine,' she snapped. 'I will give her a second chance to prove herself. But there will be no coming back this time if she fails.'

'You're not going to make it easy on her, are you?'

'He's my son. He may be annoying and arrogant and immature, but he's still my son. He deserves the best. If she can't prove herself good enough for him, then it ends here.'

Zeus nodded. 'So be it.'

PART THREE

'But Psyche, in a perfect consternation at the enormous work, sat stupid and silent, without moving a finger to the inextricable heap.'

Source: Thomas Bulfinch, *The Age of Fable; or, Stories of Gods and Heroes* (1855).

CHAPTER
TWENTY-SIX

'Four tasks?' Skye stared disbelievingly at Hermes.

He scratched his neck awkwardly. 'Yes. But once you complete them, you and Coop will be free to be together.'

'I've heard that before.'

'You failed before,' Hermes pointed out gently.

'I didn't know it was a sodding test, did I?' Skye balled her fists in frustration. 'And now I'm to be tested again? What is it with you bloody gods?'

'Skye...'

'And why four? I thought it was usually three tasks. You know, in all the old stories the hero is given three feats to perform.'

Hermes coughed. 'Er, yes.'

Skye put her hands on her hips. 'Well?'

'Well, men get three.'

Skye stared at him. 'You're kidding me? I get four because of my gender? It's harder because I happen to not have a penis?'

'I know it's not ideal.'

'Ideal?' she shrieked. 'It's completely unfair!'

'You're...' Hermes began, before faltering.

'What?' Skye snapped.

He swallowed. 'You're going to do them, right? Coop really is in love with you, Skye. He's never been like this. Not with anyone. He'd do anything for you.'

'Except I'm the one who has to perform like a bloody circus seal to prove my worth while he gets to kick back and watch daytime television.'

Hermes looked pained.

Skye sighed. 'Of course I'm going to do the stupid tasks. I promise I'll complete all four or die trying. What else would I do? I'd do anything to be with him.' She closed her eyes briefly and pinched her nose as a fleeting image of Coop flashed into her mind. 'How hard are they likely to be?'

'Well, Aphrodite is setting them...'

'Aphrodite? Coop's mother? The woman who wouldn't even bother talking to me?'

'That's the one,' Hermes answered miserably.

'Great,' she said sarcastically. 'They'll be a piece of cake then.'

Skye kicked irritably at a clod of earth. There was no alternative. The thought of never being allowed to see Coop ever again sent a bolt of pain through her heart. It didn't change the fact, however, that the foibles of these stupid gods were patently ridiculous. She wasn't a hero. She wasn't brave. She was just a typical, average, run-of-the-mill woman. How on earth was she going to complete four godly feats?

As if reading her mind, Hermes gave her a sympathetic look. 'They won't be impossible,' he said softly. 'That would defeat the purpose.'

'Oh yeah? And what exactly *is* the purpose, other than making me look like a total idiot and a weak pathetic human?'

'Proving your worth.' At her look of derision, Hermes continued hastily, 'Coop knows your worth. In fact he believes he's the one not worthy of you. But you have to understand how his mother feels. There are girls all over the place who'd give their eye teeth to be with him. She wants to make sure her son ends up with the right person.'

'He's a god. He's got to be hundreds of years old. Why can't he be allowed to make up his own mind?'

Hermes just watched her.

Skye sighed again. '"Action is eloquence."'

'Huh?'

'Shakespeare.' She straightened her shoulders. 'Very well. If this is what I have to do, then so be it. What's first?'

'I'm to transport you to the first place.'

'And where is that?'

Hermes looked uncomfortable.

'Oh, I get it,' said Skye, 'you can't tell me.'

Hermes shook his head.

'Can you give me any hints at all?'

'I don't know what you'll be asked to do. It will be possible though, Skye, even if it doesn't appear to be to begin with.'

She looked him in the eye. Hermes was facing her with a look of absolute sincerity.

'Then let's do it,' she said decisively. 'Take me to it.'

'Are you sure? You can have a rest first and start tomorrow if you wish. It doesn't have to be now.'

'The faster I complete these stupid tasks,' Skye grumbled, 'the faster I can see Coop again.'

Hermes bowed his head. 'So be it.'

He grasped her arm, instructing her to hold on tight. Skye shut her eyes, feeling a lurch of nausea. Moments later, her nostrils were assailed by the reek of manure.

'Shit,' she said softly, feeling Hermes' hand leave her. Then she opened her eyes.

A huge barn stood in front of her. A long, deep sound made her jump. Terrified, she whipped around, her eyes searching through the dusky twilight to find just what monster it was that made that noise. When she realised it was nothing more than a cow, and that she was standing in the middle of a field, she relaxed slightly. There was no sign of Hermes.

'Brilliant,' she muttered to herself. 'Now what?'

With no indication of what she was supposed to do, Skye eyed the vast structure in front of her. No doubt that was where she had to be. Wind whipped round her as she mused about what might be inside the rickety edifice. She tried desperately to recall what she knew of previous tasks from the old Greek stories her parents had read to her at bedtime. Everything she could remember involved slaying terrifying creatures. Skye glanced doubtfully down at herself. Perhaps she should have spent more time in the gym and less time reading. Then she might have had some muscles to help her in a fight. Wasn't there something about eyes, throat, groin, that women were taught in self-defence classes? She shook her head, realising she was shaking. If this really was a monster she had to defeat, then she had no hope. But there was simply no alternative.

Taking a deep breath, Skye walked forward, willing her legs to feel more like steel and less like jelly. There was a small door in the front of the barn which she tentatively pushed open. She peered inside, unable to make out anything in the dark, gloomy interior. A cow outside mooed again, making her jump.

'Don't be a wimp, Skye,' she told herself firmly. Then she stepped inside.

A rich earthy smell assailed her. The barn's interior was still too dark for much to be visible but fortunately there appeared to be no sign of any kind of monster.

Reaching behind her, Skye's fingers felt along the wooden wall next to the door. She breathed a silent sigh of relief when she found a light switch and flicked it on. For half a second nothing happened then, abruptly, there was a loud hum of electricity and the barn was bathed in a flood of light.

Blinking rapidly, Skye tensed. Her eyes darted around while she carefully took a step backwards in case a fire-breathing, three-headed, five-tongued monstrosity decided to appear. There was nothing, however. The barn was empty apart from a mountain of grain reaching up towards the roof. She chewed her lip. Okay, now what?

Keeping her back pressed firmly against the rough wall of the barn, Skye sidled along to her left, attempting to peer round the huge mound, her eyes constantly flicking around for any sign of movement. There was nothing. A large wooden ladder stood against one wall, the door was at another and there was the grain in the middle. No monsters, no gods, no anything.

Now that Skye was certain she was alone she felt bolder and left the safety of the wall to take a few tentative steps forward. When there was no sudden roar or rush of an attack to fend off, she continued until she had covered a circuit of the whole space. Her fear was dissipating and being replaced by annoyance. What kind of task was it if she couldn't even work out what it was she was supposed to do?

Just then, her eyes caught something sticking out at the top of the grain mountain. It looked like a piece of paper. Glancing around quickly again to make sure she was completely alone, she walked forward. There was nothing to do except climb up and retrieve whatever it was.

Skye lifted one leg. As soon as her foot landed on the grain, it sank in. She cursed and pulled up the rest of her body, leaning into the mound and using her hands to yank herself upwards. Mini-avalanches began to tumble down the slope, impeding her progress. It was like trying to climb up a pile of sludge. Every time she seemed to get somewhere, her body weight shifted ever so slightly and she slid back down. When she opened her mouth to gasp for air, she ended up with mouthfuls of grain and she could feel the tiny husks getting trapped between her body and her clothes, scratching her skin.

Taking a deep breath, Skye decided she would have to make a rush for the top. She tightened her muscles and fixed her eyes on the summit, then sprang upwards, her hands and feet scrabbling at the surface of the sliding mountain. Her fingers just managed to snatch the edge of the paper before she began falling back down again so, holding it tightly, she turned and jogged back down, leaving sunken footprints in the grain. The last thing she wanted was to be smothered by it collapsing on top of her.

Back on the safety of the floor, and spitting out grain from her mouth, Skye smoothed out the paper. There was a message on it, written in an elegant looping script.

CONTAINED HERE ARE *two different types of grain, wheat and oats. You have until dawn to separate each out into two piles.*

SKYE TURNED THE PAPER OVER. There was nothing else, not even a signature. She stared disbelievingly up at the huge grain mountain. Dawn could be no more than ten hours away.

She reached in and scooped up a handful, tracing through it with her fingers. The difference between the oats and the wheat was clear but there was so much. This appeared to be an impossible task.

'Well, you're not going to get anywhere by looking at it, Skye,' she scolded herself. And at least there wasn't a monster to defeat.

Realising there was little time to spare, and with the wind outside causing a few grains to fly upwards, Skye went back to the barn door, turned the latch and returned to the mountain. She squatted down and got to work, taking up handfuls and spreading them out on the floor, then picking out all the flakes of oat and setting them to one side. She worked quickly, her fingers moving through the grain and deftly separating out the different types. Her eyes stung from the dust and her neck ached but she continued, getting faster and faster as time passed.

After what seemed to be a couple of hours, Skye looked up to take stock. Her heart sank. She had barely made a dent in the heap. The two piles were tiny compared to the mountain in front of her. She rocked back on her heels and massaged her neck. Outside, the wind continued to howl around the barn. The wooden walls creaked and groaned but at least inside was warm. It was certainly more sheltered than the ruins she'd been forced to hide in during the storm she'd been caught in on the way to Litochoro. That was scant comfort, though. Dawn was only a few hours away, and she would need a month to separate the grain. She'd never get it done in just one night by using her hands.

Trying not to panic, Skye picked up a single wheat grain and examined it carefully. Then she did the same with an oat. They were clearly different sizes. Perhaps all she needed was a sieve. A very, very large sieve. She put her hands to either side of her head and thumped her temples. There had to be a way to fashion one.

Skye stilled. Fashion.

She was wearing jeans, a t-shirt and her coat. None of those would work but her underwear might because her bra was made of intricate lace. She blushed as she remembered that the last time she'd worn it was when she was with Coop. It was a kind of poetic justice if the scrap of material would also help her return to him.

She reached under her top and unclasped her bra, pulled down one strap and extricated her left arm, then her right. She yanked at the material, freeing it from her clothes and frowned at it.

The cups were rather small. Not for the first time, she wished she'd been born with larger breasts. It still might work though. Taking a small handful of the grain, she dropped it into one of the bra cups and shook, exhaling loudly as the majority of the wheat fell through the gaps in the lace while the larger oats remained in the bra. Skye grinned to herself. It wasn't a perfect method, but it had to be better than her hands.

She quickly developed a rhythm. She pushed in her bra and scooped up the grain, then shook each cup to free the wheat onto one pile and emptied the remaining oats onto the other pile. Some of the wheat clung stubbornly inside, catching on the lacy material. It was fairly easy to get hold of those husks, however, and suddenly she was moving much faster than before. Skye was aware she would never have time to separate out the entire mountain. She would just have to hope that by managing to sort a large amount of it, Aphrodite would let her off.

Skye was so intent on her task that she blocked out everything else. Scoop, shake, empty. Scoop, shake, empty. For that reason she didn't notice the wind picking up and the door to the barn beginning to strain and bang against the latch. The rusty nails holding it in place were no match for the might of the wind. She stopped for a moment to wipe the sweat from her brow – and that was when the door burst open, allowing the wind's full force to gust in. Before she could react, her two neat piles of separated grain were blown up into the air.

Yelling, Skye scrambled to her feet, waving her arms and attempting block the wind from destroying her hard work further. It was too late though. Everything she'd achieved so far had been destroyed, every separated grain pushed back against the original mountain.

Skye's mouth dropped as she stared in horror. She ran back to the door and pushed it but, with the latch broken, she had no way of keeping it closed. Swirls of grain blew up from the mound, mixing with each other. She sank down against the wall and watched helplessly. There was nothing she could do. Dawn was little more than a couple of hours away and she had failed.

Her eyes pricking with tears, she followed the movement of a few errant oat flakes, dancing in the wind as if they were taunting her. Skye cursed aloud and swiped at them but they jerked away from her, merrily sweeping upwards through the air.

'Bloody oats!' she cried, flapping her arms out towards them.

Then she stopped. 'Oats,' she said again, although this time in a whisper.

Only the oats were flying around because they were light enough to be picked up by the wind. The wheat grains moved but they were far heavier and weren't carried as far.

Her mouth was dry. Skye knew exactly what she needed to do. Ignoring the flapping barn door, she ran to the other side of the building. There was only the one entrance but, far above her, on the opposite side to the door, there was a large skylight set into the roof. It was covered in glass and Skye could make out the night sky with the stars glistening above. The tinge of purple indicated the approach of dawn. It didn't matter, though; suddenly there was a way out of her predicament.

The ladder was heavy but it wasn't far away from the skylight. She yanked it along the wall a few metres. When it felt stable and it was close enough, she began to climb. The skin around her fingers was tender from all her work separating the grains but Skye ignored the pain and pushed herself upwards as fast as she could. It was fortunate the ladder was tall enough to reach the sloping skylight; if it hadn't been, all would have been lost. But even though she managed to reach it, there appeared to be no way to open the window itself.

Without thinking, Skye pulled off her shoe and grasped it in her right hand. Averting her face, she smashed the heel into the window as hard as she could. At first nothing happened but she continued, sensing that the glass was weakening. Wobbling slightly on the ladder, Skye took a deep breath and flung her arm at the glass. This time it worked and the window cracked. She gulped in relief and hit it again. The glass broke off into several shards. Taking care not to cut herself, she gingerly broke off enough pieces to create a large gap, then quickly slid back down the ladder.

'Come on,' she whispered.

Creating a gap into the outside world worked perfectly. There was now a howling wind tunnel between the door at the far end and the break in the window. The airflow was strong enough to swoop through from one end of the building to the other. Covering her eyes with her sleeve to avoid being blinded by the flying oats, Skye ran out of the barn, her hair whipping around in all directions. Irate cows in the nearby field bellowed their displeasure and Skye shouted glee-fully into the wind.

'Do it! Come on!'

She jumped around like a mad woman while, high above her, a tiny smile played around Zephyr's lips and the first glimmers of the sun appeared on the distant horizon.

CHAPTER

TWENTY-SEVEN

'It's hardly perfect,' Aphrodite stated caustically, her eyes sweeping over the mound of oats, which had been pushed to the far end of the barn as a result of the gusting wind. 'Not all the grain is separated.'

'You are being somewhat unfair.'

'The task was to properly divide *all* the wheat and oats.'

Zeus raised a single bushy eyebrow. 'In twelve hours? Even you have to admit that she did a good job with the time she had.'

'She had help. She couldn't have done this alone.'

'Your son hasn't left Olympus for days.'

'That doesn't mean he didn't inveigle someone else into helping.'

'Aphrodite...'

'Fine,' she snapped. 'The girl passed.'

Zeus watched her, his face impassive. 'He is really in love with her.'

'The question is whether she returns the sentiment.'

'Perhaps if you spoke to her, you would gain a better understanding of her character.'

A look of pain crossed her face. 'Liking her won't mean anything.'

'Is that why you're avoiding speaking to her face to face? You're afraid you'll like her?'

Aphrodite turned away. 'I'm not afraid.'

'You'll need to let go of him sooner or later.'

'And if she proves herself worthy, then it will be sooner. There are still three more tasks to go. We'll see whether she can really come up with the goods or not. Besides, I'm hardly the only one around here who has to deal with problematic children.'

'Apollo's not a child.'

'Neither is Coop. It doesn't mean the pair of them don't act like three year olds sometimes.'

'You're changing the subject.'

The goddess didn't answer. Instead, without even turning, she snapped her fingers and vanished. Zeus remained where he was for another moment, his gaze thoughtful. Then he too disappeared.

Outside the barn, Skye was pacing up and down. She'd been too afraid to look inside to see whether her plan had worked and the wind tunnel she'd created had done its job. The thought of going back home without seeing Coop ever again was too painful to consider. She *had* to have passed.

'You did it.'

Skye closed her eyes in relief for a moment, then turned to face Hermes.

'Good,' she answered briskly. 'What's next?'

'When was the last time you got some sleep?'

'I'll sleep when I'm dead,' Skye snapped. 'What's next?'

Hermes eyed her warily. 'You're a lot more ... angry than you used to be.'

'Well, I've got a lot more reason to be, don't you think?'

'Don't let them change you, Skye. Don't let all this,' he gestured vaguely towards the barn, 'change you.'

'I'm still the same person. I'm just getting mightily tired of being treated like a toy.'

For once it was Hermes who looked embarrassed. 'The gods are fickle. And jealous. And often slightly unbalanced. Being immortal does that to you.'

'You're not like that,' she pointed out. 'Coop's not like that.'

Hermes smiled faintly. 'Not since he met you anyway.'

Skye blushed ever so slightly.

He grinned at her. 'Now that's the Skye I know.'

She squared her shoulders and looked him in the eye. 'Stop delaying and take me to the next task.'

He sighed. 'Okay. Just be careful with this one. Not everything is what it seems.'

Skye opened her mouth to ask him what he meant but before the words could form she was standing alone in a different location. There was no sign of the barn and no sign of Hermes. Instead, she was facing a gushing river and several fields, all cordoned off with barbed-wire fencing. The gods of Olympus clearly had a thing for farming.

Looking around for another note to tell her what she was supposed to do, Skye felt buoyed by her earlier success. As long as she kept her wits about her, these stupid tasks would be a piece of cake. Hermes was right that the gods were fickle, jealous and unbalanced; what he'd failed to mention was that they'd obviously underestimated her. Maybe she wasn't Hercules, but that didn't mean she couldn't pass these tests.

'Roar,' she whispered. Then louder, 'Roar!'

'I had been told to expect a young human woman,' came a voice seemingly from nowhere, 'not a lion hybrid.'

Startled, Skye whipped round her head. She was still alone, so where the hell had the voice come from?

'Hello?'

'Hello!' came the cheerful rejoinder.

Skye looked upwards at clear blue sky. There was nothing there other than a few fluffy white clouds.

'Where are you?'

'I'm here, of course.'

Skye couldn't pinpoint where the voice was coming from over the sound of the river. 'Where's here?' she asked, exasperated.

'Right in front of you. Can't you see me? See me! See! Get it?' The voice's owner laughed.

Skye frowned and took a step towards the river.

'There you go.'

She wrinkled her nose. 'You're the river?'

'The river is the river.'

What on earth was that supposed to mean? 'And the sky is the sky,' she responded. 'Except when Skye is me.'

'You're a sky god?'

'No,' she answered slowly, 'but you're a river god?' She tried and failed to keep the question out of her voice.

'Well done! My name is Asterion.'

'Hi.'

'We've already done this part,' Asterion said solemnly.

'I suppose we have. So?'

'So what?'

'Are you going to tell me what my task is?'

'Oh, that. You need to collect the wool from the sheep in the field up ahead. There's only one. You'll know the wool when you see it.'

'That's it?'

'That's it,' he replied breezily.

'How much am I supposed to get?'

'An armful will do.'

That was remarkably vague, Skye thought to herself. Then she remembered what Hermes had said. 'Is there anything else I should be aware of?'

'Ah! This one's no fool,' laughed Asterion.

Getting impatient, Skye folded her arms. 'Well?'

'I'm a river god, not a well god. They're dank and smelly. Surely even a human can tell the difference?'

Asterion brought new meaning to the phrase 'babbling brook'. Skye sighed inwardly. 'Of course I can,' she said, trying a different tack. 'You're fresh and fast. I truly admire your stunning crystal swell. And even in winter, the song of spring is evident in your river shallows.'

'Why, thank you,' Asterion said.

Thank you John Keats for writing so many poems which featured rivers in them, Skye thought.

'You're welcome.' She leaned down towards the water and lowered her voice. 'Can you tell me what I need to watch out for?'

'Sadly no. I am forbidden from revealing anything about this task by command of Zeus himself.'

Skye rolled her eyes. Typical.

'But I can tell you my sister Lethe has a very sweet tooth.'

'Eh?'

'E, I, O, U.'

Skye blinked. This was getting too weird. 'Alright,' she said finally. 'Thank you for your help, Asterion.' Such as it was.

'My pleasure, fair lady.'

Skye smiled overly brightly in the vague direction of the river, then bent down and took off her socks and shoes, rolled her jeans up to her knees and started wading across. The water was icy cold and made her gasp aloud while the stones on the river bed were slippery. More than once, she had to pause to regain her balance. But it was nothing more than a river.

Hermes had said not everything was what it seemed. Had he meant that in relation to Asterion? Skye shook her head: she really had no idea. And considering she'd just held a conversation with a river, she was probably the crazy one.

Pulling herself out, she shook her legs and rubbed them down to dry them off as best she could, then padded to the edge of the field, carefully scanning every inch of it while she put her socks and shoes back on. She couldn't see a sheep anywhere. There seemed to be plenty of cows, placidly chewing the grass and ignoring her, but she couldn't see anything else. Skye walked down the length of the fence, searching the entire expanse.

A flicker of movement caught her peripheral vision and she turned to glance at it, before being forced to shield her eyes suddenly as whatever it was glinted brightly in the morning sun. Skye squinted towards the glare, trying to work out what it was. Her mouth dropped open in astonishment: it was indeed a sheep. Sort of. It was the same size as a sheep and to all intents and purposes it was the same shape as a sheep. This animal, however, wasn't covered in a white fleece; its coat was a rich, burnished gold. The glare from the sun bouncing off it made it painful to look at. Then the sheep trotted back behind the tree it had been hiding behind and Skye's vision returned to normal.

'A golden sheep,' she murmured to herself. 'Unbelievable.'

No wonder she'd been tasked with collecting its wool; a cardigan made of that material would be a sight to behold. She smirked at the thought of Coop's glamorous mother with a pair of knitting needles. Perhaps not.

Without pausing further, Skye carefully pushed down the barbed wire fence so she could clamber over it. Sheep were hardly vicious creatures – but then sheep didn't usually have such valuable fleeces so it was entirely possible this was some kind of man-eater. She could just make out the gleaming edge of its coat from behind the oak so she made a beeline straight for it, her eyes searching the ground for something to coax it into submission long enough for her to pull off what she needed. The least Aphrodite could have done was to supply her with some shears, she thought ruefully. She didn't want to hurt the animal.

A thought occurred to her. Her skin was scratching where a few grains were trapped in her clothes. Surely a sheep, even a golden one, would appreciate some wheat and oats. Grinning to herself, Skye paused and began to shake out her jeans and t-shirt. Several grains fell onto the grass under her feet. She reached under her t-shirt to grab the flakes of oat which were still trapped in the fabric of her bra, taking a quick glance around in case anyone happened to be watching. Then she bent down to scoop up her meagre findings.

Suddenly, there was a tremendous bellow. Skye looked up, her insides transforming into jelly as she realised where the sound was coming from. The cows, which had been contentedly chewing away while she was safely on the other side of the fence, were bearing down upon her. She had just enough time to spot gleaming white fangs protruding from the beasts' large, cavernous mouths before she dropped everything, turned and ran.

Her heart was hammering against her ribcage as she pumped her legs as fast as she could. She covered the distance back to the fence in a time which any sprinter would have been proud of but, when she was barely an arm's reach away, her toe connected with a stone and she went flying flat on her face. Skye had only just registered what had happened when a sharp pain, worse than anything she'd ever felt before, tore into her. One of the smaller cows, which was clearly faster than the others, had sunk its jaws into her calf.

Skye shrieked, desperately trying to get back to her feet and safety beyond the fence. The beast's teeth tore through her flesh while the remainder of the herd thundered towards her. With an inarticulate yell, she yanked hard, freed herself from the cow's jaws and vaulted over the barbed wire. The denim of her jeans caught on the wire and ripped and Skye fell forward. She turned quickly to make sure the fence would hold the monstrous cows. As one they had stopped, frozen like statues, and watched her with huge limpid brown eyes. Then they turned and slowly trotted away.

Breathing hard, Skye stared at her leg and the stream of blood. She gingerly pulled away the torn fragments of denim but, when she saw the wound reaching through her flesh and exposing the bone, she fainted dead away.

Skye had no idea how long she'd been unconscious. The sun was high in the sky when she opened her eyes. She tried to sit up but her stomach roiled with nausea and she felt so dizzy she was sure she was about to pass out again. Gritting her teeth, she took several quick shallow breaths. The pain in her calf was intense. Not even jellyfish stings could come close to a cow's bite. She chided herself for not considering the animals might be a threat. Her success at the barn had caused her to become far too complacent; she'd almost paid for that complacency with her life.

Aphrodite didn't just want her to fail, she thought dully. The goddess wanted her dead. For some reason, that strengthened her resolve rather than weakened it. Skye shrugged out of her coat and carefully peeled off her t-shirt, wincing in pain. Before she could faint again, she bound the cotton material tightly around the wound to staunch the bleeding. Then she forced herself back into her coat and staggered to her feet.

'I will not fail!' she shouted. 'Do you hear me? I will not fail!'

Nobody answered. Feeling hopelessly alone, Skye staggered to the fence. Even if those bloody cows ripped her to shreds, she was not going to give up. She would never give up.

Despite the fact that her vision was blurry round the edges, she managed to spot the section of ripped denim clinging to the barbed wire. Skye reached out and touched it with her fingertips. Then she laughed aloud.

'You see?' she yelled again. 'I can do this!'

Moving carefully from fence post to fence post and doing everything she could to keep the weight off her wounded leg, she hopped round the field. The terrible cows seemed to ignore her presence but she was fairly certain they were aware of where she was. Regardless, she continued until she found what she was looking for. At various points around the field, golden curls were caught on the barbed wire. The sheep had obviously brushed against the fence at different times and sections of its fleece had been pulled away. In one corner there was a bush where she gathered several gleaming handfuls. Although she was moving slowly, it wasn't long before she had an armful.

A wave of agonising pain hit her and she collapsed backwards, still clutching the soft fleece. 'Told you so,' she murmured, before she closed her eyes and blackness took over once again.

Moments later, freed from the golden chains of Olympus, Coop was by her side. His hands were shaking with rage as he gently smoothed back Skye's sweat-soaked hair and brushed the blood soaking through the makeshift bandage on her leg.

'How could you let this happen, Mother?' His voice was soft, but the steel lacing his tone left no doubt as to his true feelings.

Aphrodite's face was pale. 'I didn't want her to get hurt.'

'No,' he snarled, 'you just wanted to keep us apart. So much for being dedicated to the course of true love.'

'Coop,' she began.

'Fuck off.'

He rearranged Skye's limbs and lifted her carefully up in his arms, holding her warm body against his broad chest. He gazed tenderly down at her, before sending his mother a look of absolute loathing. Then his wings unfurled and he flew up into the air, taking Skye with him.

CHAPTER

TWENTY-EIGHT

Skye wasn't quite sure where she was but she felt very warm and very safe and very comfortable. There was a slight throbbing in her leg but it was little more than an irritant. Of far greater importance was the hard body pressed against the length of her back and the arm curled round her waist.

She sighed happily. 'Coop.'

'I'm here,' he murmured in her ear, pulling her even closer against him.

Skye yelped in surprise and she sat up, twisting round to stare at the tanned contours of his face as he smiled up at her.

'It's over,' he said softly.

'I don't understand.'

He pulled himself up to her level and gazed into her eyes. 'Just know that everything's going to be alright from now on.'

He planted a long, lingering kiss on her lips. Skye moaned. This was almost too good to be true.

She suddenly withdrew. 'I'm not dreaming, am I?'

Coop laughed. 'No, you're not dreaming.'

'The fleece?'

'You got it. You collected an armful. You showed all of them, Skye. I'm so sorry my stupid actions put you through all that. I won't let anything happen to you ever again.'

She frowned. 'But there are still two more tasks.'

He caressed her cheek. 'You don't need to worry about them. You've proven your worth. My mother has agreed to let you off.'

'But...'

'Shhhh,' he said. 'Everything is fixed. We have an audience with Zeus in an hour and then you're free. We're free.' He smiled. 'So come on, get your lazy arse out of bed. We'll have plenty of time for that later.'

Skye's cheeks warmed. Coop laughed again, happy lights dancing deep in his eyes. He slapped her playfully on the thigh.

'We'd better not keep the King of the Heavens waiting.'

BARELY FORTY-FIVE MINUTES LATER, the pair of them were standing in Zeus's magnificent throne room, their fingers intertwined. Despite being next to Coop, Skye was still hopelessly intimidated. The large room was packed with people of all shapes, sizes and forms. Some, such as Hermes, were openly happy to see her; others appeared merely curious. And there were, admittedly, one or two who appeared hostile. Apollo, in particular, was standing up near the dais and glowering at them. There was a hint of mockery on his face as he watched them.

Coop squeezed her fingers. 'It'll be fine,' he whispered. 'Just don't forget to breathe.'

Skye swallowed. Her legs were shaking. She'd rather face the carnivorous cows again than stand here in this vast marbled room with so many eyes fixed upon her.

Aphrodite, draped in a long, elegant gown, glided over to them and inclined her head. 'Ms Sawyer,' she said stiffly, 'I apologise for any physical hurt you sustained during the course of your tasks.'

Skye tightened her grip on Coop's hand, aware he was on the verge of saying something he'd later regret. He answered with a reassuring caress, his thumb stroking her palm.

Skye lifted her head and looked Aphrodite in the eyes. 'That's okay,' she said softly.

Something flitted across the goddess's face, then she pasted on a smile. Skye watched her carefully, suddenly understanding why the abrupt volte-face. If Aphrodite continued forcing Skye to complete the tasks, she'd have lost Coop forever, regardless of the outcome. In order to keep her son, Aphrodite had yielded. It had nothing to do with Skye proving herself as brave or resourceful or worthy of Coop's love.

Aphrodite opened her mouth to say something else and Skye tensed. But a sudden fanfare sounded, indicating Zeus's arrival, and the goddess fell back. A trickle of self-doubt ran down Skye's spine.

'What's wrong?' Coop whispered.

She shook her head, not trusting herself to answer and turned instead to watch Zeus approach. He strode forward looking every inch the king, and towering over the assembled crowd, who knelt as he swept past in an odd mimicry of a Mexican wave. When he reached Coop and Skye, she dropped into a curtsey, feeling both foolish and clumsy. She inwardly cursed as, yet again, she began to blush.

Zeus ascended the steps in front and turned to face them. His blue eyes were looking upon her kindly but Skye still felt terribly awkward.

'So,' his voice boomed, cracking through the room like the lightning he purportedly carried, 'today we meet to smooth out the matter of the human, Skye Sawyer. What say you, Cupid?'

Coop cleared his throat and stepped forward, although his fingers still clung to Skye's. 'Skye was given four tasks to complete to prove her worth. She has successfully finished two. I petition Your Majesty to set aside the remainder of the tasks and allow us to live out our lives together. To this end, I relinquish my immortality and position.'

An audible gasp filled the room and a shiver of horror ran through Skye. Coop hadn't told her that was what he was planning. She glanced at Aphrodite and saw misery etched all over her beautiful face. Oh gods.

Zeus folded his arms. 'You can't just give up being a god.'

'Why not?'

Zeus shook his head and tutted. 'Aphrodite. The tasks were yours to set. Are you prepared to drop the matter?'

She took a step forward, but before she could speak, Skye pulled her hand away from Coop's. 'Zeus,' she said, rather more loudly than she'd intended. 'I mean, uh, Your Majesty.'

He frowned and looked down at her.

'What are you doing?' Coop hissed.

'I don't agree,' Skye said.

Clearly taken aback, the King of the Heavens blinked at her. 'Excuse me?'

Skye moved forward. 'I said I don't agree. I was given four tasks to complete. I will complete those tasks. I will not leave a job unfinished.'

Coop looked stricken. Skye glanced around from Aphrodite to Apollo and then back to Coop. She smiled at him reassuringly. 'I love you,' she said simply. 'More than I ever thought I could love anyone. You're my heart. My life.'

'So why the hell are you doing this?' The agony in his voice was evident.

'Because otherwise I'll never be truly accepted as worthy of you. I promised to finish every task and that's what I'll do. I will not have you give up everything for me.'

'I'm giving up nothing, Skye. Don't you see that? If it means I can be with you then I'm giving up nothing.' His eyes pleaded with her.

'You are aware, Ms Sawyer,' interrupted Zeus, 'that if you go ahead with the tasks and fail, the terms state you will never see Cupid again?'

She looked at him steadily. 'I am aware of that. But you have to see that I won't fail. I can't fail. I will honour my promise and see the remaining tasks through. It was doubt that caused the problems between Coop and me to begin with. I won't allow there to be any lingering doubt.'

'I rather think it is us as gods who have proved ourselves unworthy of you, Ms Sawyer,' said Zeus quietly. 'Very well. You will receive the details of the third task this afternoon. Whether you succeed or fail, know that you have our admiration.'

Without saying another word, Zeus strode down the stairs. When he reached her, he stood for a moment in front of Skye and bowed his head. Then he moved past, and walked out of the room.

'I've never spoken in front of so many people before,' Skye said shakily.

Coop grabbed her shoulders. 'What in hell have you done?'

'What was right.'

The others in the room began to walk out silently. Skye looked up in time to see a flicker of approval in Aphrodite's eyes before she also turned and left.

'Skye, if you fail...'

She smiled at him, raising her hand to touch his cheek. 'But I told you. I won't fail.' She tried to ignore the twist in her stomach which suggested otherwise.

'You know I love you, Skye Sawyer.'

She stood on her tiptoes and kissed him. 'And that's why I have to do this. I'd better go and get ready. The sooner these two tasks are completed, the sooner we can be together.'

Coop watched her go, pain and pride warring inside him and his fingertips absently brushing his lips where the taste of her still lingered.

Behind him, Apollo cleared his throat. 'You don't deserve her, you know.'

Refusing to rise to the challenge, Coop gave the Sun God a half smile. 'I know.'

'I thought that you'd be more of a man, Cupid. She's out there, risking her life to complete your mother's tasks while you top up your tan.'

'Maybe being a man means not treating her as if she's made of glass,' Coop remarked, turning to face his one-time adversary. 'If I could stop her from doing this I would, but she's her own person and I have to respect that.'

Apollo snorted. 'I wonder if you'll still be singing the same tune when she comes back to you in a body bag.'

'She won't,' he answered quietly. 'She won't fail.'

'You don't know that.'

'She told me she won't fail. I trust her.'

'How do you know she's decided she just doesn't want to be with you, eh? Maybe this is her escape route. Maybe even death is better than being with you.'

Coop lifted up his chin, a fathomless expression flitting across his face. 'I'm sorry.' He sounded as if he meant it.

Apollo blinked. 'For what?'

'For the way I acted towards you before. It was stupid and I see that now. And I'm sorry that you only briefly understood what it means to experience true love. It changes everything. I hope one day you'll feel it for yourself. Otherwise what's the point in living?'

The sincerity in his voice was genuine. Apollo, however, glared at him with distrust.

'Be happy, Apollo,' said Coop. He gave him a smile and followed everyone else out, leaving the Sun God gaping after him.

STANDING YET AGAIN outside the imposing gates of Olympus, Skye wondered whether she had made the biggest mistake of her life. She'd been given a way out and she'd refused to take it. The assembly of gods might have approved of her actions; she had definitely seen respect in many of their eyes, even those of Apollo. But if she failed the remaining two tasks, that respect would be worthless.

Hermes appeared by her side. 'Here,' he said, handing her a chunky black box covered in velvet.

Skye, momentarily surprised by its weight, turned it over in her hands. 'What is it?'

'A container,' he answered, looking troubled. 'It's made of crystal so you'll have to be careful not to drop it.'

'Thank you.'

'You don't know what you have to do with it yet,' he replied grimly. 'The tasks were set before you began, so even if Aphrodite wanted to make them easier, she couldn't.'

Skye gazed at him. 'Do you think I made the wrong decision?' she asked softly.

'You mean continuing?'

She nodded.

Hermes shrugged. 'I can see why you did it. Coop shouldn't have said what he did about giving up his immortality and status. It doesn't work like that. He was being dramatic.'

Skye gave a small smile. 'He certainly achieved that. It wasn't the reason why I said I didn't want to give up, though. It just gave me a little nudge, that's all.'

'So why then?'

'I'm not a quitter. I promised to see this through so that's what I'll do.' Skye hoped the tremor running down her spine wasn't evident in her voice. 'But more than that, I would never be accepted if I just gave up.'

'Accepted by the gods? Most of them were on your side to begin with.'

'By the gods. But by Aphrodite, in particular. The breach between her and Coop is obvious to see.'

Hermes eyed her. 'They'd make it up sooner or later.'

Skye shook her head. 'I don't think they would. Especially if she never truly likes or respects me. It means little to me what she thinks, but it means a hell of a lot to Coop.'

'It's true that he would never forgive her if she didn't fully accept you. If you do this, she'll not just say she respects you, she'll actually believe it.'

'Exactly. And Coop won't have to spend the rest of his life hating her.'

'He's immortal,' Hermes reminded her gently.

A tiny frown crossed Skye's forehead. 'Yes,' she sighed. 'He is.'

She no longer had any lingering doubts as to Coop's real feelings for her. Whether those feelings would remain the same when she was an old woman while Coop remained eternally young would be a different matter. She couldn't worry about that now. There were far more pressing matters at hand.

'You know if you fail, he'll still hate her.'

She shook her head. 'No. I'm the one who stepped up when I had the chance to back off. He'll see that.' She gave Hermes a pointed look. 'You'd better make sure of that.'

'I will,' he agreed solemnly. 'But I'm not sure it'll do much good. You'll just have to succeed.'

'I'll do my damned hardest.' Skye straightened her back. 'Well, come on then. What's the task?'

Hermes bobbed his head towards the box she was still holding. 'You need to fill the crystal container with water.'

She gave him an arch look. 'It's not going to be as simple as that, now is it?'

His mouth twisted. 'No. It needs to be water from the source of the river Styx.'

'Oh,' she said faintly. 'The river Styx. Isn't that...?'

'Yeah. You don't actually have to go to the Underworld though.' Hermes gave a short laugh. 'That would be crazy. The source is located behind Angel Falls in Venezuela.'

'Angel Falls?' There was a hint of irony in her tone.

'Hey, we didn't name it. That's entirely down to you humans.'

She rolled her eyes. 'Whatever you say. Is Styx a river god too? I mean, like Asterion?'

'Oh, they all are. Styx, Acheron, Phlegethon, Lethe...'

'Lethe?'

Hermes grinned. 'Oh yes. Word is she and Styx had a huge falling out. They're barely on speaking terms.' At Skye's glance, he held up his hands. 'Hey, so we gods like to gossip sometimes. It doesn't make us bad people.'

No,' she said slowly, 'it does make you very helpful though.' She raised her eyebrows at him. 'Do you perhaps have a kitchen I could use before we leave?'

TWENTY-NINE

ermes left Skye at the edge of the vast river next to Camaina camp, a rustic collection of tourist accommodation on the fringes of lush jungle. He wrapped her in a tight hug before he vanished, leaving her in no doubt how much he hoped she would succeed. She carefully shouldered her bag, the constricting weight of the crystal container in its box shifting as she did so. Skye had packed the contents very carefully, doing everything she could to keep them from harm.

The jungle sounds were louder than she had expected. There was a continuous hum of wildlife, from the chirrup of insects to the calls of exotic birds. It wasn't as hot and steamy as she'd expected but the humidity was still a shock after the winter chill of Greece. The verdant, emerald green blanketing the hills and mountains took her breath away. She couldn't quite see the Angel Falls from where she currently stood; she had to admit that, despite the very odd circumstances, she was excited to visit them.

Spotting a flicker of movement out of the corner of her eye, Skye turned to see an athletic-looking woman piling up several bright orange lifejackets.

'Hey!' she called out. 'When's the next trip to the Falls?'

The woman straightened up, surprised, and looked her over. 'You're one of the new tourists?' she asked, in heavily accented English. 'You arrived on the bus last night?'

Skye nodded, hoping her cheeks wouldn't betray her. She could hardly explain she'd just been magically transported here by a Greek god.

'I, um, wasn't feeling well before,' she said. Perhaps that would curtail further questioning on the woman's part. Skye needn't have worried, however, as the woman obviously had little interest in who she was and how she'd got there.

'The boats are leaving now.'

Skye blinked. 'What? Where are they?'

The woman pointed at a path leading away from the huts. 'That way. Next to the restaurant. You'll miss them if you don't hurry. There's not another trip until tomorrow.'

Alarmed at the thought that she might have to hang around and twiddle her thumbs for twenty-four hours, Skye immediately took off, speeding down the path. Her heavy bag slammed rhythmically against her back and she cursed, reaching back to attempt to steady it. When she caught sight of a long canoe up ahead, pushing away from the shore, and other boats already moving away down the river, she sprinted harder and yelled, 'Wait!'

No-one seemed to hear her above the jungle cacophony and the roar of the water. Skye forced her legs to continue pumping and tried to ignore the lingering pain in her calf then, when she finally reached the shore, she sprang forward. Water splashed in all directions as her body slammed into the large canoe and it rocked dramatically. Finally hands were pulling her into the vessel, gripping her limbs and yanking her into place.

Skye twisted round, attempting to avoid squashing the precious contents of her backpack, and sat upright. There were three tourists staring at her open mouthed while a man in the front, whom she presumed was the guide, was giving her a disapproving look.

'What did you think you were doing?' he snapped. 'The river is dangerous. It's easy to be pulled under by the current, even when it's not deep.'

'I'm sorry,' she gasped. 'I didn't want to miss the boat.'

He muttered something inaudible under his breath and threw a spare lifejacket onto her lap.

'Thanks.'

'Are you staying at the cabins?' asked one of the men behind her, suspiciously.

'Er, sure,' she dissembled, turning to give him what she hoped was a dazzling smile.

'I've not seen you.'

'I hurt my leg,' Skye said, as if that answered everything.

A woman leaned forward and punched him on the arm. 'Scott, don't be so rude!'

'We've paid a lot of money for this trip,' he grumbled. 'The last thing we need is any freeloaders.'

Skye forced a laugh. She didn't have a single cent on her. The last thing she needed was to be dumped off the boat into the dangerous current because she'd not paid her dues.

'Ignore him,' the woman said, with the obvious twang of an Australian accent. 'He's just in a bad mood.'

The third man, seated at the very rear of the canoe, didn't say anything. He was paying Skye scant attention, his eyes focused on the other couple. 'Yeah, give it a break, Scott,' he drawled. Then he flicked his gaze quickly to the woman, as if seeking her approval. She didn't notice.

Unsure how to respond, Skye smiled at them all then focused on the scenery. She wondered idly whether Coop took requests. It seemed apparent that grumpy Scott and the woman were an item – and that the other man wished things were different. Then she scolded herself for even considering the idea. She was starting to realise why Coop had become so cynical about his day job. It was far too easy to manipulate people into falling in love. And far too easy to make snap judgments about people based on fleeting conversations. This sudden flicker of understanding about his feelings made her feel closer to him, despite them being thousands of miles apart.

The long canoe wended its way down the river, with the guide expertly manoeuvring it through rocks and rapids. There were three other boats ahead, filled with people chattering excitedly and pointing out flora and fauna. The closer they got to the roaring Angel Falls, however, the more nervous dread trickled through Skye's veins. She was fairly certain her plan would work – but she'd been fairly certain it would be easy to gather an armful of shining golden fleece. The last thing she needed was to be overconfident.

The valley walls on either side of the river were getting steeper and higher. Even though it was a sunny day, the further the canoe travelled, the darker the surroundings seemed to get. The forest became increasingly impenetrable, except for the luminous flashes of colour afforded by the occasional flap of tropical birds' wings.

Just as Skye was thinking about the brooding desolation of the jungle, and feeling like she was travelling into the South American version of the heart of darkness, the canoe twisted round a river bend and the waterfall came into view, thundering its way down the cliff. Clouds of spray caught in the sunlight and hues of orange and red formed at the base of the towering force of nature. Skye's eyes travelled upwards; she was awestruck at what she was seeing. It seemed that everyone around her was feeling the same. The Angel Falls stretched up towards the heavens as if they were a mile high.

'By Olympus,' she whispered to herself, her words swallowed up in the deafening tumble of water. The waterfall next to Olympus had been pretty, but it was nothing compared to the scale of these falls. She curled her fingers tightly into her palms. If only Coop were here with her now so they could experience this together.

She glanced back at her temporary companions. The woman was reaching forward, her hands on her boyfriend's shoulders while he was extending his own arms backwards for her. Despite her previous

– and possibly very wrong – judgment about their relationship, Skye shot them a happy smile before turning back.

Using his paddle, the guide pushed the boat towards the shore where the ground was scuffed and bare from hundreds of other recent tourists. The other canoes were already emptying, people pulling out cameras and phones to take pictures which would never do justice to the imposing waterfall. Skye closed her eyes momentarily, enjoying the cool spray on her skin, then she carefully stepped back onto dry land.

The guide secured the canoe and gestured them forward to a well-beaten path leading through the jungle and up closer to the base of the falls. Skye allowed the others to go ahead of her then fell in behind them. She'd have to hope that she could sneak off unnoticed as soon as possible.

Her chance came sooner than she'd expected. Once the group came out into another clearing closer to the water's edge, they all began stripping off to their swimwear, keen to take a dip in the cool waters in such a magnificent setting. The four guides clustered together, sharing food and chatting. Fortunately, none of them had decided to quiz her about her sudden appearance. Skye figured that the last thing they were expecting was for her to abruptly vanish into thin air.

Giving one last glance to double check they weren't watching her, she swung her backpack onto her shoulders and took off, her slight figure almost immediately swallowed up by the jungle. This time there was no path, so she simply had to hope she was heading in the right direction. Clearly, finding the bloody source of the Styx was going to be the most challenging part of this quest. Skye could imagine herself getting lost in the thick undergrowth and heading deep into the jungle instead of towards the wall of water. She paused several times to listen for the direction where the water was loudest to make sure she was moving towards the right place.

Soon she was dripping in sweat. Her skin itched painfully where she'd been bitten. She had no idea how the insects managed to crawl so quickly underneath her clothes to find the choicest bits of flesh to nibble on.

Finally the trees began to thin out and the cliff wall next to Angel Falls became visible. Thanks to the continuous spray, the ground underfoot was slimy and slippery. Skye reached out, palms flat against the smooth rock surface, and began to sidle along carefully. The closer she got to the waterfall, the more nervous she felt. The force of the water was getting stronger and even though all she was feeling was residue spray, it stung her skin. At least there was enough of it to conceal her should anyone below decide to look up.

Once or twice she almost lost her footing and only just managed to cling on against the side of the rock wall. Despite the large pool at the base of the falls where the tourists were frolicking, Skye had no doubt that were she to fall, she would hit the jutting rocks long before she hit the water.

Spotting a suitable foothold, she carefully raised up one leg and forced her toe into the space. Then she reached upwards, her fingers seeking purchase in the cracks along the cliff's surface. She didn't have enough upper body strength to hang on this way for long; she had to find the entrance and find it quickly. Pulling her body upwards, she raised up her other leg, moving her foot around to find another crack. As soon as she did so, however, she shifted her weight slightly and almost lost her balance, one arm flailing around in mid-air.

With her fingers already losing their grip, she pushed all thought out of her mind and swung back towards the cliff face, finally managing to grip tightly with both hands and both feet. She remained there for a heartbeat, gratefully acknowledging the fact she was still alive, and then tried to reach higher up.

"'Faeries, come take me out of this dull world,'" she gasped, as her fingers scrabbled against the wet rock. "'For I would ride with you upon the wind, run on to the top of the dishevelled tide, and dance upon the mountains like a flame.'"

Her heart pounding, she found a space big enough to squeeze in her right hand and grip on. The trouble was, it was at least a foot above her head and in order to grasp it properly, she had to jump upwards.

'Come on then, faeries,' she muttered to herself. 'Where are you when I need you?'

Her arms were already aching and, between the spray from the falls and the sweat that kept sliding off her brow and into her stinging eyes, it was difficult to see. Gritting her teeth, she heaved her body to the right and tried to feel upwards with her fingertips on her left. She waved them around in the air but somehow, no matter how far forward against the cliff wall she leaned, she couldn't connect her hand with its surface. Skye frowned and tried a bit lower down. And that was when she felt the ledge. Her fingers curled over its edge and her eyes widened. Praise the gods. With one heave, she stretched herself up, managing to pull her elbow over the lip of the ledge so she was more secure. Then she used the toe of her trainers to bounce off the sheer cliff and launch herself upwards, finally yanking her body over the edge and rolling away from the dangerous abyss below her, her breath coming in short, heavy bursts.

After a few moments, she pulled herself up to sitting position and glanced out. A large overhanging rock concealed the cave's surface from outside view. Few people, if any, would be brave enough to climb up the waterfall's length without first knowing for sure that this cave existed. If she looked over to her left, it appeared she'd barely clambered up any distance at all. The small clearing where she'd begun her secretive ascent seemed little more than a few metres away. But if she twisted her head to the right and looked down, her stomach lurched with dizzying vertigo. The drop down to the pool on that side was perilously far away.

Without wasting any more time, Skye backed inside and turned around. There was just enough room for her to squeeze through the claustrophobic tunnel, although she had to take off her backpack and push it ahead of her. Fortunately, the tunnel was short, soon opening out into a cavernous space that stretched up through the roof of the mountain almost as far as the Angel Falls themselves. There had to be a gap somewhere above, because a cascade of white water was falling down in the centre as if it were nothing more than a shower, glimmering flecks catching the remaining dull light that was seeping in from outside. What was it with these bloody gods and waterfalls?

Clambering to her feet, Skye searched for signs of the Styx. She knew from what little Hermes had told her that she would immediately recognise the source because of its thick brackish blackness. She moved deeper into the cave, avoiding the shower of water from the falls and skirting round the edges. She hadn't gone far when a stale musky odour filled the air. Skye straightened her back. This had to be it.

'Hello?' she called out nervously. Her voice was drowned out by the sound of the waterfalls, both inside and out.

She tried again, louder this time. 'Hello?'

Skye took a few more steps forward. There, bubbling up against a collection of small stones, was a liquid black ooze. She knelt down and peered cautiously at it, then nodded to herself and opened her backpack, taking out the heavy velvet box and opening it carefully. Nestled inside was a crystal decanter with a corked stopper. Skye squeezed out the cork and laid it gently to the side then placed the crystal next to the rocks.

'What do you want?' The voice was so sudden, and so cracked and dry, that even though she'd been expecting it, Skye almost fell over in surprise.

Recovering quickly, she stood up and directed her voice down. 'I'd like some water, please.' She was amazed at how calm she sounded.

'There's water everywhere. You didn't need to call me to get some. Take a bloody look outside.' Styx sounded bored and weary.

'It's your water I'd like, sir,' Skye said quickly, before the River God decided she wasn't worth his time.

'So take some then. What do I care?'

She licked her lips. 'Well, I have a funny feeling that if I try to take some, something bad will happen.'

'Something bad? Do you know the last human who touched me became virtually invincible. Don't you want that kind of power?'

Skye had thought this through already. Sure, Achilles may have initially done well from his contact with the Styx. Things hadn't worked too well for him in the end, though. She may not know many of the old Greek myths but she was certainly aware of that one. It wasn't worth the risk.

'Actually,' she said, 'I was rather hoping you'd help me and fill my container for me.' She jerked her head down at the crystal.

A dry laugh emanated from the black water, echoing around the chamber and drowning out the sounds of the waterfalls.

'You're not as vapid as you look.'

Skye stuttered out a smile. 'Thank you.'

'Now piss off.'

'Wait!' she cried out. 'I can give you something in return.'

There was a moment of scary silence. Then Styx spoke again. 'What do you have that I could possibly want?'

Exhaling audibly, Skye reached into her backpack again and pulled out a brown paper bag. 'This,' she said triumphantly.

Styx was unimpressed. 'A bag?'

'Cupcakes!' She reached in and pulled one out. Her exertions in getting to the canoe in time, along with her other travels, hadn't done the confectionery much good. The mound of icing was smeared on the inside of the bag and now looked like red sludge on top of a very misshapen dark sponge.

'What do you get served at birthday parties in heaven?' Skye asked.

Styx didn't respond.

'Angel cake!' she answered for him, then laughed nervously.

'Is that supposed to be funny?'

Skye blushed. 'Clearly not.'

'Why, in Olympus's name, would I want cake?'

She took a deep breath. 'You don't want cake?'

'I know I don't want cake.'

'But Lethe wants cake.' The bubbling water at her feet seemed to grow in stature. Skye swallowed. 'She has a sweet tooth. Asterion told me.'

'Asterion is crazy.'

She wasn't going to argue with that. 'Give her some cake. She might be willing to patch things up with you if you give her a present.' Skye glanced down at the forlorn-looking cupcake. 'And because it's obviously homemade, she'll appreciate it all the more.'

'Have you been speaking to Aphrodite?' Styx growled.

Skye started. 'Er...'

'Bloody woman is always trying to matchmake.'

Nonplussed, she took a step back. Matchmake? That hadn't been her intention. She wasn't Coop. Something in the River God's tone had made her pause, however.

'I'm friends with her son,' she said softly. She flushed more deeply. 'Actually we're not friends. We're,' Skye took a deep breath, 'in love.'

'Cupid? And you?' The River God seemed to be mulling it over. 'Fine,' he finally snapped. 'Put the bag down. I'll take the cakes.'

Skye clutched the bag in her fingertips. 'Give me some water first.'

Styx sighed in annoyance. Then a single plume of thick black water shot up in the air. Skye jumped back, alarmed, but she needn't have worried. The water curved up through the air in a perfect arc before pouring through the neck of the crystal decanter. She hastily scooped the decanter up, rammed the stopper in as tightly as it would go and placed it back inside the box.

'The cakes,' Styx grumbled.

'Oh, yes.' Skye put the cupcake in its bag and placed it next to the dark spring. 'Mr Styx?'

'What now?'

'When you talk to her, you should be nice. You know, tell her she's looking good.' Skye glanced down. Did these river gods even have corporeal forms? 'Or that you've really missed her. Tell her the truth and she'll come round.' She chewed her bottom lip. 'You have missed her, haven't you?'

'I'll tell her,' he returned gruffly. 'Thank you.'

'You're welcome,' Skye said softly, then left the way she'd come.

CHAPTER
THIRTY

'So,' said Hermes, looking embarrassed, 'you remember how I said it would be crazy for you to be asked to go to the Underworld?'

Skye stared at him. He coughed awkwardly.

'You're kidding, right?' she said finally.

'Um...'

'Goddamnit!'

'It's not as bad as it sounds.'

'Really?' she asked sceptically. 'What is it then?'

Hermes rubbed at his collar. 'Well, I've never actually been myself,' he began.

'You've never been?' Skye screeched. 'How am I supposed to go if even the bloody gods themselves are too scared?'

'I'm not scared, per se. Just...' He flicked her a glance. 'Okay, maybe I'm a little bit frightened. Only a little bit though.'

Skye was silent for a second. Then she took a deep breath. 'Do I have to be...?' Her voice drifted away.

'What?'

'Do I have to be dead?'

Hermes' eyes widened. 'By Olympus, Skye, no. It's true that only the dead are supposed to be allowed to pass through but other people have done it. In fact, there was a guy only just last week who went.'

'Did he come back?'

Hermes nodded vigorously. 'Aphrodite doesn't want you dead.'

Remembering her ordeal at the jaws of the carnivorous cows, Skye wasn't so sure.

Hermes, as if reading her mind, placed a reassuring hand on her shoulder. 'Well, definitely not now anyway. She was really pleased when you came back with that sample of the Styx. Honest.'

'You've already said that the tasks were set from the beginning and that she couldn't change them now even if she wanted to,' Skye pointed out.

'Okay, yes, that part's true. But Zeus would never let her set a task that involved certain death.'

'No,' said Skye sarcastically, 'because that would be unfair.'

'It's the last task. It's going to be the hardest because that's the nature of these things. But do this and it's all over, Skye. For good.'

She sighed heavily. 'Fine. What do I have to do?'

'Just find Persephone.'

Skye racked her brain to remember who that was. 'She's Hades' wife?'

'Yeah.'

'That's it?' she asked suspiciously. 'Just find her?'

'Well, um, not exactly.'

'Hermes, spit it out.'

'When you've found her, you need to persuade her to give you some of her beauty to bring back to Aphrodite.'

Skye wrinkled her nose. 'Bring back her beauty? How is that possible?'

'Not all of it,' Hermes said hastily. 'Just a sample.'

'That's ridiculous.'

'Actually, it's not as hard as you'd think. It has to be donated voluntarily, but it's a fairly easy thing to do.' At her look, he quickly amended his words. 'For gods. Fairly easy for gods.'

Skye rolled her eyes. 'Of course it is.'

'I'll drop you off at the entrance. It's normally invisible to humans so I'll need to show you exactly where it is. You go through, find her, persuade her and the job's done.'

'What am I likely to come across?'

'In the Underworld? First, you need to persuade Charon to take you across the Styx, then you have to pass by Cerberus.'

'The three-headed dog? He's real?'

'It's all real, Skye.'

'"The vasty hall of Death,"' she said. 'Outstanding.'

'Shakespeare?'

'Matthew Arnold.' She sighed again. 'Let's go, then.'

Hermes watched her carefully, as if waiting for something else. 'What?'

He didn't answer, just gave her a hopeful, expectant smile. She thought quickly. There had to be something missing, something she was supposed to say or ask. Then she snapped her fingers in sudden understanding.

'Coins!' She grinned at him. 'Can I borrow some money?'

Relief flashed across his face. 'Of course.' He dug into his pockets. 'Here.' Hermes dropped a small bronze coin into her palm. 'It's a danake. It won't buy you much in the shops but I think it'll get you what you need.'

'Past Charon, you mean.'

He nodded.

Skye wondered whether she was missing any other important details. What else did she know about Charon?

'Virgil,' she said softly. 'What did he say about Charon?' She searched the recesses of her brain, her face clearing when she remembered the words. '"A sordid god: down from his hairy chin a length of beard descends, uncombed, unclean; his eyes, like hollow

furnaces on fire; a girdle, foul with grease, binds his obscene attire.'''
Unexpected bile rose in her throat. 'Oh, crap.'

'Poetic licence,' said Hermes dismissively. 'He's really not that bad.'

'How do you know? You've never been to the Underworld. Don't tell me you've met at some godly party. You know, a themed event? I can just see it now.' She deepened her voice. 'Come to the 1500's party. Dust off your favourite Renaissance outfit. Food on offer will be seasoned tripe and stewed rabbit. You will even listen to those classic hit tunes with the hurdy-gurdy, the hornpipe and the lyre!' Skye pinched her nose. 'Sorry,' she apologised. 'The lack of sleep is making me crazy.'

'Actually, that kind of sounds fun,' Hermes commented.

She sent him a droll look before becoming serious again. 'Do you think I'll do it?'

'Complete the task? Win the day and live happily ever after in sickeningly sweet love with Coop?' He beamed at her. 'Of course.'

Skye took a deep breath and turned away. 'Right. Thanks.'

Behind her back, Hermes' face immediately dropped. 'Shit,' he mouthed silently. Then he rubbed his forehead and pasted on another grin. 'Come on,' he said cheerfully, 'let's get going.'

HERMES left Skye in front of an innocuous-looking cave. She made bets with herself about how many sodding waterfalls she was likely to find inside. By the time she finished all these tasks, she reckoned she'd be an expert on them. Perhaps if she failed, she wouldn't have to go back to eking out a miserable existence as a waitress; she could become the world's foremost authority on dark spooky caves and gushing streams of water. Not to mention talking rivers and dangerous cows. She smiled grimly to herself. She was definitely letting fatigue get to her if she was contemplating failure. The only way she'd succeed was if she truly believed that she would. And regardless of what Hermes had said about the last task being the most difficult, this *was* the last task. She could be back safe and nestled against Coop in a matter of hours.

Steeling herself, she glanced backwards. Hermes had already vanished.

'Thank you,' she whispered into the empty air, 'for everything.' Then Skye nodded once to herself and stepped inside the entrance to the Underworld.

She'd expected it to be dark and gloomy. This was, after all, the gateway to the afterlife. It served no purpose other than to provide an avenue for the dead. She'd also expected the adrenaline to start pumping and for her heart to race. It didn't get more terrifying than tangling with death, after all. But she was surprised on both counts.

The interior of the cave was neither dark nor gloomy. Instead it was lit by a warm blue phosphorescence, creating an almost welcoming, albeit ethereal, atmosphere. And rather than her heart rate speeding up, it seemed to slow down. She was enveloped in a state of calm. It was possible that the sensation was being forced upon her; after all, it wouldn't do to have terrified newly-dead spirits causing problems hour after hour. Regardless, she took a moment to breathe in deeply and take stock of her emotions; she wanted to remember how it felt to not be scared or nervous.

The path she was standing on was smooth and well worn. All around her was silence but it felt oddly comforting. Skye walked forward carefully. There was a cluster of flickering images ahead which she tried to focus on – but every time the blurred images started to solidify, they suddenly slid away and dissipated into noth-ing. From time to time she shivered involuntarily, as if someone was metaphorically walking over her grave. She wrapped her arms around herself and continued forward.

To her left there was an odd, roped-off section. It looked like the lines you'd see at a theme park, or in an airport, snaking off into the distance. If she tried not to look too hard, she could see more hazy dancing images between the ropes. Skye paused. Was she supposed to queue? She shrugged. She'd spent her life following the rules and being polite. By entering the Underworld as a living, breathing human, she was already breaking some of nature's most important laws. She reckoned that not standing in line would hardly be a grave sin by comparison.

She walked on. No ghostly figures tutted or got in her way. She kept going, past the hundreds and hundreds of zigzagging, seemingly empty, queues.

After what seemed like hours, she realised that the soft blue light was starting to change hues. Up ahead it was more green than blue and if she peered closely, she could make out a figure. It had to be Charon. As she got closer, however, she realised that the boatman was nothing like she'd expected. Instead of a hooded figure with robes and a shadowy face, he was middle aged, wearing a baseball cap, Bermuda shorts and a tattered t-shirt proclaiming that he was a fan of the Grateful Dead. Skye smirked. At least Charon understood irony, if nothing else.

When she was close enough, she raised a hand in greeting. He remained motionless, watching her with expressionless eyes.

'Another one?' he said drily.

Skye swallowed. 'I'm sorry...?'

'Another live one? It didn't work out particularly well for the last guy.'

Skye realised what he had to be referring to. 'Hermes said he got out.'

Charon cocked his head. 'Aye, I suppose he did.'

'You mean he didn't?' Her mouth felt dry.

'He got out.'

'He's alive?'

Charon's eyes shifted slowly left and then back again. 'Yes.'

Her stomach squirmed. 'I want to get across the river.'

'I figured.'

She tried to smile. 'I know Styx. I met him yesterday.'

The boatman scowled. 'Name drop all you like. I'm in charge

here.'

'I didn't, I mean, I wasn't...'

'Can you pay the price?'

'What?' Skye stared at him wide-eyed.

He rubbed his fingers together. 'It's not free,' he said, leaning in towards her. 'I'm not running a charity here.'

Relief flooded through her. 'Oh, yes.' She fumbled in her pocket for the coin Hermes had given her and handed it over.

Charon turned it over in his hand, then raised it up to his mouth and bit the corner.

'I thought you were only supposed to do that with gold,' Skye said, before she could stop herself.

Charon pocketed the coin and glowered. 'Do you want to get across or don't you?'

Skye nodded, suddenly mute. He stepped aside and gestured at a very rickety boat. She hoped it wasn't going to leak. After all her efforts to avoid touching the black water of the Styx at Angel Falls, it would be ridiculous if she ended up covered in the stuff now.

She licked her lips and moved forward, climbing gingerly into the boat. Charon got in after her and sat down at the rear, starting up a small motor which sent the vessel chugging into life. With a lurch, the boat jerked across the fast-flowing river.

Skye stared into the water. It was so black here that against the green light it almost seemed purple. She leaned out, sniffing delicately, trying to see how similar the water was here to the source. As she did so, a huge scaly shape rose up. She shrieked and pulled back.

'You should keep away from the water,' Charon observed calmly.

Skye shot him an exasperated glance and scooted to the middle of the boat. It rocked from side to side, as if the monster below was creating its own tide. She clenched her teeth and hoped the journey would be over soon.

'The last lifer was a lot more friendly than you.'

Skye scowled. 'There's nothing wrong with being quiet.' She turned and looked at him. 'What's a lifer, anyway?'

'Who,' Charon corrected, making a slight adjustment to the boat's rudder.

'Fine. Who is a lifer?'

'Someone like you. Someone who thinks they can persuade Hades to give them back their loved ones.' He raised his eyebrows at her. 'It almost never works. You should give up now.'

Skye frowned. 'That's not why I'm here.'

'Really.'

'Really!' she protested. 'I just want to speak to Persephone, that's all.'

Charon began to laugh. It started off as a small sound but grew in intensity, until he was bellowing and making the boat shake.

'What's so funny?' Skye asked, stung.

The boat jerked to a stop against a small wooden pier. Charon wiped his eyes. 'We're here.'

'Wait, why were you laughing?'

'You need to get out.'

'Tell me first.'

He gave her a dark, amused glance. 'You won't get in.'

'What do you mean? I'm here. I'm in.'

'Lady Persephone doesn't spend much time in these parts. Hades likes to keep her to himself when she's here. He won't want the likes of you interrupting him.' Charon winked at her. 'The pair of them are busy.'

Skye felt her cheeks reddening. 'They can't be busy all the time.'

Charon smirked.

She drew a shaky breath. 'She'll see me,' she said. 'She has to.'

'I give you about fifteen minutes before you're running back here with your tail between your legs.'

Skye drew herself up. 'I'm not scared.'

He narrowed his eyes at her. 'You should be.'

Trying to push down her rising trepidation, Skye clambered out of the boat. 'Thank you,' she said primly then she turned on her heel and walked off the pier and onto the dark shore.

Shoving her hands into her pockets, Skye forced herself to appear as nonchalant as possible. Her previous calm had disappeared at Charon's words. As much as she tried to tell herself to ignore him and remain optimistic, she couldn't help feeling that she was strolling blithely to her doom. You didn't have to do this, she told herself. You could have quit ages ago and lived happily ever after. She smoothed back her hair. She'd been certain that she was right to continue with the tasks and make sure they were all completed; now she couldn't help feeling that she'd made the worst mistake of her life.

Spotting a dark shape and a large gate up ahead, she headed straight for it. When she was about ten feet away, the shape moved. Two red eyes were glowing at her.

Biting her lip, Skye took another step. The shape moved again. Then there were three eyes. A fourth snapped open and regarded her unblinkingly. Even though her insides were screaming at her to turn and run while she still could, she took yet another step forward. Cerberus's remaining head jerked awake. Now all three pairs of eyes were following her progress. She sidestepped to the left. The eyes swivelled towards her. She sidestepped right and they did exactly the same thing. Skye held her palms out, trying to indicate that she wasn't a threat.

'Good doggy,' she said softly. She stopped for a moment. 'Good doggies,' she rephrased.

A low growl began in the beast's throat. It was lying directly in front of the gates so there was no way she could skirt round it. She had to either find a way to pacify the three-headed dog so it let her past, or try and defeat it.

Skye thought carefully. Her wits had helped her get this far. Surely she could think of a way to get around this. It was just a dog. A three-headed dog with glowing red eyes, but just a dog.

She forced herself to calm down. Dogs could smell fear. If she acted like prey, it wouldn't hesitate to attack her. She needed to show it who was boss.

Straightening her shoulders, Skye walked forward, straight at it. All at once Cerberus leapt to its feet and each monstrous head began barking . She stared at its size. It had to be at least a storey high. Three sets of jaws opened and shut, snarling and dripping with drool. Its body was huge, with muscles rippling under its smooth dark fur. Skye spotted a studded collar around its neck. Despite her fear, she admired whoever it was who'd been brave enough to try and tame this beast.

'Sit!' she said sharply.

No matter how hard she tried to sound unafraid, her voice still trembled. It didn't matter, however, as Cerberus ignored her command. The head on the left side lunged forward, jaws opening to reveal sharp white fangs and a lolling red tongue. Skye stood her ground. Okay. That head was possibly the most aggressive of the three. Perhaps she could appeal to one of the others, whose inaction had prevented the first one from reaching her.

She pointed towards each head in turn. 'Head One, Head Two, Head Three.' Then she moved slightly to her right and addressed Head Two.

'Hi there.'

It snapped and growled. She was aware that Head One was glaring at her malevolently but, for the time being, she chose to ignore it.

'I'm here to see Persephone. I've been sent by Aphrodite.' She licked her lips nervously. 'She's a goddess. That means she's got more power than you. You don't want to piss her off. Believe me,' she said under her breath, 'you really don't want to piss her off.'

Skye walked forward two paces. Head Two reared up and howled, making her ears ring. Then, without warning, it sprang forward, fangs flashing. She only just managed to jump out of the way. Damn it. She sidestepped again and looked Head Three in the eyes.

'Tell Hades I'm here.' This time, her voice was clear and strong.

Head Three turned slowly and looked at its companions. She could almost smell the disdain. This wasn't working.

Backing away, she fumbled in her pockets. They were empty apart from her phone. She began casting around on the ground for something to help her. Keeping one eye on Cerberus, she bent down and scooped up two small stones, hefting them in her hands. Each of the heads growled. For a moment she was tempted to see whether she could aim each stone well enough to strike the dog in its separate foreheads. That was a foolish thought, however. She only had to miss once and she would end up as Pedigree Chum. There was a smarter way.

She tossed up one of the stones and caught it. The three heads bobbed up, their eyes tracking the movement.

'You want to play?'

She tried the same with the second stone. The same thing happened: each pair of eyes remained trained on the stone as it left her hand, heads jerking down as it landed back in her palm again. Skye grinned. She took a step forward. Then another. Very carefully, she unfurled her fingers and held out her palms, revealing a stone in each.

'Do you want to play fetch?'

A drop of spittle fell from Head Two's mouth. Skye shifted her weight. She had to be ready to run.

Head Three barked and Skye winced at the sound. There would only be one chance to get this right. She took a deep breath then, with all her might, flung one stone to her left and one stone to her right. Head One went one way, Head Three went the other. Skye sprang forward, shoving herself underneath Head Two while it howled in agony as the other two heads ripped it in either direction, vying desperately to be the one to run after the bouncing stones.

Skye threw herself along the ground and under Cerberus's belly. Its tail, sharp and pointed, almost like a dragon's, whipped from side to side and she rolled along the ground like an acrobat to avoid it. As soon as her hands clasped the cold metal of the gates, a triumphant smile curved her lips. Maybe she'd make a ninja after all.

Quickly, before Cerberus could spin around and react, she yanked at the gates. They clanged together but didn't open. She could sense the three heads of Cerberus reacting as one, snapping one way then the other to try and stop the intruder from entering the Underworld. Alarmed, she pulled harder. The gates still didn't open. Spotting a bolt, Skye leapt to her right and began fumbling at it. It wouldn't budge. She cursed and tried harder but no matter what she did, she couldn't raise the heavy latch to let herself through.

Something wet and sticky landed on the back of her neck. Skye slowly turned. Cerberus had managed to twist itself around. All three heads were facing her and all three of them had hatred in their cold, red eyes. Skye's stomach dropped and she could feel her legs trembling. She could feel their hot, heavy breath on her skin. Then she ran.

Cerberus leapt at her, its three heads now working in unison, all with one simple objective: to catch her and kill her. She could feel jaws snapping at her back. All she had to do was to get back to the pier; she knew instinctively that the beast wouldn't encroach upon Charon's territory. Skye swerved left, then right, zigzagging in an attempt to fool Cerberus and get away. There were ten feet to go, nine feet, eight ... she was so close. And then she felt searing pain as her body was lifted up in the air. The mouth – she couldn't tell which head it belong to – shook her violently while the pressure on her ribcage made her feel as if every bone in her body was about to break. Finally she was being flung like a rag doll to one side. Her body slammed against a wall and she collapsed, barely able to breathe. She pulled herself to her hands and knees and began to crawl, while every one of Cerberus's six eyes watched her. Her fingers were clawing the dirt and she could hear herself moaning involuntarily in pain. The beast was toying with her now.

'Please,' she whispered. 'Leave me alone.'

Then another voice filled the space, a cracked, dry voice which echoed in her brain and sounded familiar.

'Begone, Cerberus,' said Styx, a looming figure wrapped in water pulling up out of the river and pointing at the animal. 'Begone.'

Head Three whined softly. Skye jerked her head upwards and watched as the animal turned and slowly padded back to the gates. It lay down with a heavy sigh, each red eye still fixed on her.

Skye pulled herself over to the bank of the river Styx and collapsed, gasping.

CHAPTER

THIRTY-ONE

'It worked,' said Styx conversationally, as Skye forced herself to sit up. All she could feel was overwhelming misery and agonising pain.

'What?' she asked dully.

'It worked,' he repeated.

Skye glanced back to the gates where Cerberus was lying down again. 'No, it didn't.' She could feel tears pricking her eyes. 'I failed.'

Styx ignored her. 'Lethe and I are back on speaking terms. The squashed cakes were perfect. Can you make me some more? Maybe with little hearts on them this time?'

'I was supposed to find Persephone,' she whispered. 'I was supposed to be with Coop.'

'Huh?'

'Don't you see? I'll never get past that dog now! That was my one shot and I screwed it up.'

'Oh. Sorry.'

'Whatever.'

She clambered painfully to her feet, her head still ringing. Any minute now she'd start seeing little birds tweeting round her. She'd been so sure she could do it. Even with Charon's warnings and the enormity of the tasks, she had still believed she would succeed. And now it was all over. She wondered whether she'd see Coop, just one last time, so she could say goodbye. Considering the terms of the agreement, it was unlikely.

Skye pulled out her phone and studied it. The least she could do would be to call him. If she was lucky he'd be allowed to answer and she could tell him herself that she'd failed. That she would love him until the day she died and that she was so very, very sorry.

'The signal here is very good,' Styx commented helpfully. 'You wouldn't think it would be, but it is. Charon's always playing silly games on his phone or checking his email.'

Skye took a brief moment to wonder who on earth would be emailing the Underworld's boatman. It was probably just spam, she thought uncharitably.

Her heartbeat stilled. She stared down at her phone as it displayed Coop's number. 'Email,' she whispered.

'Pardon?'

'Email. Persephone. Email.' She jumped up and down and then winced at the pain.

'I don't understand.'

'What's Persephone's bloody email address?' she yelled.

'I'm a river god,' said Styx, 'why would I use email?'

'Pomegranate@olympus.com.'

Skye's head jerked up. It was Charon. He stared at her for a moment then shrugged. 'You did better with the dog than I thought you would.' He smiled faintly. 'Not bad for a human girl.'

'Thanks,' she breathed.

'Persephone doesn't know who you are,' Styx pointed out. 'She's not likely to help a stranger for no reason.'

Skye grinned. 'Maybe I'm not a stranger.'

'So let me get this straight,' said Hermes, 'you've sent a spam email to Persephone, the Queen of the Underworld, pretending to be Aphrodite.'

'Yup.'

'You told her there was a themed party coming up and that she needed to borrow some of Persephone's beauty.'

'Yup.'

'And Persephone believed this? She's sent it to Olympus?'

'Yup. In a pretty little box,' crowed Skye. She held up her phone so he could see Persephone's email response.

Hermes shook his head. 'Unbelievable.'

Skye grinned. 'I know.'

'So that means...'

'That Skye Sawyer has passed every task with flying colours,' boomed Zeus, appearing out of the gates of Olympus. His eyes twinkled at her. 'Congratulations.'

Skye suddenly felt shy. 'Thanks,' she mumbled. 'Where's Coop?'

'I'm here.' He stepped out from behind Zeus and moved towards her, cradling her cheek. 'You're hurt,' he said softly. 'I shouldn't have let that happen.' He rested his forehead against hers.

'I'll heal,' she said, losing herself in the depths of his eyes.

His arms curved round her waist. 'I'll never let you out of my sight again.'

Skye laughed. 'That's hardly fair! For most of the time I've known you, you've never been *in* my sight.'

Coop smiled down and brushed his lips against hers. 'I'm so proud of you. I'm going to spend the next millennia making sure that you're just as proud of me.'

Skye pulled back. 'I'm already proud of you. But...'

'Congratulations, Ms Sawyer,' interrupted Aphrodite. 'You succeeded. Your tenacity is admirable.' Her gaze flicked to Coop and softened. 'As is your influence on my son.'

'I love him,' she said simply.

'I see that now. I should not have put you through what I did.

Perhaps Coop is not the only one who has learnt a lesson through knowing you.'

Skye blushed.

Aphrodite looked at Zeus. 'It's time.'

He nodded.

'Turn around, Skye,' said Coop in her ear, his fingers tightly holding on to hers as if he was worried she would suddenly escape.

Skye looked over her shoulder, then gaped at who was there. 'Mum! Dad!'

The pair of them were pale and staring at the imposing walls of Olympus.

'Oh my goodness,' her mum said, with her hand at her throat.

Her dad seemed lost for words. Skye reached over and gave them both a tight hug, then smiled shyly.

'This is Coop. The man,' she licked her lips, 'the god I was telling you about.'

'God,' her mum whispered.

Skye laughed, while Coop shook her dad's hands and gave her mother a peck on the cheek. 'It's an honour to meet you,' he said.

Her dad recovered first. 'God, you say? I wonder if you might be able to help me with a little problem I've been having?' Coop raised his eyebrows. 'My football team...'

'Dad!' Skye groaned and thumped him on the arm.

Coop gave him a wink. 'I'll see what I can do.'

She rolled her eyes.

'Hi.'

Skye looked up and spotted Emma. 'Oh my goodness! Where did you come from?'

Her old friend smiled at her. 'I'm so sorry, Skye.' She shook her head. 'I should never have got involved. I should never have opened my big mouth.'

Skye hushed her and gave her a quick hug. 'It's okay.' She gazed at Coop. 'Everything's turned out for the best.'

'It's not over yet,' he grinned.

She frowned. 'What do you mean?'

'You'll see.'

'Skye Sawyer,' intoned Zeus, 'we ask you here, on the steps of Olympus and in front of this gathering of family and friends to make your vows to Cupid.'

Startled, Skye turned to Coop. He knelt down on one knee and took her hand. She was aware of her mother gasping next to her.

'We don't normally do it this way,' he said, 'but in your case I'm willing to make an exception.' His eyes searched hers, warmth, love and something that looked a little bit like nervousness reflected in them. 'Skye Sawyer, will you marry me?'

For a moment it seemed to Skye that she'd forgotten how to speak. Or breathe. Then she found her voice. 'Yes,' she said. 'Yes.'

Coop pulled her to her feet and kissed her until she felt dizzy, then he laughed.

'I can't wait to spend the rest of my life with you,' he whispered.

'Skye Sawyer,' continued Zeus, smiling, 'as the wife of Cupid, you are welcomed into the family of Olympus. The same rights and privileges are granted to you as to other gods. Your humanity, kindness and compassion leave me with no alternative but to proclaim you as the Goddess of the Soul.'

'I don't understand,' said Skye, bewildered.

Aphrodite frowned at her. 'You mean you didn't know?'

'Know what?'

'That by becoming his wife, you become one of us?'

Skye stared at her dumbly, shaking her head.

Aphrodite sighed and glared at her son. 'If you'd told me that sooner, we could have been spared a lot of time. She hardly had ulterior motives to get her hands on immortality if she didn't even know it was possible.'

'Immortality?' Skye paled.

'Can we damn well get on with this?' snapped Zeus. Everyone fell silent. 'Very well, then. Skye Sawyer, you are now a goddess of Olympus.' He extended one index finger and pointed it at her. The top of his finger sizzled and there was a crack of thunder, then several gasps.

Skye felt a warm glow spreading through her body. Her skin tingled.

'Your wings!'

Puzzled, Skye half turned, then gaped at the soft feathers extending from her back. They weren't snowy white like Coop's; instead there were many multi-coloured hues, glimmering in the sunlight.

'Oh,' she said weakly.

'Are you okay?' Coop touched her face.

'We'll be together forever.'

'That we will,' he said. 'You know, "the wise want love."'

She smiled faintly. 'Shelley? "Those who love want wisdom". I think I understand you now. I understand how you feel about true love.'

Coop looked pained. 'That's because I didn't think it was real.' He drew her close to him. 'Now I've got you, I see that it is.'

'When did you know you felt that way?'

He looked into her eyes. 'It was creeping up on me for so long, I hardly realised. But that moment at the beach when Apollo tried to hurt you then he threw you into the sea? That's when I knew. Because if anything happened to you, I wouldn't want to live.'

'We had to work for it.'

He laughed. 'That we did.'

'It wasn't just a sudden bolt out of the blue. Maybe,' she paused for a moment, then took a deep breath, 'maybe it's sweeter now because it wasn't instant. Because we had to fight for it.'

'What are you saying, Skye?'

'I helped Styx,' she said. 'I didn't mean to, but I did. He's in love with Lethe although he won't admit it yet. I helped him see the light.'

'And you did it without a magic gun.'

She nodded. 'Maybe you don't need to shoot people. Maybe you just need to help them along a little bit. Get them to make the moves themselves instead of doing it for them.'

'You mean sort of like a dating agency?'

'A bit. Just one where you know they're actually meant to be together.'

'It might work,' he said slowly. 'Let's put it to my mother and see what she says.'

'Together?' squeaked Skye.

He kissed her deeply then smiled. 'Together.'

ABOUT THE AUTHOR

After teaching English literature in the UK, Japan and Malaysia, Helen Harper left behind the world of education following the worldwide success of her Blood Destiny series of books. She is a professional member of the Alliance of Independent Authors and writes full time, thanking her lucky stars every day that's she lucky enough to do so!

Helen has always been a book lover, devouring science fiction and fantasy tales when she was a child growing up in Scotland.

She currently lives in Edinburgh in the UK with far too many cats — not to mention the dragons, fairies, demons, wizards and vampires that seem to keep appearing from nowhere.

You can find out more by visiting Helen's website: http://helenharper.co.uk

Printed in Great Britain
by Amazon

29581275R00155